THE GRAY EARTH

THE GRAY EARTH

A NOVEL

GALSAN TSCHINAG

TRANSLATED FROM THE GERMAN
BY KATHARINA ROUT

milkweed
editions

© Insel Verlag, Frankfurt am Main und Leipzig, 1999
© 2010, Translation by Katharina Rout

Published 2010 by Milkweed Editions
Originally published as *Die graue Erde* by Insel Verlag, Frankfurt am Main
    und Leipzig, 1999.
Printed in Canada
Cover design by Brad Norr
Cover photos by Corbis
Author photo by Aibora Galsan
Interior design by Rachel Holscher
The text of this book is set in Anziano
10 11 12 13 14 5 4 3 2 1
First Edition

Please turn to the back of this book for a list of the sustaining funders of Milkweed Editions.

Library of Congress Cataloging-in-Publication Data

Tschinag, Galsan, 1943–
    [Graue Erde. English]
    The gray earth / Galsan Tschinag; translated from the German by
Katharina Rout.
        p.   cm.
    ISBN 978-1-57131-085-9 (alk. paper) — ISBN 978-1-57131-812-1 (e-book)
    I. Rout, Katharina. II. Title.
    PT2682.S297G7313 2010
    833'.914—dc22

                                                        2010040470

For Dshokonaj,
My brother and teacher,
Who had to go
So I could stay.

CONTENTS

THE GRAY EARTH

THE SPIRIT

At my feet lies a miserable, mute, and fearful sky. It must submit to my battered brass ladle each time my ladle dips into the clouds. Then the sky shivers and shudders and the clouds blur. Sitting above the sky, I shamanize and fondly consider the sheep whose fleece I am plucking.

With each scoop from the river the verse also rises, answering my need. The water streams into the aspen-wood pail with a bright streak and a dark rumble and then, once the pail has filled up, sparkles and splashes over its brim.

Meanwhile the verse sinks softly and quietly onto my tongue, and word after word rolls into my throat where it turns into song. I keep the bright, fluttering melody from the prickling, almost piercing splashes of the gushing water and draw out and savor each line's last syllable.

How fortunate that I have bush standing behind me firm and thick to hide me from other people's eyes and ears.

Here I can shamanize as long and loudly as I like, and dally as much with the spirits as my desire and courage allow.

I am determined to become a shaman, even though my parents are against it. They say I lack the roots. There has never been a shaman in our family; the one shaman we have—a woman named Pürwü—is only related to us through marriage. When they hear me shamanize, they get angry with me. But Pürwü has given me permission to follow her example. She said so in our own yurt, in front of Father and Mother and a handful of other people.

This was years ago. Brother and Sister were still at home, my dog Arsylang was still alive, and Grandma was still on this earth, close enough for us to see and touch her. I had been sick and bedridden for days, and so the shaman had to come. As she was shamanizing, and slapping me with her *shawyd*, the colorful whisk made from strips of fabric, I suddenly—so I am told—reached up and snatched the *shawyd* from her hand. And that was not all. Apparently I also jumped up and raced around the stove, whipping myself with her *shawyd* and singing about a white sheep that alone would save me.

At first they tried to catch me and quickly tuck me in again, but I fought ferociously and insisted that a sheep be consecrated on the spot if I were to be kept alive. The shaman, who had lost her place in the chant, stood confused and then decided to do as I wished. So the sheep I had demanded was brought and consecrated. I cannot actually remember any of it. Only dark, shadowy shreds of memory have stayed with me—I must have been delirious with fever.

Soon afterward I recovered completely. But for a long time the strange behavior of the child I was remained a topic of conversation. The farther word of it traveled through time and space, the more impressive and lavish the story became. And when I told my story to other children, I embellished it with even more details, making it even more beautiful and significant. I can't say whether this was the reason, but I sensed that everyone knew and admired me.

"He is Ish-Maani's youngest," strangers said when they referred to me, and the respect they had for this particular youngest child could be heard in their voices. Ish-Maani, "Oh-You-Poor-Soul," is my kind and empathetic father's nickname.

All of this led me to butt in a second time when one day Aunt Pürwü was shamanizing again. But this time I knew what I was doing. Without any warning I jumped up, tore the scarf from the head of the next best person within my reach, and, screeching and waving the scarf, followed the shaman. Cooing and snorting and stomping and waving wildly about, she stepped out the door to tackle something invisible in the darkness of the steppe. In the flickering light of the dung fire the faces around me looked rigid with fear, which gave me a prickling satisfaction. A man's voice hissed through clenched teeth, "Hey, come back, you bad boy!" But by then I was almost through the door and obviously in no mind to turn back. Instead, I was surprised the stranger would not know who I was. He made me smile. But then I put on a serious face, stepped forth, and, drawing on everything I had, supported the shaman in her struggle to drive away the evil spirit I believed to be hidden in front of me in the dark.

Later, when I had returned into the yurt under the shaman's wings, I heard the same reproachful voice brazenly raised against my parents: "You're not the only people with a youngest child."

Another voice agreed: "Yes, this has gone too far. Who knows where it will lead." I recognized the voice; it was Tuudaj. Tuudaj always showed up when we butchered a large animal. That it was her, of all people, annoyed me somewhat, and I asked myself what I would do the next time she popped up at the edge of our *ail* with that greasy, shiny goatskin bag under her left arm. Would I run toward her as fast as before to restrain our dog? But then the shaman interrupted her chant and said, "Let him be. He has his reasons, or else he wouldn't do it."

I was grateful to her, but I had lost the courage to carry on and instead crouched and hid behind everyone at the back, while a heavy silence weighed upon them.

The following night wolves attacked our *ail*'s flock. We soon lost sight of the animals the wolves had chased away. But somehow we managed to stay connected with the victims until dawn, firing shots in their direction, banging pails and basins with sticks, and calling out after the sheep and goats, pausing only to listen. The animals knew each of these sounds was meant for them, and baaed and bleated in reply.

At dawn, we saddled the horses and loaded the dung baskets to bring back the dead and the wounded. More than a dozen animals had been killed—there were whole piles of remains. The dogs howled for several days and nights, their helpless cries born from shame and rage.

Every misfortune demands a culprit. This time, the verdict fell on me. Had it come from only one side, I probably would have tried to defend myself. I could have said the attack was part of life and our *ail*, having been spared for so long, was due.

But too many people, everyone really, went to battle against me. Even Mother did. She accused me of a brazenness not even a madman would allow himself, and she claimed that with my twitching and screeching I had scorched her face for all the world to see. Father agreed with her: with my performance I had done worse than bring shame to the family—I had enraged the sky. The bundle the sky had given me at birth simply did not include shamanizing. Their voices were cold and hard, as if I were no longer their baby child. Other people came and behaved as if demanding damages from Father and Mother since I, their child, had awakened the evil spirits and lured them close with my insolence. Soon my defiance collapsed. I remembered whom I had named in my verses:

Ary börü, asa gooshu . . .
Greedy wolves, ghostly devils . . .

Of course I had tried to drive them away instead of luring them close. But the fact remained that I had called their names. And maybe they had heard their names, rushed toward us, and slipped past me. I had been insolent and, unfortunately, blind as well.

I shrank down to the size of a tick and waited in agony for someone to hurl the fateful line from my verse at my head like a rock. Fortunately, no one did. But things were bad enough already. There was no way of knowing when—if ever—the flock would recover from the loss. For the longest time I could not shake my remorse and melancholy. Time after time I swore to myself never again to shamanize.

Time passed. Among shamans and their nightly performances, I kept my word. I was just one of their spectators and listeners, and a very mute and quiet one at that. Whenever I watched one of the shamans rise up against death and the devil, my plight returned. I felt the sharp pain of remorse in my diaphragm. The wound might have formed a scar, but it was far from healed.

Then the bad year arrived. It ended with me rising up against the sky and flinging at him my best weapons—my words. I denounced him. Instead of replying, Father Sky stayed as unreachable and invulnerable as ever. That provoked me the most. What exactly was the sky? I had to find out. In the beginning, I was afraid. I feared he would strike back. But absolutely nothing happened. First I was thrilled and encouraged, then disappointed and affronted.

Curiosity awoke in me like in a suckling that stirs, stretches, and waits for his mother to come and feed him, and then starts to cry when no one comes.

My way of crying has always been to sing the shaman's chant. So I started to shamanize again, even more than before.

Ever since that awakening, I have been calling out for the sky. My language is poetry and song. My poetry is mostly pleas, sometimes threats and scorn. When I feel the urge to take on the sky, I flee from people. If people overhear my shamanizing, it is because I have made a mistake. Then I must accept rebuke. But people's passing remarks are tolerable. They remind me that no one can train his mind for the work of a shaman the way he can train his hands for the craft of a tanner, that the sky alone calls one to shamanizing, and that, when he does, the call is by no means a reward. It is a heavy burden, almost a punishment, and impossibly hard to bear for a human being with an eye of water and a heart of flesh. Anyone who is truly a shaman feels condemned to carry this heaviest of burdens through the years as his or her fate. This is how our aunt, the shaman, puts it.

Nevertheless, since that worst day in that bad year I have not been given a beating. I can tell my parents are treating me more cautiously. That is probably best for all of us, for every so often I feel the urge to run away. I would love to fly away like a bird or swim away like a fish, away from all these powerless people and animals and away from these unreliable mountains and valleys, which dish out we never know what from one day to the next. Away from the mute and pitiless sky that supposedly knows all, sees all, and hears all, but pretends to be deaf and blind the moment I need to be heard and seen.

I envy the winds, the water, and the birds whenever I think of them. They blow, flow, and fly; they all get to leave, whereas, in spite of my two quick legs, I am condemned to stay among the mountains and the river valleys, not much different from a tethered horse. I grow restless whenever I imagine the world beyond the mountains. I want the gusts of wind, floods of water, and birds of passage to take me wherever they go. I would gladly go to the end of the world, look into the gaping abyss, lose my way, and face the furies of everlasting night and hell's roiling, toxic sea. How often I wish I had spirits to take me there and bring me back. Because this feeling is so strong, I am ready to give up whatever I have and to do whatever it takes to become a shaman.

"Watch out," Mother warns me one day. "Others have dabbled in shamanism against the will of the sky, who had not given them such powers. Quite a few paid with their lives."

Father is usually quick to support her: "Anyone chosen by the sky is seriously ill and needs to heal before becoming a shaman. It is difficult."

I do not reply, but mull over their words for a long time. Eventually I decide to ask the shaman herself. She says more or less the same thing as Mother and Father, but when I dig, I learn more: in rare cases a person with pure bones can get infected with shamanism by a shaman. Such an infection can be brought about by different means, but most often results from a blood transfusion.

This is a fateful bit of news. I decide to try, or rather force, a blood transfusion between the two of us. Some time later I go back to our aunt's place. In the birch-wood sheath on my belt I carry a small dagger with a horn hilt that Father keeps ground and honed. Soon my opportunity comes: the woman is sewing, and when I see her struggle with a dull knife to unpick an old seam, I jump to help her with my dagger. Now she holds the two sewn-together pieces in her hands to stretch them apart. All I need to do is touch the yak tendon with the grimly sharp blade of my dagger, and the two pieces of sheepskin spring apart with a soft crackle. When my aunt praises me, I grow unsure of my plans, but promise myself not to miss the opportunity that is within my grasp, making my fingers prickle. Just before we come to the end of the seam, I twist the dagger slightly. We both cry out. I am surprised how easy it was, how fast the desired, precious—sacred, even—blood spurts out. The blade has touched the tip of my aunt's right ring finger, and bright-red blood runs over the fleece and the blade.

While Aunt Pürwü sets about plucking a tuft of wool from the back of the sheepskin so she can burn it and press the glowing ashes into her wound, I dash from the yurt. I hear her shout after me, "Make sure you wash the blade carefully."

When I have reached the hiding place I sought out

in advance, I open my *lawashak*, drop my long pants with their wide legs, and pierce the thick, soft flesh of my left calf with the blade I have carried, bloody side up, in my outstretched hand.

Fortunately, I have no time to think, and everything happens fast. The wound hurts badly. I cannot help but cry out, and my whole body begins to shake. But otherwise I don't move. My face is twisted with pain, but I am determined. I stare at the blade. The bright silvery steel is stuck two-fingers deep in my flesh, and its knobby goat-horn hilt trembles ever so slightly.

I wait to make sure that the alien sacred blood gets absorbed by my flesh and travels through my body. Meanwhile, my leg feels heavier, and a dull pain begins to extend to the tips of my toes. Finally, I pull out the blade. That hurts even more than thrusting it in because the steel is stuck. My wound begins to bleed, which worries me mostly because I am afraid the sacred blood might leak out. I lick the wound until the bleeding stops. Then I bandage it with a strip of fabric I tear off my belt.

Now I have a limp. When people notice, I explain that I hurt myself on a branch jutting from a tree. As time goes by, the pain only increases. The wound turns an angry red and begins to fester.

All that happened in the summer. Now it is autumn, and still the wound has not healed. It is the reason we had to take our yurt on a detour along the dangerously wild Homdu

River instead of traveling across Borgasyn and battling straight through our mild, milky-white mother river, Ak-Hem. The day before yesterday we arrived in this place on the far side of the district center and the large water, and yesterday the doctor came to look at my wound. He brushed on a pungent liquid and told me to take off my old puss-encrusted pants and go to bed. At first I enjoy lying in bed. I even fall asleep in the middle of the day! But then I decide to get up. Many lines of poetry come to mind. Bite after bite, they slide over my tongue. I can neither make them stay nor make them go silently—they demand to be chanted aloud and released into the wide world.

I have no choice but to get up and steal away from the yurt.

> Worn thin are my soles
> Like the shoes of a camel yearling.
> That is how much I have looked for you,
> o-oh-ooj.
> Threadbare is my throat
> Like the opening of a bag.
> That is how much I have called you,
> u-uh-uuj.

I am calling for the spirits even though the words, jumping dumb like fish from the flood, run effortlessly together as lines, and the voice that nets them has already found its own strength. So far I am no more than a neighbor to the clouds and a brother to the fish, but I sense I am being transformed and on my way to water and air, ready to rise above myself and become the fish's throat and the clouds' heart. If I succeed, I will also succeed in becoming a counterforce and a counterweight for the sky and the earth.

> For anything that needs to be poured,
> Here is my brainpan.
> Round and rooted with soot-black hair
> Take it, a-ah-aaj.
> For anything that needs to be bound,
> Here is the thread of my life.
> Red and braided of eight springtimes
> Take it, e-eh-eej.

I take my time as I call out to the spirits whose presence I sense as clearly as the sun and the wind. Incessantly I plead and relentlessly I lure, for today I want to see them in the flesh.

And then I catch sight of something: a blurry figure in a pale, fluttering cape stands before me in the ladle. I am startled, and as the ladle slips from my hand, I believe I see the figure shrink into something round, like a stuffed first stomach of a sheep, its rumen, before bursting and dissolving. I quickly turn and jump: someone is standing right behind me.

He is an elegant, foreign-looking man. His body is angular and chiseled and his face light-skinned and smooth.

Luscious glittering hair flows out with a flourish from under his ash-colored peaked cap. His long coat is as green as bile and unbuttoned, and his narrow boots have high legs and heavy heels, and are made from leather polished to a mirror.

A muffled groan escapes me as I stare at the man who seems more likely to have fallen from the clouds than squeezed through the dense willow bushes—he seems so celestial. Nevertheless, his pale chiseled face with the narrow flat eyes and the bony crooked nose looks familiar. Suddenly I recognize Brother Dshokonaj. Yet I cannot believe it is him, or why it is him.

I cannot help thinking about the figure I saw in the water. Still, I have my doubts. That figure was stripped bare both above and below the waist, was it not?

Until now the man has stared at me in silence, but now a greeting escapes him: "Come here, little man, let your big brother sniff you."

I finally stand and, relieved because it really is his voice, walk toward him.

Close up, I am hit by a wave of the sharp smells I recognize from the goods sold in the store. I take them in with relish and am reminded of sweets and especially the red-and-yellow striped candies I was once given as a present. I feast on the man's smell as if it were exuding from crackling white candy wrappers.

But then I stop and think again: the two hands touching my cheeks are cool and wet. Again I remember the figure in the water. He must have been wet and naked.

The figure had trembled before it shrank into a rumen and then fell apart and dissolved.

A cold shiver runs up my calves and spreads across my belly and my back, and I feel my hair rise and turn into awls piercing my skull through the skin.

BROTHER

"What were you doing?" he asks me.

I think it better not to tell him. But when his gaze drills through the already tight skin at the top of my ringing head, I can't hold back: "I was chanting."

He doesn't reply. But once we are back in the yurt, he says what I dreaded hearing all the way home, limping behind him, ladle in hand. After putting the water pail down in front of the kitchen shelf abruptly, he lets fly: "Do you know why the rascal wouldn't come home? He was shamanizing! Fooling around with the spirits!"

Father and Mother wince as these words pelt them like rocks hurled at animals.

"All the while you are sitting here, innocently thinking he's too young for school," he rages on. "He's played the baby long enough—it has to stop. Anyone who makes rhymes on death and the devil and fills the sky and the earth with his shouting can learn a few measly letters and numbers."

Father and Mother cower in silence. I sit motionless, not saying a thing. Occasionally our eyes meet. See, their eyes say to me, that's what happens when you don't listen to us. At least be good now, please.

I hold on a little longer, but my eyes ask, Where has he come from? And why?

They do not know. I ask why they sent him after me. They did not, I read in their eyes. He went of his own accord. I should not have stayed out so long.

It looks as if he wants take me with him right then and there. My eyes plead and cry, but neither Father nor Mother is able to resist. Instead, they want to know what they should prepare for me.

They don't need to prepare a thing, he announces. Everything will be provided by the school. Mother mentions the doctor, who will return the next day. No longer necessary, the brother growls. I will be taken for treatment today.

Suddenly I realize I am not wearing any pants. To my annoyance I learn there is not a pair of clean pants around. Of course the doctor will not want to see me in the old dirty ones he had pulled off me with his own hands.

I make a face and try to suppress the tears. It makes me deeply miserable that I am no longer allowed to do anything, not even shout and cry to my heart's content. How I would love to jump and run around and yell until I wear myself out.

But I feel so heavy and mortally cowed I can no longer find legs to run away. I have to accept that everything around me happens exactly as he, and he alone, decides. And so I have to put up with not having any pants to wear.

What had to happen happens: he takes me away. As tiny as lice and as dumbfounded as I am, Father and Mother stand there stunned. All they can do is release me to go my separate way by sniffing my right cheek and leaving the left one for later, for our reunion. And talk about how I am to gain knowledge and how I must not cry when I am leaving for school with my big brother.

I cry anyway. The milk I am allowed to sip for the farewell cannot wash away the salt that fills my throat.

Father and Mother stay behind, along with our yurt and our flocks, the meadows and the bushes. I can see them blurred through the tears. Behind the saddle, glued to the horse's back, which presses against my naked bottom as narrow and as hard as the back of a knife, I begin to grasp my situation. My threadbare *lawashak* barely covers my private parts as I stick to the horse like a tick and withdraw into myself, away from a suddenly incomprehensible world.

I feel ambushed. No one ever said a word about my starting school this fall, and I have been treated without respect or love. How different everything was when Brother Galkaan and Sister Torlaa left for school: they looked dazzling, wrapped from head to toe in colorful brand-new clothes Mother had sewn throughout the summer. Father himself led them away. And how do I look? I am in rags. My head scarf is frayed and stained with squirrel blood and fish slime. And I am supposed to be the beloved baby? No one would believe it. Considering my lot makes me lose control, and I begin to sob loudly.

Meanwhile we have reached the ford, and the horse starts wading through the river. The brilliant reflections and dull roar around me only make things worse: I feel abandoned and at the mercy of forces whose names I have yet to come up with.

"Hey, what's got into you?" Brother admonishes me. I sob louder in reply, whereupon this man who is said to be my brother, lording it in the saddle in front of me, goes wild. I feel him twitch and writhe on the other side of the stiff coat I desperately cling to. Then he hisses, "Stop right now or I'll push you into the water!"

His words hit like the crack of a whip, terrifying me. I shout for all I'm worth against the hiss and roar of the river: "Don't, dearest Brother, please don't. I'll stop, I promise!"

I whimper and dig my nails into his terribly stiff coat, which, no matter how hard I try, stays as unyielding as smoked leather. Experience has taught me never to look down when crossing a river, but I can't help myself. Instantly our horse shoots upstream.

Even more frightened, I try to look away from the seething current, but my stubborn gaze is as rigid as my body, and I can't look away from the river's whirling surface.

Frozen with fear and wet with tears, I wriggle to brace myself against the rushing waters, like a cowardly dog who groans and cries just to stay alive and seated. If I had more courage and daring, I would rage and fight and drown, and then float away from the injustices hounding me so mercilessly and shamelessly.

I crave a few comforting words—Don't worry, little man, you don't believe your big brother would push you off the horse, do you?—but they do not come. Instead I hear "Shut up, will you?" These words sound hardly less ominous than Brother's earlier ones. I am stiff with fear, but I try hard to clench my chattering teeth and throttle the cries of pain.

Below me, the water is rising. First my right boot feels wet and shortly after my left one as well. Then I feel the cold water at my calves, my thighs, and my bottom.

The horse loses contact with the bottom and starts to swim. Lying at an angle, it floats like a piece of driftwood and no longer darts against the current.

I remember Father once calling my big brother hard-hearted. While I cannot remember the occasion, I do remember that Mother did not like hearing it. She tends to quickly take offense because my big brother is her son by another man. Everyone knows it. It is why Brother has never lived with us. He used to come and visit from time to time, but he always quickly left again, like some distant relative. Eventually, we lost track of him. People say he's pursuing the path to knowledge somewhere far away from us.

Now he has returned, a bolt from the blue that has hit me like lightning.

My suffering continues for what seems like forever, until at long last the vast wild water lies behind us and I can let myself slide down the side of the dripping-wet horse. I feel relief, even joy, at the feeling of solid ground beneath my feet. The sensation comes with a new awareness: from now on, if I don't watch out for myself and my survival, in whatever place and by whatever means, no one else will. However, only later will this awareness become a conscious thought.

Something confusing happens next that gives me cause for much thought. Brother steps close, wipes off my tears, and says, "Don't cry, my dear little shaman. Now you don't like what I'm doing, but one day you'll be grateful for your new life. At home you may be the baby, but you can't be the baby the rest of your life. That's why, sooner rather than later, you must take on the burden of what we call knowledge. Knowledge has been waiting for you. And unless you accept its burden, you won't be able to carry it into the future. Knowledge is the fire that illuminates our darkness and destroys our backwardness. Now go and wash off your tears and snot, and dry your clothes. I have to dry mine as well. See? I got wet up to my belt. I should have gone to the ford rather than try to find a shortcut."

Half a pail of water pours out of each of my boots. I pull the felt lining out, wring them as best I can, and pull them over two narrow, pointy rocks. I keep on my *lawashak* and realize I have to stand still, arms and legs spread wide apart like a scarewolf's, to make sure the bottom seam stays smooth and straight in the sun.

Brother has taken off everything but a pair of briefs that barely covers his private parts. At first I glance at him quickly, but then I can't help myself and keep peeking. His skin is as light as a newborn's, but with a bluish tinge. Maybe this is what scares me. His feet, their long toes spaced apart, suddenly remind me of the figure in my ladle. His coat, spread on the ground next to his other pieces of clothing, attracts my attention: it could be the cape I saw. I try to calm my pounding heart: in the ladle I saw a bald pointy head not at all like his, which is shaggy and shaped like a yak bull's. The difference strikes me as significant, and I decide it is his long and wavy hair that makes him so different from anyone else I know, and hence so unapproachable. Will I be allowed to wear my hair like his once I have acquired the knowledge everyone talks about? The idea shakes me, but also brightens and warms my inner world with vague hope for a future lying in wait behind the rust-colored eastern mountains. Today—so the voice I sometimes hear inside me whispers—some of that future may still be a large lake or a high mountain. But every day a part of that future will split off and become a bright, sunlit morning, and all these mornings will move toward me, facing an unknown path. And they will treat me well.

My brother steps into the river, vigorously splashes himself with water, and equally vigorously rubs his wet parts with his palms. He crouches and then stretches his slender body so it sways and floats in the current like a piece of aspen trunk. I cannot take my eyes off him. He washes differently than we do. We avoid stepping into a river when we wash but remain at the bank, kneeling on the dry gravel and scooping up the water with our cupped hands. We always make sure the water we take from our great mother river to wet and wash our head, face, and hands never runs straight back into the current.

Finally he stands up, puffs and blows, and steps out of the river. Dumbfounded, I stare at his briefs. Their bottom droops and water runs out of them in a bright stream. He goes over to his coat and pulls from its side pocket a piece of fabric that is folded into a square. With two fingers he pinches one of its corners and elegantly shakes it open. Then he dabs his face.

The cloth is brilliantly white and gossamer-thin. I know such cloths from Brother Galkaan and Sister Torlaa; they are called handkerchiefs. I have heard that every civilized person carries one in his or her breast pocket. Brother and Sister are civilized because they attend school. Father and Mother and I are not. We are primitive country folk. Sister Torlaa said so, and Brother Galkaan confirmed it. Brother and Sister showed us how to use a handkerchief: you blow your nose into it. The three of us were speechless. Then Father and Mother decided they would rather remain primitive country folk. But when I tried to follow their example, Sister told me to shut up. One day I, too, would go to school. Later she gave me a square, blue-mottled cloth to practice with, so I wouldn't be a calf trying to shit like a bull.

Father and Mother bristled when they heard her say that. Father asked where she had learned such language, and Mother commented that the snot blown into a cloth must conjure up the shit that soils your mouth and other people's ears. Their words did not stop me from carrying the cloth in my breast pocket and practicing with it for a while. I did it a bit differently, though, than I'd been shown. I blew my nose into the open steppe and then wiped my nose with the cloth. Until one day I lost it.

And now another snow-white, gossamer-thin cloth! Brother slowly lifts it to his light-skinned, smooth forehead and dabs off each drop of water. Knowing the proper name for the cloth does not leave me any less fascinated. Maybe one day I, too, will pull a handkerchief out of my side pocket and even use it properly.

THE WORLD
BEYOND THE
RIVER

The images change as quickly as in a dream. I see yurts pushed into a clump like chased lambs. These yurts are so dark that if they were real lambs, they would belong to the Kazakhs. Black with soot, they are stooped from having been put up long ago. Other snow-white yurts glow and form a straight line. A hill separates the dark from the white flock of yurts. Four lines of smooth rocks gathered from the steppe form a square around each flock.

At one corner of each square, four posts lean toward each other to form the corners of an equally square if cock-eyed shed. Standing out bright against the dark steppe, the sheds' bottom halves are patched together with plywood and cardboard, while a strip of sacking is stretched around the sheds' upper parts. A tousled head peeks out above the upper edge of one of the sheds, and soon Rabid

Buura, also called Blue Tooth, comes limping around the corner, his *lawashak* of bright-yellow silk flung wide open, his hands on the string holding up his pants.

Here and there I see a few dogs, but none barks at us. Sniffing the rocky ground, they slink around busily but soundlessly. The few people I see look sluggish and drowsy. They stand or crouch in front of the yurts, yawning and stretching. Occasionally someone walks to another yurt.

At the far edge of the bare rock-strewn steppe stands a lone horse. Apparently tethered, it must have grown tired of searching for occasional blades of grass and fallen asleep. Its head, mane, and tail hang lifelessly. I can see no herds, and no other living beings, in this endless gray-brown barrenness.

But here, now, begins the district center of which I have heard so much. I see houses. A house is bigger than the biggest yurt and more beautiful, I suppose, since it is square and has an equally square shining eye between the two corners of each wall. The eyes reflect us and the horse.

I am in awe of the people who have created all this and who dismantle and put it all up again with each move. These *dargas* must have countless strong camels to carry off even one house. And there are so many houses!

Here even the fence is powerful and altogether different from our fence of interwoven willow and birch branches that staggers like a drunk in a bumpy circle around our haystack. Here, young larch trees stand dead straight in a row, tightly nailed together and mowed level at the top.

Our horse stops at one of the fence corners. "We've arrived," says Brother.

"Is that true? Is this the school? It's huge!" I prattle on as I get off the horse.

Brother maintains the silent composure he assumed as we approached the settlement. I notice a man walking toward us. Brother has descended and waits with the lead in his hand instead of tying it to the fence as I would. The man hurries so much he almost breaks into a run. When he reaches us, he takes the lead from Brother. I hear him pant and talk, but cannot understand anything besides "Comrade Principal." He speaks in a foreign language, probably Mongolian.

Brother first asks a lot of questions. Then he continues without interruption, loud and fast and for a very long time. His head tilted, the man twists and kneads the lead, listening carefully before he turns to me. When he realizes I do not understand, he asks me in Tuvan whose child I am.

I am so intimidated I lower my eyes and scratch my neck. Then I reply: "I am Ish-Maani's son." I use Father's nickname because I dare not say his real name.

"I understand!" the man replies quickly, stroking a tuft of hair that pokes out where my head scarf has slipped. His voice is quiet and reverent. Brother grabs my hand and says something I can only guess at. Most likely: "Shall we go?"

With a burning throat, my hand limp and powerless in his, I hobble along beside Brother. As we walk through a gate, I realize that the world I have known is about to end once and for all. The gate is so tall even a fully loaded camel could pass. A moment later I enter the school yard and with it an entirely new world. This is the square world that I have only had inklings of. And from here on out, I will encounter it in ever more polished versions.

Seen from inside, the fence seems even taller and very steep. It pierces the sky that silently looks down on this impudent world, pausing over all that has come about or is still to come. Three houses, covered with clay and whitewashed, aim for each other in a triangle, while a small fourth one, made of wooden boards and lacking a roof, is shoved into the southwestern corner. Although there is not a soul to be seen, the sight of the little house reminds me of Rabid Buura with his wide-open coattails and his hands on his string belt. Now I, too, feel the urge. But I know that for now I must try to ignore it, and probably other urges as well.

So I hobble on, towed by the hand that clasps my fingers ever more tightly. We hasten toward the northwestern house, where I climb my first stairs to the doorstep, a larch beam thick as a thigh that countless feet have worn thin in the middle and hollowed in places. A cave opens up in front of me, square and surrounded by steep walls, and before I can make sense of the echo of our steps across the creaking floorboards or the tinny female voice ringing from the end of the hallway, I feel as if I hear the beats of my heart no longer coming from my chest, but from one of the walls.

"Take off your scarf and don't shuffle so loudly," Brother urgently whispers into my ear. "Class is in session." His words make me unsure of myself and nervous I might slip and stumble on the shiny creaking boards, and so I no longer dare to bend my knees.

By then we have reached the end of the hallway. There are light-colored doors on both sides. The woman's voice now sounds even shriller and more threatening. When Brother drums with the back of his bent index finger against the upper half of one of the doors, the loud bangs startle me. Footsteps ring out and the door opens.

I see a man who looks frighteningly like Brother. Behind him, children's heads sit frozen in straight rows. They all look in the same direction and are set in the same position. Instinctively I pull back. Were it not for the hand that holds mine, I would take off and run at the sight. But instead the hand jerks me into the room, and the flock of children jumps up and stands with trembling nostrils and shining eyes, swaying lightly like a forest. Brother yells a longish word, and the children answer in a booming chorus with a shorter, more impressive word. Standing in front of them, Brother looks as grand as a fully grown larch tree in front of saplings. He casts a quick scrutinizing glance at the children and shouts something else. In response, the human forest noisily crashes down as if mowed by a storm.

Brother talks with the man. Even though I don't understand what they say, I know it affects me. Indeed, a moment later a name is called out and a girl leaps to her feet, walks to the front of the room, and grabs my hand. She leads me to the back row, pushes me into an empty seat, and says something. I quickly sit down and, because the girl walks back to her seat, conclude that I didn't do anything wrong.

Later I will learn that the girl, Ishgej, the oldest student in the class, has just assigned me a seat and that I do not have the right to exchange it for any other seat unless I have her and the teacher's permission. Brother leaves the room, and the lesson continues.

The man drags a white stone over a square black board. The stone leaves behind white tracks, which the students copy into their exercise books. They are funny-looking tracks, not at all like the animal tracks I know, of fleeing rabbits or playing squirrels. I would like to join in and draw tracks myself, as well I could if I had an exercise book and a pencil. Already my right index finger is copying on my desktop the white stone's movements on the black board.

It must be envy and admiration I sense under my skin like a warming, though it feels more like caustic fire when I squint at my neighbor laboring over his exercise book. He has fat lips in a moon-shaped face. The pencil in his round, brownish-black fist struggles to scratch back and forth on the white paper and leaves behind shaky black tracks. Will I ever succeed at this?

The man at the front stops drawing, grabs a willow branch from atop the board, steps aside, and watches the students copy his tracks. I furtively study him and wonder how I possibly could have thought he resembled Brother. The man has a stocky roundish figure with a fleshy head, while Brother is long and slight. The man's bulging eyes are suspicious and spread a greenish tinge across his face. But it was his hair, shaggy like a yak bull's, along with his clothes—the same pointy black boots with narrow tall legs; the same ash-colored suit with a snow-white shirt— that made two such different bodies and faces look alike at first glance.

The tubby man with his burning-green eyes lifts the stick, points at the white squiggles on the black board, and says something. A few hands fly up. The elbows stay propped on the desks, the lower arms stand up straight, and the hands above look like bright wings in mid-flight.

The green eyes aim at the back, and there is a shout: "Sarsaj!"

The boy next to me jumps up and calls out words like *san-sam* or *sar-saj* or maybe *saj-sar*. His eyes follow the tip of the stick wandering sideways along the tracks. Is he identifying or explaining them?

After a sharp *ssuh* followed by a jerky signal from the stick, the boy sits down. *Ssuh,* I whisper, wondering what it means—sit down, perhaps? Whatever its meaning, the word flows through me like *ssug,* the word I know for water.

The stick is put aside. Again the green eyes aim at the back row, but this time they focus on me. The man says something. I don't know what to reply, so I keep quiet. He repeats himself, but he could repeat it a hundred times and because I don't understand, I keep quiet, wondering what he wants from me. Then a few words slip out of my mouth: *"Dshüü didri ssen aan?"* What did you say?

Hearing the agitation in my own high-pitched voice makes me want to cry. The herd bursts into raucous laughter—mockery has won out over fear. But their delight is short-lived: the man with yak-bull hair and horsefly eyes shakes his fists and yells something that sounds like a grown bull plunging his horns between a young challenger's ribs. The neighing dies in the throats. Everyone twitches and shrinks. The mockers implode and cower frozen in their seats. I, too, am terrified, but because I haven't yet learned the rules, I don't shrink back from the man with the yak-bull head and the waving fists. Instead I plead and try to explain that I honestly don't understand him, calling him *höörküüj Aga*, dear Brother.

The man listens. But instead of answering he makes the girl who had taken my hand and led me to my seat stand up. She translates: "The teacher says he asked you for your name."

I quickly give my name: Dshurukuwaa, Fur Baby. The girl's lips hint at a smile, and a tiny bright light flits across her round, bright-red cheeks. The ducking heads and bent backs in front of me quiver. I learn that we must not speak Tuvan at school. The girl translates: "The language itself, like your Tuvan name, is behind the times and cannot be written. For that reason, both must remain outside the fence. We must leave behind everything that is backward.

Instead, we must learn the civilized Mongolian language, which will lead us to the bright pinnacles of learning."

Finally, I learn not to address anyone as Brother or Sister, for here we are teacher and students.

At that moment a rumbling starts up as if a horse were farting after eating its fill. I jump with fright, but the others come alive with anticipation. At first deep and hoarse, the sound slowly becomes a high-pitched wail. It lasts a full breath before fading away and dying out.

The students rise, but wait for the teacher to leave the room before following him row after row as if tethered to a rope. When it is finally my turn and I am about to walk to the door, some have already snuck back in. They nudge me into a corner.

They want to know everything: Why have I arrived only now, when school began a whole month ago? What year was I born? What do I have in my breast pocket? Since they all talk Tuvan with me, I am relieved: so speaking Tuvan is allowed after all, at least sometimes. "My leg is injured," I tell them obligingly, and point at the offending dagger I carry in a sheath on my right thigh. The half circle between me and the door lets out oohs and aahs of admiration. I give my year of birth as the Year of the Horse and am told I could have easily waited another year. Most of the students here were born in the Year of the Snake if not the Year of the Dragon.

To show them what I have on me, I pull my head scarf from my breast pocket. As I do so, my pipe drops on the floor with a thud and gets picked up quickly. This time the circle around me groans with even louder oohs and aahs. Carved from a sheep's shoulder blade, my pipe has turned yellow and is worn along the edges.

"Do you also have tobacco?" The boy who wants to know is so tall that I attribute him easily to the Dragon, or perhaps even to the Rabbit or the Tiger.

"I don't," I say. "But I have *erwen.*"

"Are you a shaman?" a weedy boy snickers.

I ignore him and add, *"Erwen,* mixed with rabbit dung."

"Of course. Rabbit dung tastes best, much better than horse manure," the tall boy agrees. "But *erwen,* well . . ." He purses his lips and pretends to swallow his spit.

"I'll tell the teacher," announces a boy whose big head sits atop a skinny neck and body.

"Don't you dare, you tiny pup of the Widow Deshik. Or have you forgotten about this one?" The tall boy raises his fist to brag and threaten the skinny guy.

Someone else wants to know where precisely I have my injury—apparently in an attempt to throttle the imminent fight. Eager to help, I open my *lawashak* and show my wound. It is the size of a palm and has a blood-red edge. Another round of oohs and aahs wells up, and in the eyes around me I discover a fear born from admiration. I feel faintly proud.

At that moment a girl's voice I had never heard before calls out from the door. The witch must only just have pushed her stupid head through the door, along with her prying eyes and her shameless, merciless, and bungling tongue. When the conversation had turned to the pipe, the students pulled the door shut and made sure it stayed.

But there it is, her high-pitched, deadly loud voice: "The boy isn't wearing any pants!"

Everyone jumps, most of all me. I quickly drop the seam of my *lawashak* and turn toward the voice. A tall girl with a sallow face and long heavy braids stands at the door and grins. Her head is tilted sideways and her mouth is half open. Later I will learn she is called Sürgündü and was born in the Year of the Tiger. She is a bit slow, and her round tongue cannot pronounce the *s*. Soon my sharp tongue will repeatedly and mercilessly bring tears to her dark-green, good-natured eyes.

But it has not yet come to that. We have only just met and are sizing each other up, her fox eyes filled with ignorance and scorn, my calf eyes with shame and despair. In a corner of my heart I am hoping that the group, or at least the boys with whom I have had such a manly, naughty conversation, will stand up for me. With that in mind I turn to the tall boy whose ready fists hold such power to terrify and control. He'll show the girl once and for all. She'll never again poke her nose into other people's pants.

What happens instead floors me. The tall boy turns his bull's eyes on me: "First a pipe and a sheathed dagger, and now a bare ass—boy, you are some character!"

Laughter rings out and swells to a roar, taking my breath away.

"Weirdo, weirdo, weirdo!"

"Fur Baby, Fur Baby! Fur Baby goes to war!"

"What a man! A snotty brat with a bare ass!"

They pat and paw me all over. I don't resist. Blindly I stare at a spot somewhere above their heads. Too bad I haven't gone deaf and numb as well. Or maybe I have. I no longer feel shame rage under my skin and torment me like a bunch of wild fire ants. Instead I feel hurt and disappointment, killing me bit by bit.

"Don't you realize you'll get your pants pulled down and your skin torn off? You have it coming!" Big Head pipes up. "Teasing the principal's little brother will really get you into trouble."

His words hit home and the room falls silent.

The principal is my brother? I wonder and pause, but I don't feel relieved. Instead, I am inconsolable. Suddenly I see what has been done to me. I am a stone that has been moved. I cannot possibly return to the place where I was dropped, when I first began to be.

NUMBER
ONE HUNDRED

Sit? *Ssuuh!*
Stand? *Boss!*
Turn? *Äh-regh!*
Sshuuh—boss—äh-regh!
Sshuuh—boss—äh-regh!
Sshuuh—boss—äh-regh!
We are doing drills. Uncle gives me orders, and I crouch,
jump, and turn. Later I learn that Uncle's name is Arganak;
he is to be addressed as Comrade Arganak, and crouching,
jumping, and turning is called obeying his commands. So I
should say Comrade Arganak gives commands that I obey.
However, I am still not saying it quite right. I am no longer
really myself. I have almost become a student—as soon
as I get out of here, I will be one. I should probably put it
this way: Comrade Arganak gives commands the student

obeys. Maybe I will even have to be addressed as Comrade Student?

Sshuuh—boss—äh-regh!
Sshuuh—boss—äh-regh!
Sshuuh—boss—äh-regh!

I am sweating. My leg hurts badly, but I keep going because Comrade Arganak will not stop. Why won't he? Surely he sees I have learned his lesson ages ago. The man is unyielding. His thick smoker's voice babbles on tirelessly, so I, too, keep going.

Sshuuh—boss—äh-regh!

I feel sick. I am hot in these clothes. But apparently I look nice. The uncle, Comrade Arganak, whistled through his teeth when he saw me dressed up. Then he knit his brow.

Boss—sshuuh . . .

Why does the damned stuff have to be so tight? The skin over my wound is burning so badly I am scared it will burst. If only my brother, Comrade Principal, would come back!

Boss . . .

I can no longer stand it. Why won't he shut up? I am just going through the motions anyway, no longer needing to be told . . .

The grind started at sunrise, when Comrade Principal dragged me here and delivered me into the hands of this man. He talked to the man for some time and then left. Once I was crouching stark naked, my head shaved, in a huge trough of slimy black planks, Comrade Principal returned.

With my bare hand I tried to protect my wound from the boiling-hot water that was poured over my twitching body. Comrade Principal touched me here and scrubbed me there, told the other man I don't know what, and then left again. The man began to lather and scrub me from head to toe. I jumped and screamed when he scrubbed my wound, but he was unruffled. He pushed me to my knees and continued to manhandle me. The man was just a head with no ears and no eyes! Eventually he dried me off with a rough rag and dressed me in things I had never seen, not even in my dreams. At the time I did not have the slightest idea what they were called or what they were good for. Mainly they were a jacket and a pair of pants, both of Manchester corduroy the color of brown leather, and a pair of pointy black boots with long narrow legs.

"Stop whining. Enough is enough!" Comrade Arganak wheezed again, and then again in Tuvan. "I hope he knows how nice he looks. And I hope he remembers that not everyone has a principal for a brother."

It was almost as if he was thinking aloud. He spoke more quietly now and in no particular direction. The triangular eyes in his wrinkled face gleamed inwardly, their light almost vanished.

And now all these commands I obey. At long last Comrade Principal returns. I am about to crouch down for the umpteenth time, but I stop myself and remain standing even though I have second thoughts right away. His eyes sparkle and shine, and his hot face glows with joy. In a loud voice he offers to Comrade Arganak what must have been praise because a small trembling beam of light flits across the man's gaunt, furrowed fox face. I don't think Comrade Principal noticed. He turns to me and takes my hand, and I feel a heavy burden fall from my shoulders.

My relief disappears quickly. As we walk away, I feel a leaden weight and a dull pain in my leg. Worse still, as soon as we step outside I am told not to limp nor stare at my new clothes. I find it hard to avoid doing either, but I try.

Suddenly I am startled: a forest of people, straight rows planted in squares, rises in front of me. I recognize children's faces, like countless little fires. At the far corner of each square, a few steps apart, stands a teacher. The teachers catch and hold my eye. Increasingly I have trouble keeping up with Brother, who walks even faster as the checkered crowd approaches us with blazing faces. I am aware of how badly I limp, but can no longer pay attention to my miserable leg. Brother's strong hand pulls me forward like a horse pulling a sleigh. And so the man-horse storms toward the people-forest, breaks through between two teacher-larch trees, strides with undiminished speed past the inner edge of one of the squares, and comes to a stop at the upper end of the overall formation.

Hanging on to my hand, Brother turns around with a jerk, quickly surveys the faces with their shining eyes and trembling nostrils, and shouts into the morning like four dogs barking all at once. The children's eyes continue to shine and their nostrils to tremble, yet their bodies remain wooden and their faces stony, until suddenly they twitch and their mouths spring open. Out flies something like a short, roaring *ssen*, or "you."

Again it is Brother, or rather Comrade Principal, who barks in the same pinched voice though a little more quietly now, hurling a torrent at each face. He sounds like a long whip snaking out violently and breaking into hissing snippets. Finally, his hand lets go of mine, and briefly I feel some small relief. But then I get pushed forward. I try not to budge, but fail and end up that much more embarrassed. Now all eyes are on me. My face feels as if the faces across from me were flamethrowers, and my gaze wanders to flee from their intrusive eyes. I wish I could stop myself, but I can't help noticing that none of the other children are in clothes like mine.

At last Comrade Principal falls silent. The familiar sounds of life stop as the crowd reverts to an icy silence. But not for long. Steps disturb it, like a flattened club crashing down with long swings, making the morning air and the silently expectant crowd tremble and shake. Now I can see a figure step out of line and approach me. Its gait is strange: the head keeps flinging back toward the neck; the arms take turns flying up and down, and each time one arm flies up, a leg lurches up as well, only to whip down the next moment and pound the bare ground with the boot's broad sole; at the same time, the upper body plumes and swaggers. The whole body moves with wooden stiffness.

The figure approaches in a straight line, and then I recognize a tall girl. On her right shoulder I make out the broad strap of the square, light-blue bag swinging by her hip. The closer she comes, the more unpleasant, even scary, are her angular movements. They cause clouds of dust to balloon and merge with the sunshine and air to form a reddish dust devil. When she arrives before us, one of her boots smashes into the other with a dull thud. In this way she positions herself—not in front of Comrade Principal, but in front of me. I was already stiff with fear up to my neck, but now I am frightened nearly to death.

In between these waves of terror, I can feel the bag I saw dangle next to the girl's hip now hang off me. Out of nowhere I hear my sister's voice. It startles me from my trance: Torlaa stands in front of me. But I come to understand what just occurred and what it was all about only much, much later.

The school had ninety-nine students, Sister told me later. This fact struck different people differently. Some were happy because in their eyes ninety-nine was a sacred number. They were the backward and superstitious people. Or at least that was what other people thought, Sister said. These other people lamented that so little was required in order to bring the number up to one hundred, just a single head, even if it were to contain more water than brain, still . . . Whoever held this view was of course progressive and modern.

Then there was the question of the school uniform. At the beginning of the school year, each school was allocated one complete sample uniform. The sample was modeled on the uniforms worn in the capital, and all schools were asked to duplicate it as closely as possible, by handing out free uniforms to their special students.

The special students—that is, the top students and orphans—have to get special treatment from the State and the People, always and everywhere. The State is embodied in our school, and the People in us, the students. The students are led by the Comrade Teachers, who are led in turn by Comrade Principal. This means Comrade Principal is the leader for all four teachers, one hundred students, one man cook and one woman cook, and finally for Arganak, janitor. Thus Brother Dshokonaj is the leader for all in our state school.

Soon I would be overflowing with the knowledge that had been poured into me, but this cold morning it had not yet come to that. At this point I was still an empty vessel, a dumb creature. I stood at the threshold, marking the end of my world and looking ahead helplessly to what was coming.

Sister stands in front of me, staring directly at me as if I were a dog about to attack her. She yells something that pounds on my eardrums and makes me pull a face. I understand nothing and feel even more intimidated. And I wonder: Why is Sister Torlaa showing up only now, when I haven't seen her since the summer? Why, instead of holding my head in her hands and sniffing my cheeks and whispering "Bitsheldej! Dear little one!" in her gentle voice, why does she have to yell at me in a foreign language? And where is Brother Galkaan? Where have the two been hiding since yesterday, while I have been looking and listening for them all that time? I am crushed.

Quickly I turn to run away. But a burning sensation awakes in my hips and, like a fire caused by lightning, races in opposite directions through my flesh and sinews. Nevertheless, I hobble away, dragging behind me my poor leg, which is numb with the sharp pain of my wound. I scream with pain and fury. I am enraged because, hobbling toward the gate in the sky-high fence, I already know people will catch me and lug me back like a mangy lamb. Covered with tears and snot, I will be made to stand again where I stood before.

This is exactly what happens. I get caught before I even reach the gate. Nothing helps, though I fight with what little I have. They already took my dagger and its sheath. The bone pipe, which would have come in handy as a weapon, was left behind in one of my boots. The ground beneath my feet is no longer like the steppe it once was: there isn't a single rock I could pick up. The only weapons I can draw on are my voice and my tears. I use them as best I can. I call upon Father and Mother, upon the Blue Sky and the Gray Earth, and I call upon my spirits: the Reddish-Brown Eagle with the Whistling Feathers, and the Stone-Gray Polecat with the Flaming Carnassials. May they come to free me from the fangs of the violent! And if that is impossible, may they come and sever the red thread of my life, freeing me from this wrong, from this neither-life-nor-death.

But no one comes, and nothing helps!

Dressed to kill, I am sweating. As if to mock me, my

snappy clothes are so tight I can barely breathe, let alone drop to the ground. I want to roll in the dust of the steppe like an *asa* rolling in the ashes before shifting shape. But here the steppe is swept bare and trampled colorless, and two tall boys grab my arms and carry me off like a sacrificial lamb. Squished between the boys, both as unyielding as larch posts, I am drowning in snot and tears. Although I have given up hope, I can't stop fighting and screaming, stabbed and spurred on by the human herd that seems to relish my pain and shame, like a stick teasing an animal before hunting it to death.

Sister Torlaa has beaten a retreat and blended into the sea of people behind her. Brother Galkaan is glued to the spot, but he looks pale, bleak, and bewildered. I can just make out a twitch in his cheek muscles. Like a flayed animal, I think of vengeance and can almost taste the bittersweet satisfaction.

Suddenly Comrade Principal shouts something over the tops of the heads. Row after row, the human snake backs away. Coarse, with shades of gray like yak-hair rope—it winds its way back until it slithers into the dark jaws of the school building.

Ropes of animal hair, if they are left in still water for seven-times-ten days, become snakes. The thought makes me shake with nausea. When the end of the snake's tail has disappeared and the door has been shut behind it, Comrade Principal springs back to life. He turns in the opposite direction. Just before the fence he veers sharply to the left and heads straight toward the house I was in earlier that morning, where my old clothes lie in a corner, rolled into my *lawashak*. The two boys follow him in lock-step. They continue to hold me as tightly as before, even though I no longer fight or scream but cry with abandon.

Comrade Arganak's fox face shows no trace of sur-prise when he sees us coming or, for that matter, when he sees me in such a state. He must have heard me shout and scream, and he probably watched from his window. Comrade Principal hastily starts to bellow, and then quickly disappears. One word sticks in my ear: *shorung*, prison. Comrade Arganak and the two boys, who let everything wash over their bowed heads, stay behind with me. The boys finally let go of me but continue to stand at attention, while Comrade Arganak nods toward the little pile that sits in the corner as I left it. His nod and subsequent short hiss reveal contempt and a touch of malicious pleasure. But this is another insight I will gain only later.

I stand there motionless, thinking about my situa-tion. The man hisses in Tuvan, "Stop standing there like a dummy. Are you expecting others to undress and dress you because the principal is your brother?"

I start to undress, but his scolding continues: "A worth-less dog's stomach can't even digest yellow butter, people say." Why yellow butter, I wonder, while I struggle to free my foot from the narrow boot. Yellow butter is melted but-ter and therefore has more fat, I conclude, and turn to the other foot.

I am not the least bit sorry to give up my new clothes. To the contrary, I am relieved. In my old familiar clothes I'll be able to move again with ease. But I wonder whether to keep the white long underpants. The fox eyes pursue me, and I get caught as I try to throw my *lawashak* over the underpants.

"Pants off!" he hisses. And then comes an even more threatening, murderous hiss. For one leg of my underpants is stained with blood.

"Look at it: beautiful, brand-new underpants and he's already made a mess of them."

The underpants are pushed under the boys' noses. Both boys start back with anxious disgusted expressions. "This is a matter of state property. I am accountable to the People and the State. And I couldn't care less who happens to be your brother. I shall report your case and make sure the State gets compensated."

With these words Comrade Arganak throws the underpants in my face. I wait a bit before I pick them up off the floor. A little later, assuming I have wrecked them so badly I will have to replace them anyway, I try to put them back on. But they are so brusquely ripped from my hands that I expect a thrashing as well.

So I button up my *lawashak* and reach for my belt.

"Aren't you going to wear underpants?" the man asks, a bit more gently this time.

"I don't have any," I say quietly.

"You have no underpants!" the man hisses, craning his thin neck. His skin is wrinkled and flabby. He further screws up his already narrowly slanted eyes. They have a yellowish-green gleam. He tiptoes toward me.

I remain silent and look at the floor, embarrassed in front of the boys. I hate this man so much that if I had a cup of steaming-hot tea in my hand, I would fling it right in his face.

The man turns to the boys: "This is the son of Shynykbaj and the grandson of Khylbangbaj, and he is not wearing underpants. Do you know what that shows? It shows miserliness. And it is precisely miserliness that makes a *baja* and distinguishes him from other people."

Turning toward the slighter of the two, he continues: "You're Tenekesh's son, aren't you? I thought so. You have ears like a summer hamster and a bony nose with sunken nostrils like a thirsty goat. That tells me whose child you are. Your grandfather Güsgeldej was one of Khylbangbaj's many laborers. Ask your father if I'm right. He will tell you. And tell your father that today a grandson of the famous *baj* has shown up with a bare ass, and that Arganak, the grandson of the have-not Sidikej and the son of the have-not Dojtuk, has given him a pair of underpants."

With these words he turns to me and dangles the underpants in front of my nose as if teasing a dog with a bone. His left thumb and index finger seize such a tiny corner that it looks as if he's about to let go.

I stand there motionless.

But when I feel one of the underpants' legs softly slap my face, I snatch the garment and fling it at the wall as hard as I can.

Suppressed laughter rings out, lonely sickening laughter. Neither boy joins in. I glimpse nervous curiosity in their faces, which is vaguely comforting. Like a beast of prey facing its hunter, I have a liberating sense of determination.

The man still will not leave me alone. He inches closer. His size terrifies me, and I hear a voice inside warn me: Watch out and hold tight!

For now I concentrate and keep my eyes on the crumpled underpants in his bony black fist as he waddles toward me. But the moment he shoves his fist with the underpants in my face and gives me a rough punch on the nose, my jaws snap shut and bite down. Something hard and soft is between my rows of teeth; I taste blood and hear a crunching sound that clearly drags on.

Again I hear the voice inside: Spit it out!

I spit. A blubbery dark mass like dog crap shoots at the gaunt old face, which is contorted with fear. It hits the face on the right and turns dark red as it spreads across the man's eye, nose, and chin.

Because I can taste the blood more distinctly now, I go to spit again. But before I can, I am throwing up.

THE PRISONER

Did I really live through all this? Or was it all a dream? I feel as if I have been beaten and crushed, and died and gone to hell. But I have my things on me: my head scarf is in my breast pocket and my bone pipe tucked in my boot. A dead sheep gets its wool plucked, a dead yak its skin flayed. All things are taken from the dead so they may stand naked and bare before Erlikbej. Hence I cannot be dead. That I am in pain is yet another sign that I am alive. My head rings, my ribs hurt, my ears burn. I seem to recall punches and kicks. But I am just a child, and he is a grown man, strong enough to kill a dog, or even a yak.

Some time ago, I sensed a strong brightness. I must have been outside. Then it turned dark again. Wood squeaked and iron clanked. There were other sounds as well, and there seemed to be other bodies along with something I sensed most distinctly: raw meat. It was no longer fresh and had a pungent smell. And there was no breeze to carry away the sweetish smell of the blood trapped in the meat.

Beneath me I feel damp cool gravel. A small clump of earth under the gravel is slimy. A musty smell assaults my senses and makes my eyes water. I shouldn't lie here any longer. I should try to escape. I lift my head slowly, prop myself up on my elbows, and slowly sit up. The darkness around me spins. My mouth feels sticky, and the skin on my face is taut as if covered in glue. When the spinning stops, I decide to explore my environment. Stretching my arms sideways, I bump into a wooden log panel on my right and recognize peeled larch beams stacked on top of each other. I feel my way along the wall and reach a corner where another wall starts, this one cooler and smoother but also made from larch beams.

So I did land in prison.

I have heard of prison. Everyone fears it. Prison is where enemies of the People are sent. In the beginning there were many enemies, now not so many. Most of them have been eliminated, a few reeducated.

Samdar is one who went to prison and returned. Once he stayed overnight at our yurt and talked through half the night. He spent ten years in prison, the first three of them alone in complete darkness. His cell was narrow and built of stone, and he was allowed outside for just ten minutes a day. Just long enough to finish a bowl of hot tea, he said. Prison tea comes without milk or salt and is drunk from a tin cup instead of a proper bowl. Along with the tea, prisoners get a piece of black bread no bigger than two matchstick boxes. I have had tea without milk or salt, but I have never had bread. I would love to try some — ideally, right now.

After that night Father and Mother's fear of prison seemed to grow. As we say in our family, any yak cow that fails to calve and any sheep whose wool gets lost can land you in prison. So far we have fulfilled our quota, if barely.

And as for me now?

I feel a light but insistent pressure from my bladder. What to do? I must explore my cell and find out what I have here. Samdar said he had a plank bed and a tin bucket. I may have a bucket, too. If I don't, I'll have to find a corner to relieve myself in, at least for now.

The beams lead me farther. My prison seems big compared to Samdar's. Its floor drops. The farther down I go, the eerier it seems. First I think of a cave, then again of hell. Maybe I should turn around. What if this gaping mouth has no end, or if an abyss opens up suddenly?

My hand touches something soft, and I quickly pull back. Then I reach out to touch it again. It must be flour — many sacks, piled on top of each other. One sack contains something grainy. Is it rice? Rice grains are not this small and round. It must be millet. The discovery brightens my spirits. Now I think I can see what towers in front of me: a heap of white sacks, filled to bursting with powdery snow-white flour. Not even Father has ever seen this much flour. He brings home flour in a small rumen bag I can easily carry over my shoulder. In exchange for the pelts and small intestines he takes to the trading agent he receives not only flour, but also brick tea, salt, rice, gunpowder, lead, primer, candles, and wolf poison. When she stands in front of the provisions Father brings home, Mother always gets a little shaky before solemnly proposing: "Let's have a look at the flour and the tea."

If I were to show her this heap of flour and say "You can have a whole sack," she would probably pass out. But if she didn't, I'd say, "Have as much as you like, Mother. Take not only flour, but millet as well!" Then she would say, "Really? This is such fine food—but I won't eat, my dear child, unless you will, too," and then she would pause. Once, a long time ago, I ate so much cooked millet that now I can no longer stand it. So Father stopped buying millet. At this point I would say, "I'll find something else to eat. You go ahead and have the millet. You like it, don't you?"

I am burning with curiosity as I feel my way forward. I can feel shelves with more sacks. Salt, I realize. And onions. Finally I come across the meat whose sweetish-foul smell is making my prison unbearable. It is leftover meat from a goat's spine. I shake my head: why would pieces of marrow that should have been used up first be left while the haunches and ribs are gone? I can hardly believe what I discover next: a heavy wooden box full of sugar cubes. The box has been torn open and it is almost full. What would happen if I were to haul out the heavy box and open it in front of our clan's children? They'd probably cry out in shock and then fall silent for who knows how long. In the end they might tear into the box. After much hesitation I take four sugar cubes and tuck them into my breast pocket.

At that moment I hear a sound like a pebble rolling across a stretched hide. It seems very close, almost inside my right ear, and makes me jump. Is it a mouse? I hold my breath and listen, but all I can hear is my own heartbeat. My whole body is shaking. No matter how hard I try, I don't hear the sound again. But then I think I can actually see the mouse. It appears and disappears, runs away and back toward me. It is a hideous long-tailed mouse with bald skin and a bloated belly. Its kidneys shine bluish through its thin skin.

"One of your clan's chieftains was devoured by mice," Camel-Lips Shunu told me one day while he watched me hunt them. Why, he wanted to know, was I not afraid of mice? Of course one doesn't believe everything Shunu says, particularly since his camel lips made a strange laugh after he asked me. But he was basically right. Father can't even bear hearing about mice. If he happens to see one, his hand instantly reaches for the dagger on his belt. Mother doesn't go so far as pulling a knife when a mouse crosses her path. But she uses language she would never use otherwise, which is bad enough. Everyone in the *ail* finds mice disgusting. And disgust is worse than fear.

The pressure from my bladder, which I had forgotten, reasserts itself. I lose interest in my treasure and turn away from the shelf. Arms stretched out and head tucked in, I trot forward. Going up feels better than down, and I feel relieved because I imagine the exit is close. Instead I soon run into the log panel. No matter how carefully I grope to the right and to the left, my paths are blocked by walls of big hard beams, as solid as rock.

I keep trying to find an exit or at least a nook, but in the end I give up and pee on the beams.

The mouse I see in my mind's eye lingers close by. It stares at me with bulging glassy eyes full of insolence and suspicion, so I don't dare sit on the ground. Each time it gets close, I make the whistling and snorting sounds I would use to drive a herd. The mouse backs off, but soon comes scuttling toward me again.

When I see the animal becoming more brazen, I realize I must kill it. I pick up a handful of the larger pebbles and wait. Soon the mouse appears, smirking and squatting on its hind legs, its glassy eyes fixed on me. I move a pebble from my left to my right hand and hold it with three fingertips the way one pulls an arrow from the quiver to nock it on the bowstring. Then I take aim: the tip of the index finger of my outstretched left arm aims at the mouse while I pull my bent right arm back to propel the pebble. Missed!

A little later the animal is back. This time it senses my plan as soon as my right hand reaches for the pebble in my left one. There—the mouse is gone! I position myself for another attack and wait once more, my left arm stretched out, aiming for its target, and my right arm lifted, ready to hurl the pebble. For quite some time the coward stays away. When it finally returns, I immediately fling my pebble, but miss again. Enraged, I curse myself: "May my eyes go blind and my hands lame! I'll never hit a marmot, let alone a mouse. Try something better!" Next, I take all the pebbles into my right hand. However, I don't want to rely on any old number. There must be exactly thirteen pebbles. Holding them close to my lips, I breathe into them and implore, "May you each be a shard of the stones of the Altai's thirteen *ovoos,* and may you all carry their holy spirit!"

Then I straighten and ready myself to hurl them. My right arm is up, its hand clenched in a fist. And so I wait until my arms, neck, back, and legs are paralyzed and almost numb. At long last, the wretched creature reappears. I fling my fist forward with such force that it jerks my body forward as well and I stumble a couple of steps. By a hair's breadth I miss knocking myself over, but I have hit my target. I see, I hear, and I know I have hit the beast. It is dead.

Feeling very calm, I sit down. Tiredness envelops me like fog. I fall asleep and some time later, still aware of my circumstances, curl up on the ground like a dog and succumb to the sweetest dream I have ever been granted in my whole life.

I am awakened by a light but do not rise. Instead I let the person, whose steps I hear, come close and pull me up. Above me, I see a tall yellow-faced man in a short white cape. He looks at me sternly.

"Did you pee?"

"Yes."

"Did you take a shit?"

"No."

"Did you steal anything?"

"No. But I did take four sugar cubes."

"Did you eat them?"

"No."

I take the four sugar cubes from my breast pocket: "Here they are."

I try to hand them over, but he does not take them. Instead, he closes my fingers around them and gives me a glance. I quickly put the sugar cubes away again.

He walks ahead, and I follow. We walk through two doors and climb a number of steep steps in between. At the top, on the ground, the stout man with horsefly eyes from the day before is waiting for us. He says something I don't understand, but because he gestures with his head, I realize I am to follow him. The other man stays behind. His face with its yellow hair radiates something I feel on my back for a long time—something filling me with warmth and light. He must have followed me with his eyes and thought words he could not say to me.

I feel his gaze on my back as intensely as the sun, which now burns brighter than ever ahead of me in the southern sky, blinding my eyes. I am curious where exactly the prison is located and what it looks like from the outside, but I am scared the horsefly eyes will keep peeking at me, and so I dare not turn. Besides, the man is moving so fast I have to struggle hard not to fall behind.

Children stop their play and scatter as we pass. Each child moves alone, and they all look down and avoid us. But I can hear them whispering behind our backs.

One says, "There's the runaway," and another, "Looks as if he's been beaten." And a third one says, "From the cold, dark hell into the bright white one." Maybe the man really does not understand Tuvan, I think hopefully.

Some time later my mind must have stopped working. All of a sudden I see in front of me a woman who, with her hair twisted and piled high, seems to have two heads. She must be the one who just dragged me across the doorstep. From her manner I recognize her as the woman with the shrill voice from the day before. Strangely, now I understand everything she carps on about. When I realize I am sucking on one of my fingers, I quickly take it out of my mouth, let my hand drop, and press it, like the other one, on my hip. Then I try to get my bearings: I am in a room with many different red colors and a mirrorlike finish. High up on the walls hang satin banners the color of lungs and as wide as the span of a hand. They display white letters and frame the room. Below them, large-faced and clean-shaven men look out from square frames of various sizes.

Brother Dshokonaj sits behind a large table, writing. Besides the woman and the man who brought me here, two other men are in the room; in contrast to the first two, these other two men and the woman all wear *lawashaks*. But all four wear the same narrow black boots that gleam like mirrors, and all four remain standing even though there are benches. They face Comrade Principal and wait for him to stop writing.

At long last he lays down his quill pen, looks up, and casts a quick but thorough eye on each of the four. He says something, and everyone sits down. Only now does his gaze fall on me, and it is as if a whirling storm were blowing toward me. Yet instead of letting myself get blown away, I stiffen my neck and hold my ground. Or rather, I quickly gather the breezes inside me and send my wind to battle his storm because I hear that voice inside again: Stand up for yourself!

Immediately the storm breaks and a warm veil appears in the gap. "What's happened to you? Has someone beaten you?" Brother asks. I am unprepared for this. My wind falters, I lower my eyes, and tears well up.

Enraged, Brother Dshokonaj snaps at the stout man. As if stung, the man jumps up. His horsefly eyes pop even more and shine as he glares at me and yells in the coarsest Tuvan, "Did I so much as touch you? Hey! Speak up, boy, loud and clear, so your brother and the comrades can hear!"

I shake my head.

Apparently that does not satisfy the man. He charges at me, inspects my head close up, and, pausing on and off, goes on to list all my bruises and scars, and even the grains of sand clinging to my head. He concludes in Tuvan, "Boy, you have been beaten black and blue!"

I whisper more than speak, "I don't know."

"You do know!" shouts the principal. "Was it the old man in the bath shed?"

"Yes," I say with a loud sob. Someone is sent off and returns with Fox-face. In the meantime, I have a chance to compose myself because they ignore me while conferring with one another. They sound agitated and seem to be of one mind.

Comrade Principal turns to Arganak and speaks down to him as if from a great height. His face is rigid and his voice strained. Arganak must have seen it coming because he immediately lets rip. He talks loud and fast and steps up his efforts until he screams and stammers as if he is being whipped. At the same time he waves his right hand wildly, his thumb wrapped in a thick white bandage. Brother seems unimpressed and listens, his face impassive. When he tries to interrupt, Arganak gets even wilder, throws himself at me, grabs my *lawashak* and lifts its bottom. Through it all, he continues to jabber.

Later I learn what he said. Since I did not have any underwear of my own, he said, I had refused to return the State's pair. Dutiful Party member that he is, he tried to reclaim State property. At which point I bit into his thumb. The story of the underpants impresses everyone. They immediately seem to turn against me.

Fox-face harps on for a while. *Darga* is the one word in his tirade I can pick up now and again, and I know what it means. Barricaded behind his desk, Comrade Principal shrinks before Comrade Arganak. In the end, little is left of Comrade Principal's rigid face and strained voice. Having first ordered him to appear, Comrade Principal now respectfully asks Arganak to leave. And in the end, the man leaves without having calmed down. He turns around at the door, waves his hand some more, and points his heavily bandaged thumb at the principal. The gesture seems threatening.

The people left in the room now speak Tuvan, apparently because of me. The people who forbade any use of their native tongue now violate the rule. From their speech I gather which tribe each comes from: the stout man and the man next to him with the narrow light-skinned face and the bushy eyebrows are Ak Sayan; the woman is Hara Sayan; while the quiet man with the broad shoulders who went to get Fox-face is Gök Mondshak, like Brother.

"Listen carefully. This is all about you and your future," Comrade Principal says to me. He has repositioned himself behind the desk and gone back to his rigid face and strained voice. "That we are both sons of one mother," he adds, "is now irrelevant. This is the Teachers' Council, and the Council will decide your fate. The Council has the right to make decisions on behalf of the school, and hence of the State. In its decision the Council may or may not consider what you have to say and how you conduct yourself."

Then he changes into the official language. What he says is short. I take it to mean: Now it is your turn to talk, and ours to listen.

The woman demands to know why I fled. I don't know what I could possibly tell her and remain silent. When they all press me to answer, I say, "I don't know."

"Were you ashamed?"

"I think so."

"Don't you like going to school?" asks the stout man.

"I don't know."

They all get edgy and exchange glances and words.

The light-skinned man asks, "Don't you think that one day you'll want to become a teacher like the rest of us, or even a principal like your big brother?"

What can I say when what I really want is to become a shaman. So I ask, "Can a teacher be a shaman?"

Buttocks shift nervously in seats, and again glances and words fly.

"What's that? Are you actually thinking of becoming a shaman?"

"Oh yes."

Silence descends.

Brother's eyes glare threateningly and his cheekbones twitch. But it seems to happen somewhere far away, leaving me strangely unaffected.

The silence spreads to the walls and corners of the room, blanketing everything with an invisible veil of ice. I feel chilled, and when the broad-shouldered man breaks the silence, I can hear a soft clinking.

"I understand you are a boy who loves to sing," he says. "Is this true?"

"It's true."

But the man with the light-skinned face interrupts: "You did say shaman, right?"

"Yes."

Comrade Principal slams his fist on his desk and jumps up. "Nonsense. You're a snot-nosed little squirt. Don't you lie to us."

"I'm not lying."

I can say that with complete peace of mind and look

him in the eye to remind him: You have seen me with your own eyes. But I worry about the others. Will they believe me? Hardly. Then I remember my shaman's pipe. Once they see it, they will realize I'm not lying. I bend down and pull the pipe from my boot.

"See? This is my pipe. I smoke it before I shamanize."

I can tell everyone is shocked. For a short moment, Brother forgets he is the principal. He looks helpless and swallows. Then he pulls himself together, marches up to me, and waves his right hand, his index finger as stiff and pointy as a raven's beak: "And to top it all off, you're a smoker? You spoiled-rotten fool!" And with these words, he rips the pipe from me. "What else do you have?"

"My scarf." I slip my hand into my breast pocket and pull it out. Something hard falls out in the process—a sugar cube.

"Where did you get that?"

I pause, stutter, and then admit: "In prison."

"Well, well, well! Do you have more of them?"

My hand slips back into my breast pocket and fishes for the other three: "These are all I have."

"Put everything over here."

I put my scarf and all four sugar cubes on his desk.

"What else do you have?"

"Nothing."

"There's no point in trying to hide. Don't even think about it. We'll strip you and check everything."

"I don't have anything else." By now I can no longer help myself. With a trembling, tearful voice I say, "Everything I

have said is true, dearest Brother. I really don't have anything else."

But I am questioned and scolded further.

The stout man asks, "Were those sugar cubes perhaps
lying under the gravel in your prison?"

"No. They were in a box."

"And did they jump into your pocket on their own?"

"No."

"How did they get there?"

"I took them."

"Wrong. You did not take them. What you have done
is called something else."

"I put them in my pocket?"

"Try again."

"I stole them?"

"Yes, that's exactly what you did. You stole them! And
so you are a thief."

The light-skinned man lists my misdeeds: "So you dis-
rupted the assembly, you bit and injured a man, you are
underage and you smoke, you want to become a shaman,
and you have committed theft. Do you know what all that
adds up to?"

Because I don't know what to say, I wait and remain
silent.

The stout one summarizes: "You have violated five
State laws. What do you have to say?"

I still don't know what to say.

The woman concludes: "These are more than enough
reasons for the school to expel you."

It dawns on me suddenly that I may not need to go to school after all.

"Do you realize what that would mean?"

I shake my head.

"Well I do. If we don't admit you, you'll always be a primitive nomad, like your father or any man who tends his flocks, hunts marmots, and gathers dung."

This prospect does not frighten me in the least. Quite the opposite, in fact: I am relieved. If that is all there is to it, I will go home singing. Now that I have tainted his reputation, Brother will have to take me back across the river.

But the stout one pipes back up: "That would be much too easy. Everyone in this room is a State schoolteacher. We all fight for the cause of the Party and the State, and some of us wear the blood-red membership booklet over our heart. So I don't see how we can possibly avoid reporting your case, which — to me, anyway — appears to be very grave indeed."

"That's right!" the light-skinned one interrupts. "And if we report your case — and I think we have no choice — you will go to the colony. You do know what the colony is, don't you?"

I do not know.

"It's a prison for youth. People like you are sent there. Young people who have broken the law. You won't find bright, warm rooms like this one in there. Or teachers like us, who plead with you and explain. No, my young friend, in there it's all barbed-wire fences and massive stone buildings, as hard as iron and heavy with rock. Nothing but truncheons, sharp spears, and loaded guns."

This sounds like a pretty big deal. I need to know more: "How far away is this prison for youth?"

"Very, very far. If your father wanted to visit you, he'd have to ride his horse for months just to get there."

I am very impressed. Hadn't I already thought of going away on my own?

"Is that in Ulaanbaatar by any chance?"

"It is. But don't kid yourself and imagine you're going to be sightseeing. You'll be a prisoner, and prisoners aren't allowed to take in the sights of our glorious capital. You will be taken there blindfolded, in a prison on wheels, and you'll be thrown into a concrete-and-iron cell. You won't see anything but a dark brick wall and a fence with barbed wire on top."

It still sounds intriguing. I ask if prisoners are allowed to acquire knowledge.

"Sure," the man replies offhandedly. But then he adds ominously, "In there you're not just a student. First and foremost, you're a prisoner who has to pay for his misdeeds."

This does not scare me. With the world of the unknown opening in the distance, I feel a longing to go there. "All right," I say, "then I shall pay for my misdeeds."

Brother, who has silently watched as if none of this has anything to do with him, finally speaks: "So you think this is going to be easy, eh? In that case we'll do something different: we'll send your father or mother to prison because they have raised you poorly, and keep you here instead. You'll have to study and spend your spare time in our local prison, serving the balance of your sentence."

Now I am shocked: Father or Mother sent to prison because of me! Good heavens! Brother must have observed me closely because he continues: "Now you're getting it. Your father or mother will go to prison unless you repent your bad deeds and ask the Teachers' Council for forgiveness. And you must promise to be obedient in the future."

At last I understand what I am expected to do. But to my own detriment something inside me hesitates to give in to the pressure, for I fear making a promise I may be unable to keep.

The teachers remain seated, and I remain standing. Nothing new is said. What was said before gets repeated. It is the same as circling a rock: standing still or walking makes no real difference. Eventually someone notices it is late. Everyone agrees. And then the meeting is over.

Before they leave the room, the light-skinned one has another go at me. "Do you know why you drown if you fall into a river?" he asks as he walks past. I do not know. "Because you're fighting the current," he says, not sounding unfriendly. I know what he means: I am stubborn.

"It's a pity you're not in my class, my dear. Every day I'd pound you and make you a little softer. You and your stiff neck." He laughs as he grasps the back of my head. His grip is rough, and I feel as if he is going to rip my head off. But I stand firm and clench my teeth, pressing my tongue hard against them. "Still," he adds before letting go, "I hope we'll bump into each other from time to time."

That evening, I get dragged through another meeting. Sister Torlaa, who now insists on being called Dsandan, chairs what she calls the "Council of Siblings." Brother Dshokonaj makes no comment. What is worse, I don't even know if he is listening. He lies on his bed and stares at the poles supporting the yurt's roof. Brother Galkaan, whom we are now to call Gagaa, is a quiet, attentive listener. He limits himself to regular if brief affirmative responses.

Sister really takes off: "Brother Dshokonaj has acquired that most valuable of all treasures: knowledge. He is the first in our clan to have come this far. Our clan, supposedly rich with herds, children, and fame, was in reality caught in darkness and as ignorant and pathetic as everyone else. Not every clan can produce a teacher, and not every teacher becomes a principal. Our brother has achieved both. We should be proud of him and pleased with his success. Pleased, in particular, because as the eldest he shows the rest of us the path to knowledge.

"Yesterday," she continues, "urged by myself and Brother Gagaa, Brother Dshokonaj crossed the wild river, risking his life twice. As the Council of Siblings we had decided to fetch you and bring you here to live with us. Now we four can stand surrounded by the winds that blow from the four directions, warming and supporting each other. You're the lucky one who could have brought the number of students to exactly one hundred. You would have complemented both us and the whole school. And, as Number One Hundred, you would have been honored with a reward: you would have got a complete school uniform for free, a style no one here has ever seen, let alone worn. What a re-lief that would have been for Father and Mother! They suf-fer under the burdens of livestock taxes and quotas. How they would rejoice over any lamb they could save!"

So far, in spite of her superior, unshakable manner and her fighting spirit—her grandmotherly tone, as Father always called it—she has been relatively restrained. But now comes the about-face. Just as I have anticipated and feared, she loses it: "You must have been possessed by the devil, you miserable snot! Your brother Dshokonaj put good fortune on the tip of your tongue like a drop of sweet cream, and you spat it out. Why didn't you swallow? You made us all look like fools."

She bursts into tears, shakes and twitches, and screeches as if in great pain.

Brother Gagaa agrees: "Yes, Galdan. You've broken something and you'll never be able to put it back together again."

His words make Sister cry even harder. She sobs as if struck by terrible misfortune. Brother Dshokonaj lies mo-tionless and stares into space. In the flickering light from the stubby candle his wide-open eyes have a terrifying shine.

Oh heaven, oh earth! I think. What have I done to cause my sister and both brothers such misery? I try to look inside myself and find only a dark void. I listen for sounds outside and hear a distant dull roar. The cursed voice that so readily spurred me on to all sorts of imper-tinent remarks has fallen silent. Has it abandoned me? Why?

Sister has finished crying. "Worst of all," she says calmly but firmly, "your foolishness is putting others at risk. Envious people have been given ammunition. What if someone hears about what happened today and uses it to go to battle against Father or Brother? Father is the son of a *kulak* and not poor enough, and Brother is new at his job and not yet in the Party. Neither sits firm in his saddle."

I am not sure I follow everything she says, but I do understand "going to battle" and "not sitting firm in the saddle." I get what that means.

I recall Arganak's fox face and manner. And I see Brother Dshokonaj lying in front of me, with his pale expressionless face and his shining eyes, looking lost.

"What do you think I should do?" My voice sounds alien.

Sister flares up: "Stop acting crazy!" But this time she calms down quickly and starts sewing me a pair of pants.

"And listen to us, your brother and sister," Brother Gagaa speaks up. "Above all, listen to your eldest brother. The State has entrusted him with leading a whole school. If he knows how to lead a hundred, he knows how to keep the three of us on the straight and narrow."

Suddenly I become the most attentive listener. Our big brother—head of our tiny State yurt with its four scissor-grid walls—lies flat on his back and grieves, but things around him are happening. Sister is sewing, younger Brother is cooking noodles, and I am the nimble errand boy flitting about, doing what I am told. I poke the fire, peel the onions, wash the pots, and am once more the baby whose small, nameless services are available to all. But in truth I am weighed down with worries. Fear as cold as ice clings to my inside like a tick: what if . . . ?

When my much maligned, hapless bottom is finally clad in a pair of pants, I feel a quiet joy warming me down there and inside. But Gagaa and Dsandan, whom I secretly keep calling Galkaan and Torlaa, have to leave for the night, and that prospect casts a dark cloud over my joy. It is hard to spend another night with the man who is more Comrade Principal than a big brother to me. And the prospect of many more such nights is very discouraging. The dormitory, on the other hand, which I have not seen but have heard quite a bit about, seems more bearable. At this point, though, I don't even know if I will be readmitted to school at all.

Brother Dshokonaj, brought back to his feet by the noodle soup, figures that the rule forbidding students to spend the night away from the dormitory applies especially to any relatives of the teaching staff. I am left behind with him and have no idea how this or future nights will unfold.

Later he says, "If you want to get ahead in life, you must first promise to learn."

Then he asks if I understand.

I nod.

"How can I know if you really understand?" he says.

I think about it for a while. Then I say, "I promise that starting tomorrow I'll do everything I'm asked to do."

The Onset
of Winter

Already at the beginning of the last month of autumn we get snow that stays. It starts snowing while the sun is still up and continues late into the night. The next morning the Altai lies transformed, a brilliant flaming white. Only the caves and crags and the river stand out black against the sea of white. The air is still and the sun shines mild and timid. Around noon the surface of the snow begins to melt, and soon the Altai is barely visible beneath a layer of fog.

But the sun is not warm enough to break through the snow cover; the day is too short, and soon the sun abandons the earth to the night. Everything cools off and freezes. The snow forms a crust of ice over the mountain and steppe. Any wind would be too late now. It would only further seal the cover of snow.

Rumors, mostly bad, abound. The snow is said to have

had a bluish tinge first and a greenish one later. I saw neither a bluish nor a greenish gleam, but later I remember that there were grains of sand in the snow I scraped off the roof of our yurt.

The shaman Shalabaj is rumored to have announced that a great upheaval is coming, both for Mongolia and for our small home country in the Altai. The shaman Ürenek is said to have confirmed this, and even to have predicted early spring as the precise time for the upheaval. I have met neither of these two shamans, but I have heard that they are enemies, and that Ürenek is not even a real shaman, but only reads oracles. "And even then I wouldn't exchange Ürenek for three Shalabajs," Mother once said in an argument where she took Ürenek's side against Father. Referring to the women's latest quarrel, Father had praised Shalabaj's art a bit too loudly. Worse, he called her beautiful.

My wounds have healed. I am no longer Limpy. Instead, I am now called the Runaway. The whole class uses this nickname, and half the school knows it means me. Yes, I have become a student, and a good one at that. Learning comes easily to me, say people who would know. It took Brother and Sister no more than a few afternoons to teach me the letters and numbers. Letters and numbers have long stopped being lines and circles, pliers and hammers. I have learned their meanings and can drive them toward each other like sheep and goats. Animals get milked and letters get read; the latter make words instead of milk.

Each word contains a meaning, as each chest contains a heart and each belly a stomach.

The teacher praises me, even when he scolds others, such as Billy Goat. The tip of Billy Goat's tongue always sticks out, and most of the time his face looks unwashed, particularly around his eyebrows. When you look at his face, you really are reminded of a billy goat during mating season, all spent and sticky. On the class list Billy Goat's name is Ombar. Even though he is in our grade for a second year, he has trouble with numbers. He cannot tell you what seven ankle bones plus five adds up to. Other people have other problems. Some students cannot keep the different letters apart.

Sürgündü, who is nicknamed Old Woman, has been through first grade twice before. She disappeared both years soon after she was warned that she would have to repeat the grade. Her tongue is so lazy it would be covered with rust and notches if it were a knife.

"If you aren't too embarrassed, Old Woman, ask the little guy. He grasped in three days what you haven't learned in three years." The teacher has started to play us against each other. At first this flattered me, I have to admit. It was then that I changed from calling him the Stout One to the Teacher. But the greater gain of that day was something else. I decided to behave differently toward the girl. Seeing the poor thing humiliated by the teacher—hence by the school and by the State it represents and the teacher embodies—and seeing him get away with treating her so mercilessly made me forget the pain she had caused me. I had kept it alive like embers under the ashes, but now I feel increasingly sorry for her as she stands there groaning, her quiet green eyes filling with tears. As I watch how she fails to remember some small thing—something insignificant, really—I no longer understand the world. I wonder whether to whisper the answer, which is on the tip of my tongue. But I can't make myself do it, mostly because I don't want to cause her any more pain.

But the teacher doesn't only praise me. I have made my bed and now I often have to lie in it. When I do anything wrong, he reminds me I have been a bad egg right from the start.

Most of the criticism I receive comes from my sister. Arganak, she whispers into my ear, has submitted a formal complaint about Brother Dshokonaj to the District Administration. She pulls a face as if she has eaten a mouthful of salt. Shortly afterward I find out this really is a bitter lump: since Arganak is a Party member and the principal is not, things easily could go wrong for us.

Brother seems downcast. He spends most evenings flat on his back with his mouth shut. His eyes shine, not angrily but helplessly. I still live with him. Once or twice I cautiously ask about the dormitory. He says they don't have an extra bed unless someone moves out to live with relatives or friends. Then he declares it better for me to stay with him anyway. But he doesn't say why. If that's the case, I ask, why don't Sister Dsandan and Brother Gagaa live with us as well? They are fully registered and settled at the dormitory, he says, and already were before he even arrived at the school.

Some time later he says, "One day someone may drop by for a visit. It'll be better if Sister weren't here, what with her loose tongue and strong opinions." When is one day? I ask myself. Who might come? And why? But I keep these questions to myself.

Another time he says to me, "After all, you're my brother." It sounds as if he were saying I was family and the others were not, and I feel badly for them.

Before this conversation takes place, a bad storm comes up in the afternoon, followed by a cold evening, and our yurt gets warped out of shape and turns freezing cold inside. I come home that day and immediately sit down to my homework, secretly waiting for Sister Torlaa and Brother Galkaan to come and take care of the stove and the dinner. But no one comes. Instead, the wind, which has been strong all day, develops into a storm. The yurt flaps and squeaks, swaying and creaking ever more dangerously. Some of the roof poles come crashing down. I race over to the neighbors to ask for help, but they are busy securing their own yurts. So I run back and start to weigh down our yurt. I put gravel into everything that has a round belly—every bag and sack, bucket and bowl, even the round tin stove. Then I tie all these things to the end of a rope whose other end I tie to the roof ring. Finally, I take whatever else can serve as a weight, tie ropes around it all, and drag the pile into the middle. Our yurt, which normally looks so tidy and orderly, is a terrible mess. But I successfully defend it against the storm.

That evening Brother comes home late. The storm has eased a bit since sunset, but the sea of dust outside still rages and whirls, which is why I have not lit the candle. I am sitting on the mountain of stuff with my arms and legs curled around the rope. The pile must have had a considerable weight already, but after a while I had decided, prompted partly by boredom and partly by thoughtfulness, to add my own little weight as well. Then I fell asleep..

I wake up when Brother lights a match and calls for me: "Dshuruunaj, where are you?"

"Up here," I say sleepily. I yawn and climb down. I expect to get into trouble for falling asleep or for making such a mess, or most likely for both. But instead I am praised for my efforts: "I see you've worked really hard, little man. You turned the yurt into a fortress and barricaded yourself in. You've put up a real fight!"

He tells me quite a few yurts have been blown away or flattened by the storm. "But you saved ours. That's amazing! The yurt is our small country. I can tell you're going to be a great fighter." He adds that he, too, would have expected Brother and Sister to come and take care of me and the yurt.

It is freezing cold in our rescued yurt. But because the storm is not over, we don't dare light a fire. So we get ready to go to bed. Then Brother says, "Come over. We'll sleep in one bed—it'll be easier and warmer, won't it?"

His suggestion leaves me trembling with fear—and joy. I have never shared a bed with him. In the past, when he would visit and ask Mother if he could take me, his little brother, to his bed, I always whined that I wanted to sleep with Father and Mother.

I don't respond. But I take off my clothes, climb on the bed with its shiny iron frame and billowing feathers, and crawl under the downy quilt, between the snow-white sheets. They feel smooth and cool. This is my first time on a high bed under a soft white quilt. Earlier that day, before starting my homework, I had climbed on this bed with its velvety covers and silky curtains and fluffed the feathers a little to make them billow and sing. When will the day come, I wondered, when I could sleep in such a bed? And now I'm about to do just that!

Brother's body is colder than mine. While I have goose bumps all over, his skin is smooth, as cold as ice and as slippery as a fish. We have snuggled into each other and are shivering and talking. I tell him about the grades I got in class and about my battle to save the yurt. He mentions a meeting, but doesn't say what it was about. I do learn, though, that the meeting took so long that in the end everyone had a headache. One man—the doctor, of all people—even passed out. Brother, who had learned first aid at the teachers' college, helped to revive him. "I felt that I had a special duty to save the man," he says. "After all, he fainted at a meeting that was called because of me." He doesn't elaborate. The next morning the whole school will know.

Suddenly he says something that shocks me: he has never shared a bed with a brother or sister. When I hear this, I feel really bad inside. I am ashamed for all of us children, and I am ashamed for Mother for never giving me a slap on the bottom and telling me to share the bed with my big brother. Most of all, I am ashamed for Father. After he married Mother and our big brother was sent off to be raised by his grandmother, Father never found a way to bond with him, nor helped the rest of us to do so.

Outside the storm is calming down, and yet the yurt still trembles like some creature that reaches in vain for a handhold, but grasps only air and cannot rest. Our bodies warm, and as I snuggle with Brother, I feel incomparably happy about the night that stretches out ahead of us, about the soft bed that quivers under its fluffy quilt even when I scarcely move, and about the joy a mother's two children are finally giving each other. Anticipating good dreams, I drift, doze, and sink into sleep . . .

The next morning it is clear that winter has arrived. This winter is as bright as ice and shimmers from all sides of the Altai. The mere sight of all the ice in the distance makes one shiver. A current of cold air flows briskly, and the river that only yesterday was as smooth as a mirror and stood out as black as night against the white snow is now full of ice floes, clustered like so many lichen-backed folktale characters.

Brother struggles to get a fire going. But once it takes off, it warms the yurt in no time. We cook slices of meat in our milkless tea and realize only when we start eating that we were both starving. Everything tastes the better for it, and we are that much happier. While we solemnly eat our breakfast, Brother says, "I don't know what they are going to say to us brothers this morning or in the future. But I do know that we will be fine in the end. We must never forget to do whatever we are asked to do. Otherwise we'll perish. That's life."

He casts a quick glance at me. His eyes look empty and melancholy. I believe I understand what he is saying and assure him: "I'll do everything you say, Brother."

On the way to school we are dreadfully cold. When we arrive, we are not allowed in. The light-skinned teacher blocks the door by pushing his back against it and shouts something of which I understand only the words *party cell* and *school assembly*. He doesn't even let the principal pass, and I notice Brother is the one who offers the first greeting. Has Brother lost his position?

We walk over to the assembly. People arrive and quickly line up in rows. Brother Dshokonaj seems not to be needed at all, so he stands aside and waits silently. He seems thinner and smaller than before. Meanwhile, the other teachers bustle about and bark commands into the freezing-cold morning.

It is a long time before anything happens. The student body—class after class, row after row—stamps the icy, rock-hard ground in an attempt to keep their feet from getting frostbitten. Finally the man everyone has been waiting for appears: Jadmaj, Secretary of the District Party Cell. I have seen him and his chrome-tanned leather bag with the flashing metal clasp before, and I know what people call him: Hos Haaj, Hollow Nose.

He comes waddling along, wearing a Kazakh black coat as tall as the man and as wide as the steppe. His chrome-leather bag dangles at his side from a shoulder strap made with polished metal rings. Arganak and Oksum trail about three paces behind him.

Oksum is the father of my classmate Orgush, and I have seen him before. I have also heard that Oksum is an *udarnik*. I am not sure what it means, but I believe an *udarnik* is a tireless worker. Some of the adults I know also work very hard, but they all get tired eventually. Oksum, on the other hand, is rumored to have worked nonstop for months and years. When his story made the rounds, Uncle Know-It-All burst out laughing and said, "We know Dugdurak's boy, don't we? As far as I remember, he used to eat, drink, shit, piss, slack off, and sleep just like the rest of us."

When he heard that, Father told off his older brother: "Let people say what they want. Better you don't pay attention to what comes out of their holes. And keep your own shut. Or better still, act as if you don't have one. Master that art, or you'll end up in the Black Yurt."

The teacher who had kept everyone from entering the school building now rushes to the *darga* and his entourage. He catches up with them, leads them to the front of the assembly, and plants himself beside them. Indecisively, Brother Dshokonaj stands a few steps off to the right. The *darga*, his legs wide apart and his hands deep in his coat pockets, wearily lifts the lids over his slanted eyes toward the morning sun, blinks a few times, and then shouts sternly, "Comrade Dshokonaj, over here!"

Brother hurries over and stops next to Arganak. Together with his fellow acolyte Oksum, Arganak has positioned himself half a step behind the *darga* and the teacher. Both are standing at attention. Not bothering to turn toward Brother, the *darga* grumbles, "I said, over here. Where I am." Brother quickly moves forward. Only now does the *darga* take his hands out of his pockets and begin to open his bag. He undoes the clasp and pulls out a sheet of paper. His every movement is leisurely, but each gesture feels progressively more important.

At long last he starts to speak. Although he holds the sheet of paper up, he does not read from it. I can't hear anything he says, so I observe the five men in front of us that much more intently. They have lined themselves up like targets and almost made us—and themselves— freeze to death on this first winter morning.

Oksum looks like the stone man of Akhoowu. He stands solid as a rock, with a dreamy smile and short straight nose in his round dark-reddish face. His eyes gaze into the distance.

Arganak tries to imitate him, but he cannot stand still. His boots are worn down at the heel and falling apart, and the mere thought of his feet makes my own toes feel colder.

No smile lights up his fox face; his skin is too creased. The only thing he manages to pull off is the wooden posture of his upper body. The light-skinned teacher and Brother jump at the same instant, one worse than the other. The teacher's face pales and Brother's reddens. Both men's eyes fill with tears. In fact, everyone's eyes brim with tears, but with these two it is different. The only person who does not appear to be freezing is the *darga*. During his talk, he warms his mouth and his hands, which he waves a great deal, and even after he has finished and called upon others to speak, he looks entirely comfortable. I can't take my eyes off the bright steam rising from his gigantic nostrils.

Oksum is the first to speak, and so he takes a step forward. He maintains his solemn and dreamy demeanor. "Dear children," he says in Tuvan. "I am a simple worker. My heart may beat incessantly for the Party and the Motherland, but I am still an uneducated man. I don't know any Mongolian. That is why, unfortunately, I can only talk to you in Tuvan."

I understand everything he says. He is a kind man, and powerful. In one year he accomplished work that would have taken others more than three years to finish. I'll never understand how that was possible, but I always admired him for it.

"Studying is work, too," he continues. "For me, someone who studies hard is a school *udarnik*. I consider him or her my friend. Two of my own children are among you, but neither of them studies the w-w-way I had l-l-l-longed t-to."

He begins to stutter. Small giggles surface here and there. The teachers' raised eyebrows are enough to silence them, but the speaker has noticed. "G-g-go right ahead and l-laugh, d-d-dear children. G-g-go and laugh. Yes, I d-d-do stutter at t-t-t-imes. Your p-p-parents g-g-gave me the nickname Stut-t-t-ter Oksum. But I d-d-didn't care. I only worked harder. I am t-t-telling you: D-d-don't worry if you have a nickname. Just s-st-study harder. B-b-become a s-school *udarnik!*"

The *udarnik* seems to be coming to a rousing finale. All of a sudden he throws off his good-natured dreaminess and adopts a revolutionary spirit: "If you do extra well with your studies," he shouts like any *darga*, "then you will, one d-d-day, study to b-b-become a t-t-teacher! Here in our magical c-c-c-capital, U-laan-baa-tar, or over there, in C-C-C-P c-c-country!" He first points east with his stretched arm, then redirects it north.

Loud laughter erupts, first from the *darga*, who is quickly joined by the teachers. They are also clapping their hands.

The next one to speak is Arganak. He talks in Mongolian. What I get from his speech is *sahilga bat*, discipline, because he says it at least ten times. I also pick up *nam* and *ulus*, party and state. All through his speech he waves his right fist. It saws back and forth through the air.

Then it is Brother's turn. He is nervous and his voice is small and shaky. I understand *haer* and *itgel*, love and trust, and then party and state again, and several times, discipline.

The light-skinned teacher begins to take on the expression of a child who was forgotten when all other children were given presents. His forehead and temples are icy gray. While Brother is speaking, I watch the teacher closely. He presses his lips together and closes his eyes — he must be feeling dizzy.

Everyone there seems thoroughly frozen, and impatient for things to end. Even the teachers, who are there to maintain order, stamp and drum their boots on the icy ground along with the students. The speaker must stop! But the *darga* won't submit to the general longing to disperse. Stubborn and steadfast, he maintains his lofty pose, in stark contrast to his two shadows, who are now back in the second row and who have stopped acting their parts. The *darga* demands to see the undisciplined student. My heart jumps into my throat. My premonition was right! Brother yells, "First grade student Comrade Galsan, step forward!"

I am startled, but immediately spring forward. My feet are numb, but I feel something like needle pricks on the inside of my thighs. Tears fill my eyes.

"Are you learning Mongolian?" the *darga* asks. His face is blurry in front of me.

"Yes I am." My voice sounds weepy and thin.

"Let's hear what you've learned."

"The school, the teacher, the student, the desk, the chair, the book, the exercise book, the pencil, the blackboard, the chalk, to read, the teacher reads, to write, the students write . . ."

I reel it all off in one breath. If I had not been

interrupted, I would have rattled off the whole textbook up to where we left it on page 113, right up to the sentence "Now it is noon, and the cows have come." And I could have added all the words I absorbed by listening to the teachers talking to us and scolding us day in and day out. Like chunks of cheese set out on a board to dry on the roof of a yurt, their words and phrases are set out inside me one after the other, just as they came to me.

"Well done. I can see you're a bright boy. How are your grades?"

"One Three, two Fours, and the rest, Fives."

"Not bad at all. And what do you want to become in life?"

"A teacher or a *darga*."

The last bit slipped out. We are taught that all students should aspire to become teachers.

I don't understand at first what follows. The *darga* must have noticed something because he asks, now in Tuvan, "I understand you've wanted to become a shaman?"

I realize quickly that this is important. I wait a moment and then say decisively, "No, I want to become a teacher."

But the *darga* presses on: "Have you wanted to become a shaman or not?"

Furtively I glance at Brother. His lips are pursed, and his nose is even more crooked than usual. Its tip is a ghastly white.

"I may have said that at one time. But then I was just a country boy. Now I'm civilized. I've become a student and want to become a teacher."

The *darga* nods, but he still seems unsatisfied. "I'm warning you, you little shit! If you ever again blather on about shamans, I will single-handedly have you arrested. I am warning you. I'll throw you into prison, and I'll have you executed. You got that?"

As he concludes his right hand reaches for his bag, and in this fraction of a second I remember that people say this man used to work for the Secret Police. If indeed he did, it means that he once carried a pistol right where his bag rests today. The thought scares me to death. I moan and whimper, "Dear Uncle, I don't want to go to prison and get executed. I want to study in school; I want to study very hard for the Party and the Motherland!"

He has reached his goal. Almost instantly he leaves me alone. He finishes with a broad smile on his sallow face with its sunken cheeks and bloated nose: "I'd like to believe you. But I have to warn you, little Comrade, the Party has eyes and ears everywhere."

With these words I am dismissed, and the assembly is finally over.

Later that day something happens that fills me with wild joy. Brother Galkaan and Sister Torlaa leave the dormitory and move in with us. The four of us living together makes me think of the four directions and of the four legs of the steed Argymak in the old epics. I feel light and elated, as if I had the wings of the fabled horse. Something warm starts to sparkle in my throat and my heart. It must be the chants whose words can't wait to burst from my chest as song or prayer to reach the sky and the earth and comfort man and beast. But I now know I must not chant again.

In the evening, as we sit around the glowing stove, overcome by the yurt's cozy warmth and the lingering smell of food, I learn why I must follow this rule and all the others from now on. As a result of Arganak's report, the District Administration investigated Brother Dshokonaj and found him guilty on several counts. The uniform I was to wear as Student Number One Hundred was found to be an attempt to misuse State property for personal gain. Besides, making his two siblings reside at the dormitory even though the opportunity existed for them to stay in their brother's yurt showed him fraudulently taking advantage for his kin. And the business with me wanting to become a shaman only incriminated him further. After all, how can a man unable to keep his family from religion possibly be entrusted with leading a school?

The previous evening the District Administration had as good as decided to replace Brother with a Party member. But during the night something must have given them pause. For in the end Comrade Principal—as he was informed at the assembly—was not dismissed, but rather severely censured and warned to fundamentally change both the workings of the school and his own attitude toward State property. If he didn't heed this warning, he would be dismissed.

Brother Dshokonaj seems wide awake tonight. Leaning over a board, he draws endless lines in a thick exercise book. Plans, he explains. A job worth doing must be planned.

From now on all work will be done properly. This applies not just to him but to all four of us. We are each a strand and together must become a strong cord, and the school with its one hundred cords must form a rope.

"Mother's *mala* has one hundred and eight beads," I say.

"Don't ever mention the *mala* here again," Brother Galkaan warns me. He will no longer answer to his own name and is busy cutting rolled-out dough into wide noodles. Discouraged, I swallow the rebuke. Shortly afterward I speak up again: "Everyone has one hundred and eight bones."

"Where on earth did you get that from?" asks Sister. She is bent over one of my boots, repairing its worn-through sole.

From shamanistic chants, I think, but judge it wiser to keep that information to myself.

"I just know," I say.

"What's that supposed to mean? You must have heard it somewhere," she insists, piercing the raw yak skin with her awl. I have to come up with an answer. Brother Galkaan is faster: "Have you counted the bones in a corpse? If you have, you've got it wrong. Some ribs or back bones would be missing, or bits of the hand or the ankle joint. Birds and other animals always carry off some unchewed pieces."

"Stop it!" Sister Torlaa interrupts. "Your gruesome stories are scary." Later, when he drops the noodles into the simmering broth, I whisper in his ear: "What else?"

He has to think before whispering, "Vultures eat the bones," he whispers.

During the meal Brother Dshokonaj says, "I've been given six months. That should be enough time to change the school from top to bottom. But I need help, especially from the three of you. At home we are family, but at school we are superior and subordinates, principal and students. As your big brother and principal, I am now giving you my first important order: You must each get good grades. Now tell me if you will succeed!"

Sister is sure of herself: "Of course. No question."

Brother Galkaan turns shy: "I'll do my best."

I don't know, and so I say I don't know. But Brother Dshokonaj knows. I *will* succeed.

"Starting tomorrow, you will bring home to this yurt one grade, and one grade only," Brother-Principal says "From here on out it is nothing but Fives."

"Three top students under one roof!" Sister says longingly. "Quite a few of the Arganaks will burst with envy."

"Don't talk like that, Little Sister," Big Brother says, sounding conciliatory. "Do you know what the *darga* told me today? It was because of Arganak that Danish's appointment as principal fell through. Arganak accused Danish of even worse offenses than mine, and lined up even more witnesses. The District Administration rewarded Arganak for being so loyal and vigilant for the Party and the Country by getting him elected as one of five members of the Bureau of the District Party Cell. Now it'll be even harder to work and live with him, let alone go against him. On the other hand, I should ask myself—and you too, Dsandan—do I actually have to go against him? Wouldn't it be easier to go along with him or, easier still, simply let him go ahead?"

Sister pauses, turns half around, and appears to stare intently and with bated breath at her own shadow. Cast black and wide across the doorstep, her shadow suddenly jumps, becomes angular, and climbs up the right door jamb. She relaxes, looks straight at Brother's face, and says with determination, "You're right. Let the devil go ahead. He takes such pride in being a have-not, and after all, he has nothing but his Party membership book and the fox-face of a born snooper. Running ahead he'll quickly wear himself out. But watch out. Make sure you don't get hit when he flies to pieces."

"But Dsandan!" Brother begins, waving his right hand as if to fend off something. Sister is faster: "You always agreed when Father called me grandmotherly. Don't turn around now and remind me I am still a child."

Our big brother tolerates her reprimand silently and sinks into deep thought. Meanwhile the younger of my two brothers is enjoying his food. He slurps and chews noisily. Sister, in turn, enjoys having been right once again. And I pretend that I neither heard nor noticed a thing, enjoying my food, the quiet warmth in the yurt, and my special rights as the youngest.

In reality, however, I am a long way from enjoying myself. I am wide awake, pursuing a train of thought. Torlaa called Arganak a devil and she may well be right, but if so, what does that make her? A she-devil? The more I pursue these thoughts, the more restless and frightened I become. Yet I have to play the part of the dumbest, most carefree one— the youngest child, in short. So I say, "Brother Dshokonaj, may I sleep next to you again tonight?"

Brother emerges from his thoughts and quickly says, "You're always welcome. But maybe Dsandan and Gagaa would like to have you close for a change?"

"You sleep in one bed with your big brother?" Sister sounds astonished. She looks meaningfully at Brother Galkaan. When I nod proudly, she turns to Brother Dshokonaj: "It's time you stopped pampering the boy or he'll never turn out well. After all, who is to blame for the whole disaster? He's eight years old, and he still thinks he's the baby and can do whatever he likes."

Brother Dshokonaj gently demurs: "You may be right, Little Sister. But please don't forget that even lambs and calves need some extra kindness when they get separated from their mothers and herds."

His words are music to my ears. The bridge of my nose starts to hurt, and the rims of my eyes turn hot. Succumbing to tears, I am flooded with bliss and vow to myself to improve. I will do better, if only for the sake of this man I misunderstood for so long. Not until last night's storm did I recognize him for who he truly is: my brother and my protector. In the course of his life he has already grown from a pebble into a mountain.

Wrong

Question

"The mother . . . leads . . . the child by her hand."

"Good. Sit down. Any other examples? Who else leads?"

This is pointless. No matter how often I raise my hand or how well behaved I am, the teacher simply will not call on me. I badly need the grade. I have not earned a single one today, but yesterday and the day before, I scored three of them. Once last week I managed to walk away with four in a single day. Every single one of my grades is now a Five.

The teacher cannot make up his mind. His eyes scan the class from side to side. The gaze from his bulging eyes, bright and burning, passes over the students' hands, held up in the precisely correct way next to their heads: elbows propped on desktops, fingers close together, stretched flat,

like fixed bayonets. His gaze lingers and burns threateningly when it comes to the gap where the one hand has
failed to rise from horizontal to vertical.

"Sürgündü!" he finally hisses.

Naturally. She gets called on about three times in every
class, and each time she comes up with something stupid.
The teacher says so himself. So why does he keep tormenting her? Sürgündü jumps up, groans, and stutters, "The
mother . . . the mother . . ."

"We've already covered the mother," snaps the teacher.

"The father . . . the father . . . leads . . ."

No matter how much she stutters and pulls at her
nose or her chin, nothing but stupidity comes out. The
teacher sneers.

Someone has to help out: " . . . the horse by its lead."

"*To lead* is the root of *the leader,*" explains the teacher.
"Comrade Lenin is the leader of all progressive mankind."
He writes the sentence on the blackboard and makes the
class repeat it aloud several times. The name is hard. The
students tend to pronounce it either Lelin or Nenin. I fail
two or three times before I divide the word into halves:
Le-neen. For many of the students, his name remains un-
pronounceable. But none of them could have guessed at
the time that their difficulty in pronouncing Comrade
Lenin's name was but a foreshadowing of the insuperable
obstacles his name would cause for years to come.

So who is this Lenin? The teacher tells us a lot about
him. Lenin hated the rich and loved the poor. That is why
the Russian emperor, who is called the Czar, first threw him

into prison and then sent him into exile. But Comrade Lenin was strong and triumphed over the Czar. He smashed up the Czar's evil empire and in its place created a kind empire in which all people now lead happy and contented lives.

I have heard many similar stories of heroes. But in those, the noble young hero is a warrior and not a comrade. And he ends up as a king, not a leader.

During the break, we enter the staff room in groups of five, in order to look at Lenin's portrait. I am surprised and even shocked at the sight of the foreign-looking warrior. Unlike our warriors, who slay the huge eighty-five-headed black monster, the person who triumphed over the Czar and broke up a whole empire is just a bald old man.

It is true, though, that he has a warm and dreamy expression. And really, he must have been something. The five of us are crowding around like the five fingers of a hand, gawking at Lenin's picture, when Brother Dshokonaj joins us and stares rapturously at the leader. "Any time you feel like drawing strength from the luminous presence of the great leader," he says, "you may come in here. He loved children more than anything and always had a simple message for them: Go ahead and learn!"

After the break the teacher gives us more names to use in sentences.

"Stalin!"

"Stalin, too, is a leader."

"The sentence isn't exactly wrong. But it's not a good one. Comrade Stalin is not a mere leader. He is the Great Leader."

"Teacher! Who is greater, Lenin or Stalin?"

"Lenin, of course."

"Stalin is the lesser leader?"

"You can't put it that way. Stalin was Lenin's student. That's how we put it."

"Was Lenin a teacher? Like you?"

"Not like me, no. But he made knowledge available to ordinary people and showed them the path to happiness. That's why we call him our teacher. And that's how he was Stalin's teacher. Comrade Stalin continued his teacher's work, and today he is the leader and teacher of all peoples."

"Who is 'all peoples,' please?"

"The Mongolians are one people, the Russians another, and the Chinese still another. That alone makes three different peoples."

"Are there many other peoples beyond those three?"

"Oh yes. Many, many more."

"Don't these other peoples have their own leaders?"

"They probably do. Why do you ask?"

"Well, if Stalin is the leader of all peoples . . .?"

"Of course Stalin is the leader of all peoples."

"Are the Kazakhs and the Tuvans peoples, too?"

"No. They are minorities."

"Do minorities have leaders?"

"No, they don't. Let's move on to the next name: Mao Zedong."

No one knows how to make up a sentence with this name. The teacher comes to the rescue: "Comrade Mao Zedong is the leader of the Chinese people."

How about that? Even the Chinese have a leader—
and we don't!

The teacher is moving on: "Choibalsan."

"Is he the Marshal?"

"Of course. Who else could it be?"

"Teacher! Why does that man have two names when
all the others have just one?"

"Don't ever call him 'that man,' all right? He is our Sunlike Leader. By the way, 'Marshal' is not a name but a title.
He is our commander-in-chief. The other leaders, Comrade
Lenin and Comrade Stalin, have additional names, too. We'll
get to them later. Let's stick with Choibalsan for now."

"You said he is our Sunlike Leader. Who does 'our'
refer to?"

"'Our' refers to the Mongolian people. Kazakh or Tuvan
doesn't matter—we all belong to the Mongolian people.
That's why today we'll learn this complete name and title:
Marshal Khorloogiin Choibalsan."

A murmur goes through the class. His name is getting
longer! *Khorloogiin* reminds me of *Torlaa.*

"What's Khor . . . loo . . . giin? Is it his patronymic?"

"His mother's name was Khorloo."

"What was his father's name?"

The teacher pretends not to have heard the question.
Together the class keeps shouting the difficult name until
we are able to pronounce it correctly.

No one has ever heard the next name: Rym. Again the
teacher has to explain. Rym is the leader of our province,
and a Kazakh. The following name is Dugurshap. Many of

us know him because he is the leader of our district and also a Tuvan—more precisely, an Ak Sayan. In his case it is easy to come up with the correct sentence. But then someone asks a question that has been on the tip of my tongue as well.

"Teacher! You said the Kazakhs and Tuvans have no leaders. But these two are a Kazakh and a Tuvan, and they are leaders."

"Well, that's not quite right. They are not the leaders of the Kazakhs or the Tuvans; they are the leaders of the province and the district."

I have often heard that acquiring knowledge is hard. It must be. I am getting very confused.

"All right. Who is the leader of our school?"

Everyone knows that the answer is Comrade Principal. I have to admit I feel flattered. I am the youngest brother of a leader.

"Who is the leader of our class?"

The leader of our class is not the teacher but the student Baatar, whom everybody calls Semisek, or Fatty.

"Right," the teacher says. "And which girl is leader of the class?"

"Ishgej."

"Right. Put it this way: Comrade Ishgej is the girl leader of the first grade of the State School of Tsengel Khayrkhan District."

Another murmur goes through the class. Ishgej, the girl leader we whisper about with envy and admiration, shyly lowers her head and her round black eyes. Her embarrassment is charming and her round cheeks are glowing. I suddenly feel the desire to reach out and stroke her.

Then the teacher reveals something both amusing and shocking: Comrade Choibalsan, who needs no father, is father to all of us—and so also, by the way, is Comrade Stalin. In need of clarity, I raise my hand and ask: "Is Comrade Choibalsan my father's father, too?"

"Of course."

"That would make him my grandfather, wouldn't it?"

"No, he is your father."

"I don't understand. And another thing: no foal or calf has more than one father. I would've thought it's the same with human beings."

"It is the same."

"But based on what you've said, we all have three fathers."

Another murmur goes through the room. The class is getting restless. At first the teacher is embarrassed and then suddenly he is angry.

"You've been a bad egg from the start. Now I can tell you'll always be one."

"You said we should ask if there's something we don't understand."

"But your questions are wrong!"

How can they be? I wonder. I begin to worry and decide to say nothing.

The teacher is still upset.

"Wrong questions don't get answered, understand?"

Now I understand how it works: never ask a question the teacher can't answer. Before I could say anything, Gök jumps in.

"Teacher, how can we tell if a question is right or wrong?"

Oh dear, that was dumb. Too late now. Gök can be stubborn. Once he gets his teeth into something, it is hard to pull him off. Because he is left-handed, he had to sit in class with his left sleeve tied in a knot at the beginning of the year. During that time he started to wet his bed, and since then he has learned to write with his right hand. He still prefers to use his left hand for everything else, and he still wets his bed.

The teacher explodes, screaming, "Learn to raise your hand and stand up before becoming such a big mouth, Son of Hunashak."

Gök stands up slowly. I can make out a tiny suppressed grin in his narrow face.

"Teacher! You've just said 'Son of Hunashak.' But shouldn't you have said 'Son of Stalin' or 'Son of Choibalsan' instead?"

"Shut up," the teacher screeches. "Just shut your face." He shakes his fists, struggling to contain his rage, fearing what will come out of his mouth. At last he is able to croak that this is another wrong question.

Slowly regaining his composure, he whispers ominously, just loud enough for us to hear, "Wrong questions don't get answered. Wrong questions get reported."

That's it! I think, suddenly alert. I know this word, and so does everyone else. You don't have to go to school to learn it. It is one of those words that surrounds us from the moment we enter life—like gales, cold, or lightning. By now everyone knows to be on guard. But here is Gök, this left-handed son of a bitch, scrawny, bed wetting, foolishly brave, and even now he can't stop rattling away!

"Could it be, Teacher," Gök continues, seemingly calm, "that only fatherless people choose a stranger as their adoptive father, or at least as some sort of substitute father?"

As a result of this question, the whole class is paralyzed with fright, especially because only the day before Big Lip Uushum told everybody that the teacher had no father and that his father-in-law was related to Gök's mother. The insolent implication of this cheeky relative's question takes the teacher's breath away. His eyes rolling, he makes several attempts to say something, but while his mouth stays open and keeps twitching, no words come out. When he finally gets his voice back, the whole class hears the punishments: Gök is to be stripped and dragged through all the classrooms, I am to stand in front of the blackboard and hold the teacher's stool above my head, and the rest of the class is to stand with their arms raised.

Though he has been looking shorter and stouter by the day, the teacher is very strong. He quickly breaks the spirit of the tough, skinny little Gök by boxing him on the ears and punching him with his fists. Soon Gök is crying. Gök undresses down to his long underwear. Then the teacher slams him against the door, which flies open with a bang, and follows Gök into the hallway.

The rest of us, having started serving our sentences without the slightest resistance, are left behind.

With the door wide open, we can hear everything that happens in the hallway: the floorboards creak, a door opens and shuts, the teachers talk, the door opens again . . .

Anxious and obedient, we continue to serve our sentence. The crude larch-wood stool is heavy. I strain against its weight with all my strength, but soon my shoulder joints hurt, the skin on my underarms burns, and the tips of my fingers go numb. Bit by bit the stool sinks, until the seat bears down on my head and two legs hang in front of my face. For a short while I feel some relief, but then my neck starts feeling stiff. While I am fighting the stool's weight, I see in front of me that the arms of the students no longer reach straight up. They are bent, sagging at the elbows. My classmates' faces show enormous strain. But we carry on without complaint, and the room remains silent.

Again the door at the end of the hallway opens, and the floorboards creak. Instantly the elbows straighten and the arms shoot back up. I, too, brace myself anew against the weight. The stool goes up but does not stay where it should. Instead, it swings sideways, pulling me with it. I stagger and slam into the blackboard. The fright brings me to my knees, and I fall on my bottom before getting pulled farther sideways by the stool. Oddly enough, I hang on to the heavy stool through all this. Then, with a loud bang, it crashes against the edge of the square tin stove.

As I tilt to one side on the floor, I notice that the students' feet in front of me, next to the teacher's pointy black boots, are naked and frozen blue. My eyes instantly fill with tears, but before I get up I clench my jaw so that only a whimper escapes. Now I see what has happened to Gök. He is shaking like a leaf, crying silently, and tears streak his face and neck, then run right down his front to the underwear he is holding up with both hands. On his shoulders and back the skin has turned a dull blue color, spotted by dark-red patches shaped like hands with spread fingers.

I feel paralyzed, but I try to gain control over the tears gushing from my eyes. Should I grab the stool, which I left lying next to the stove, and thrust it back over my head? Should I wait and rest until I am forced to continue? Because the teacher is rushing around the classroom whacking bent arms straight with his pointer, I decide once more to tackle the stool's weight. But my arms are numb and no longer obey me. What if he turns around and beats me with his pointer? I am as scared as a hare with an injured spine, crouching and staring at the approaching hunter, my eyes big and helpless.

Something unexpected happens next. The teacher tells me to go to my seat and join the others. Relieved, surprised, and ashamed, I follow his order. It seems unfair that Gök, who basically did nothing but defend me, gets punished so severely while I, the main culprit who started it all by asking a wrong question, am allowed off the hook before he is.

My guilt lingers. It begins to subside only when I decide to befriend the boy who took my punishment upon himself. Instead of going straight home after school then, I follow Gök. As soon as I get a chance, I get right to the point: "It was my fault."

"How's that?" he asks. His eyes red from crying, he quickly turns away.

"If I hadn't asked that stupid question, the whole thing wouldn't have happened."

Gök shakes his head fiercely. He looks as if he wants to be left alone, so I get to the crucial question: "Do you want to be friends?"

He looks at me again, longer this time. In spite of his swollen eyes, his gaze is bright and clear.

"I don't know," he replies, softly.

"I do," I say decisively. "The time will come when you need help, and when it does, you can count on me."

Gök says nothing. He looks into the distance, with a look suggesting that my words matter to him. Then we part ways.

The next morning Gök has run away. When the teacher tells us, his voice is unusually gentle. Later the principal enters our class without knocking. We learn that the search party has returned. Gök never made it home and there is no sign of him. Now the whole school is to go and search for him.

The four teachers take their classes in the four main directions. The north falls to us. All twenty-seven students of our class surge forward in a floating row, the teacher at the center. We are told to look for tracks and for shapes in the distance, and to report anything unusual.

The wind is rough and short of breath as it blows across the hills and snow-swept hollows. The snow has hardened into shining blue ice that stretches to the edge of the mountains. Every so often a slender column of snow rises into the air, collapses, and trails off like a flaming bright mane. In spite of the gusting wind, the glass-clear hoarfrost from the previous night sticks to the skin of the steppe. Like interwoven threads of silk, its tiny snow crystals submit to the slightest pressure. We recognize all sorts of tracks, reading the steppe like our textbooks, rich as it is with the lives that defy the deadly cold. But there is no sign of Gök. At sunset we return home, chilled to the bone and exhausted, only to find that the other classes have returned as well, and the futile search aborted.

Later in the evening I stumble upon Gök. He has been waiting for me, and he emerges quietly just as I am fetching onions from the shed. When I see him I utter a cry of surprise. For a moment I believe it his soul wanting to be close to his friend while his frozen body lies undetected in a fold of the Altai. But when I feel his moist warm breath in my face, I realize it is Gök himself, and he needs my help. I quickly pull him into the shed and take his ice-cold hands in mine. They feel lifeless, shrunk to mere skin and bones.

"The whole school is looking for you," I whisper.

"I know," he whispers back. "I need something to eat."

I feel for the bag of *aarshy*: "Take as much as you want."

He takes a generous helping and fills his breast pocket.

"Where are you? I'll bring more tomorrow."

"I'll be close. I can't tell where exactly."

"Do you need anything else?"

"No. I think my feet got frostbite."

"Take my felt soles. They are new and warm."

I take off my boots, pull out the insoles, and put them into his hands.

From over in the yurt, Sister Torlaa is yelling, "What on earth are you doing? Are you glued to the onion bag?"

"Coming!" I shout, then whisper to Gök, "Watch out, or you'll freeze to death. Keep moving. Don't stop." I hear Sister's scolding faintly. It worries me that the *aarshy* for my friend, who is already so cold, is hard as a rock and as cold as ice.

The next morning my own feet get terribly cold, and my soles are numb before I get to school. Once in class, I take off my boots and rub my feet to warm them. The other students say my soles are so white they must be frost-bitten. Sürgündü reaches into my boots and says, "Pretty clear why! No insoles!" Then she hands me her quilted mittens. As my feet rest on their softness and warmth, I fall into a solemn, joyous trance, which is deepened by the fact that the class talks only about the vanished Gök. Each student reports what he or she has seen. The general consensus is that the boy cannot possibly be alive still. Yet the search continues. Today it is the district clerks' turn to go out and help, and when school is out, teachers and students will pick up the search again. I just listen, rub my feet against Sürgündü's mittens, and watch the teacher. He is even more gentle than the day before.

As usual, the students leave the classroom during recess. But today the teacher stays in his seat and calls me back. After dismissing the student on classroom duty and telling him to make sure the door stays shut, he turns to me. To my surprise, he speaks in a low voice and in Tuvan: "I have to find Gök or I'll go to prison. Do you think your shaman aunt could help me?"

I am stunned and speechless. Not waiting for a reply, the teacher continues: "I know she's your aunt as well as your teacher. Would she receive me if you went with me?" His voice goes weepy: "Your big brother will be punished, too, if something happens to Gök. You must help me, dear little brother!"

"The woman you have in mind is a long way from here," I say. Or is something inside me speaking? "If you went to her, you'd lose too much time. I could help you and your student, but you said you'd send me to prison and have me shot if I ever so much as used the word *shaman* again!"

The man eyes me with suspicion. I watch the expression in his bulging green eyes go from doubt to anxious curiosity, and then eventually to anxious hope.

"I didn't say that, little brother," he replies with sudden fervor. "It was the Party Cell's *darga* who said it, Jadmaj,

Höjük Dshanggy's son. And he only said it to frighten you."

"Oh well," I say. Or is the voice inside me speaking again? "I have to take your word for it. Our witnesses shall be the black sky and his servant—the one you mentioned, Teacher."

"What do I need to do in order to count on your help, little brother?"

"I need fire, juniper, tobacco, and a dark room."

"When?"

"Right now."

"Impossible. How about tonight?"

"What if Gök is still alive? Do we have to wait until he's definitely frozen to death? Then you will no longer need my help."

The conch is blown to signal the end of the recess. The door opens, and the students, who must have been waiting there, surge back in as one solid mass. With the teacher rooted to the spot and unsure what to do, I take my seat. Feeling all the curious eyes on me gives me a prickling satisfaction beneath my skin.

I can tell the teacher is trying to work things out. My mind is churning, too. Where will Gök be? Why didn't he tell me? Doesn't he trust me? Does he actually have a place to stay? Where did he spend last night? What if his feet really are frostbitten? Has he frozen to death by now? And if he is still alive, how will he survive the night?

The more I think about Gök, the more restless I get. Perhaps I am picking up the teacher's edginess, or he mine.

He is obviously getting increasingly anxious. After he has covered half the blackboard with writing, he tells us to copy it into our books and then to read on in our reader. The eldest student in the class is to supervise if he is not back soon. Then he leaves.

Ishgej is a good, if strict, substitute teacher. She takes her seat at the teacher's desk and organizes the reading. The class obeys, although a few students make remarks.

"Did you notice? The teacher's scared shitless."

"He'll go to prison for sure if something happens to Gök."

"Gök's father is wild. Hunashak won't wait for the law."

Big Lip turns around and asks me in a loud whisper, "Hey, Runaway, what does he want from you?"

I poke the tip of my tongue out of the left corner of my mouth, signaling that I won't tell. She doesn't quit: "Go on. Admit it. He wants you to take him to your aunt, doesn't he?"

I stick out more of my tongue and squint.

Billy Goat keeps pushing. "He wants your help, right? He wants you to give him an oracle, doesn't he? Are you going to shamanize for him?" I feel caught, and my heart is thudding in my throat. But I try to deny everything: "Come off it! What you are making me out to be . . ."

Billy Goat won't back off: "Son of Shynykbaj, do you really think we've all got our ears plugged?"

Ishgej tells him to behave, but Billy Goat mocks her: "Teacher's pet! Is that pretty little mouth going to tell on us? Go ahead. Today he's not punishing anybody."

The conch is blown to signal the next break, and the teacher finally returns. Again the students leave, I am held back, and we talk in private behind the closed door.

"I've got everything. You can start at the end of the break," he says, flush with excitement. I nod.

"Should you use the toilet before I lock you in? I won't be able to let you out again before the next break."

"You want to lock me in? Where?"

"In your prison. You know, the storage area in the cellar. Just till the next break."

"Who's going to be in there with me?"

"Nobody. You'll be on your own. You'll find everything you need."

"That's not going to work. I need someone to light the tobacco for me, to put the hat on me and take it off, and to remember the words."

"I haven't got anyone and I can't join you. I can't possibly leave the class for another hour."

"Then I can't help you, Teacher!"

This hits him hard. He frets and then says with determination that I am to go now.

"After the break," he says, "I will be where I picked you up last time."

The moment I leave the classroom, the other students crowd around me. I walk past them quickly. At the entrance to the cellar, the yellow man who allowed me to keep the sugar cubes, whom I now know as Itikej, is waiting for me.

"What did you do wrong this time, little fellow?" he asks when he sees me. He sounds friendly and caring.

"I don't know."

"You don't know?" He shakes his head. Everyone says Itikej is Kazakh. But because he speaks Tuvan so perfectly, I think he belongs to the Hara Sayan tribe.

"Itikej *Aga,* are there mice in the prison?"

I only ask in order to say something. I find it unbearable to be silent in the presence of someone like Itikej.

"The prison," he says and pauses. "You mean the storage area. No, there aren't any mice. Why do you ask? Are you scared of mice?"

"A little bit. That first day I thought a mouse was running around."

"It was probably a pebble that fell and tumbled down a board. The pit hasn't been dug that well, so the gravel keeps falling down. Eventually the whole roof could cave in."

At that moment the teacher shows up. He walks so fast he is practically running and immediately turns to Itikej: "Where's the fire?"

"In a basin, down there. It's yak dung and will burn a good long while," the sunshine-yellow man says. He sounds accommodating and kindhearted.

"Good." The teacher sounds relieved. Lowering his voice he adds gravely, "This time you have to lock us both in. Don't open the door until the next break."

Itikej's eyes grow big. "You're going in there too, Teacher?"

"You heard right. Don't say a word to anyone. Nobody needs to know."

"Itikej knows to keep his mouth shut, Teacher."

The heavy, metal-clad prison door opens before me a second time. I can tell from the teacher's movements that he is unfamiliar with the place, so I go ahead. Filled with intense smoke, the dank, dark earthen cave smells a little like a yurt. Then I see the fire. It fills the basin, casting a soft yellow light on the bluish-gray ground.

I begin by pulling my head scarf from my breast pocket—during the winter, it serves as my neck scarf—and holding one corner tightly: this will be my *shawyd*. I take my fox-fur hat off and turn it inside out. When I say "Incense!" the teacher pulls from his coat pocket a bulging pouch I recognize as a ram's scrotum. He unties the string, reaches in with his right hand, and sprinkles juniper from his palm over the basin. While the flames crackle and flicker, I wave my scarf over the fire and mumble "Alas, alas, alas," to myself. Then I say loudly, "Headgear!"

Quickly the teacher grabs the inside-out fox-fur hat from my hands, puts it over my head, pulls it down over my face, and ties the laces at the back of my neck. He seems to be familiar with shamans.

Quietly, as is the custom, I begin the opening chant. It calls upon Father Sky and Mother Earth, and I have sung it a hundred times. But today my voice is shaky and my stomach heavy, and I get stuck in a groove. No new lines and no new melody rise from my throat and tongue. I realize I am going to have a difficult time of it. Turning from the light, I crouch, take the *shawyd* into my left hand, and wave it gently while simultaneously putting my right hand on my back, spreading my fingers. Instantly something gets pushed between my fingers. I bring my right hand forward, lift it to my mouth, put what was placed in it between my lips, and inhale: it is genuine, acrid tobacco, rolled in stiff paper with a cardboard mouthpiece—not something I have ever seen, let alone smoked! I take one drag after another, suck the burning, stinking smoke into my mouth, force it down my throat, and push and press the choking mass deep into my guts. With each gulp I feel more nauseous and heavy headed. But the essential jolt that would shake me to the core fails to materialize. I mutter in vain, shiver and quiver, waiting. Then I change horses in midstream. I drop the solemn chant in favor of a skipping and bucking one:

> Little son of Süsükej,
> Grab me.
> Truncheon of the State,
> Hit me.

The man I have named and begged does not comply. He stays glued to the side of the basin as if deaf and dumb from old age.

I fly into a rage, jump up, spin around, and pelt him with insults I would never otherwise dare to let pass as verses out in the open among the mountains and waters:

> Trunk without head,
> Head without ears.

Lump that you are,
I gave you words
Not farts.

At last he begins to connect. His eyes are wide open
and cast two tight green beams of light at me. It still does
not occur to him to take my request literally and do what I
demand, namely, to hit me. I have to push harder and lure
him into a corner where he can no longer control himself.

Little son of Süsükej
Little fool of Sojakaj,
Did you really think
I would help you?
Ha-ha-ha-haa!

He jumps with a jolt, waves his fists, and yells, "I can't
believe this!"

You do not hear much more
Than what foolishness deserves.
Give me at last
What I deserve, hey!

"Watch out, boy, or you'll get a good hiding!"

A good hiding? Oh no!
You lack
A man's courage

As you lack
A father's name!

He whacks my shoulder, knocking me off balance. I
feel relieved, but this half measure is disappointing.

That's your best shot?
More like unsalted tea.
I can tell
You lack a lot!

The next blow lands on my right temple. This one
is harder and better, a more genuine blow. All along he
must have been filled with the desire to kill. I am flung
to the ground and, just when I feel the damp, cool gravel
against my face, my head starts to buzz. Screaming full
throttle, I try to get up. Although I pity myself bitterly, I
feel satisfied—apparently, this is what I tried to achieve.

At that moment I see Gök in front of me. Tiny, his face
as blue as ice, he is crouching in a corner. Quickly I forget
my self-pity and try to run to him. My path is blocked by
obstacles: walls, walls, and more walls are both separating
us and locking us in—him, me, all of us—and there are
dark beams and light beams, each harder and higher and
more impossible to overcome. Everything I see and everything I think turns into chant. I can hear my own voice,
muffled and distant . . .

Suddenly I find myself back at the basin. It no longer
contains fire. Without light or crackle, two bits of ember

glow wearily like exhausted, dying eyes. "Incense!" I demand, unsure whether I will be obeyed. There is a rustle
and the sweetish, warm scent of juniper. "Headgear!" I say
with more confidence. The hat is plucked from my head,
and a heavy burden lifts from my body and my heart. I am
aware of my hat fanning the juniper. A drawn-out yawn escapes me, and I shake myself. My whole body feels utterly
relieved and deeply tired.

"*Eej tümen eej dshajaatshy!*" the teacher says, addressing me as one addresses a shaman. "Oh, you ten thousand
spirits! I saw the world with blind eyes and listened with
deaf ears, and I acted disgracefully when I was unable to
make out the true sense of your verses. I beg your forgiveness ten thousand times." He puts my hat back on my
head, this time the right way around.

"It is I who should ask for forgiveness, but there seemed
to be no other way," I say. Then I add firmly, "I hope you
paid good attention to what came afterward?"

"Oh I did, I did," he says. "There was a mention of
someone crouching in a corner, and of walls made of dark
and light beams that block the way to that corner. And
also of a stinky place."

"A stinky place?"

"Yes, those were the exact words. That's where Gök is
supposed to be, blue with cold, crouching in a corner."

Itikej comes back sooner than expected, before the
roar of the conch. Later it occurs to me that he must have
been eavesdropping.

"The sooner, the better! Let's hurry back to class so

I can send the big boys to check the corner sheds." The teacher is visibly agitated.

A sea of eyes greets us with burning curiosity. "Did you have to go back to prison?" Sarsaj whispers as I squeeze back into my narrow seat. I shake my head. "You look like you've been crying," he says. Indeed! I think. I am shaken, but I try to look calm.

Only then is the conch blown. The teacher keeps the class in their seats. He picks first Ombar and then five more boys and tells them to check each outhouse from top to bottom. All eyes are blazing, and during the break the whole class crowds around me, wanting to know what happened. I keep insisting I know nothing. Soon, at the beginning of the next and last class of the day, the six boys return. No sign of Gök.

Suddenly the teacher asks in Tuvan, "What sort of places are stinky around here?" His question perks up the class and makes us laugh.

"Toilets!" comes from all sides.

"What else?"

Now the answers come one at a time.

"A bed when you fart."

"Places with dead animals, in the summer."

"Classrooms, when classes are over."

"Blue Tooth Buura opening his mouth."

"Hospitals."

The teacher jumps in: "Why's that?"

"Medicines stink."

"That's right. And medicine for animals really stinks."

"It stinks wherever Doctor Shööke goes."

I prick up my ears. The teacher does, too. He looks up. "Do you just think so, or do you know?"

"I know," says Hünsegesh, who made the comment about the vet.

"Everywhere he goes. It's worst where Uncle Shööke fumigates the camels. I was there the other day."

The teacher's round eyes squint. "The other day? I thought the shed was kept locked."

"No, it's not," the boy shouts. "It's not locked. The door is high up, but we managed to pry it open, didn't we, Arash?"

Arash jumps in and confirms the story.

"Quick! Run over and check. Go!"

Both boys dash off. A little later Arash returns. "Teacher!" he screams. "He's in there! Gök's in there! He's in the shed!"

Then he adds that Gök is asleep, curled up on the floor. The teacher goes pale. Before he can rush off with the boy, I take a chance and ask if I may come too. The teacher pauses, then nods.

"Everyone else stay here. Carry on with your readers."

Quickly we reach the narrow camel-high shed with the tent roof. Hünsegesh opens the door from inside. Gök is squatting, tiny and pale in a corner. He looks at us silently, and seems exhausted.

"What's up, Gök? Get up!" the teacher pleads in a whisper.

"He can't get up," Hünsegesh says. The teacher bends

down, puts his arms under the boy's armpits, and lifts him up.

"Where to, Teacher?" I ask.

"To the hospital!"

The teacher carries the boy the way a father carries his child, one arm supporting his bottom, the other cradling his shoulder. Gök is limp and indifferent to what is happening, but we can see that he is breathing. When his eyes meet mine, a tiny smile flits over his thin pressed lips.

LITTLE BLUE
MOUSE

Gök is in the hospital for a whole month. Every day we visit him in groups of three, always bearing gifts. The gifts are small and turn up almost by themselves. One day he gets a pair of knee-high socks. We call them foot sacks and laugh our heads off. They are the first socks any of us has ever seen. Sürgündü made them out of black sheep wool after a Kazakh woman taught her how to knit. The woman explained to Sürgündü that instead of wrapping your feet in fur or cloth you can stick them into sacks so they are cozy and snug in your large wide boots.

Another time Gök gets an oversized wooden spoon that Ombar carved for him out of aspen. Ombar says he figures a big mouth that brings nothing but sorrow needs to be fed with a big spoon. Then it won't have time to waste on anything other than what is most important:

shoveling it in. We also bring Gök lots of drawings. Our pictures are full of people, animals, trees, and yurts, and everything in the pictures runs or skips toward the viewer on strong, healthy legs.

Gök's feet are frostbitten, but everything would have been much worse if we had not found him that day. His whole body would have frozen, along with his thin red thread of life.

One day he shows us his feet. They are swollen, raw, and blood-red. The color, he explains, comes from the medicine. A hundred thousand ants are madly racing about in his feet.

We ask if he realized what was happening to him. He did. Why didn't he leave his hideout? At first he was afraid he would get caught and punished worse than before, this time with his underpants down. Later, when he tried, he could no longer move.

What did he think about during all that time? About home, his parents, his brothers and sisters, the animals, and about the mountains. Sometimes about us, too. Then he hoped we would find him.

The teacher asks me to teach Gök the lessons we cover in class each day. I have a great time playing teacher, perched on a stool beside my friend's sickbed. Kinder and more devoted, I don't seem to be a bad teacher, and Gök, a skinny boy who did poorly in class in the past, now makes good progress. But the teacher and the other students don't know this until Gök returns to class.

One Saturday, while we are in class, we hear an

unfamiliar clatter in the hallway, and shortly after a tentative knock on the door. Then Gök stands in front of us, shy and flushed, on his two crutches. Something like a hiss from a gigantic chest cavity escapes the class. Gök has just been discharged from the hospital, and he wants to see his friends before classes finish and the students scatter. For the teacher, too, it must have been moving to see the student he had put to flight on two healthy legs return on crutches. Since that fateful day the teacher has become milder, and now he looks as embarrassed as a dog that has accidentally been attacked by a dog from its own pack. I, too, am filled with ambivalent feelings. Seeing Gök on his crutches, I can't help but feel shamed and dejected, as if I destroyed him. But immediately afterward I notice the glowing cheeks and sparkling eyes in his narrow face, and I take satisfaction in having saved him. Eventually a third thought will sink in and brighten my kidneys and warm my bones: I am his friend and his teacher.

But that will take time. Now, Gök is simply presenting himself, but soon he will prove himself to everyone in the class. For not only is the teacher a changed man who now expects only the best of his charges; Gök, this formerly puny, stubborn, left-handed bed wetter, is transformed as well. He has fully caught up with the lessons and participates right away. But that is not all. With his forked willow-branch crutches under his armpits, he moves confidently through the classroom, the school, and even across the yard, affectionate and delightfully cheeky wherever he goes. In all he does he radiates softness and light. And as

Gök improves, classes are better, and the other students grow closer.

Sürgündü begins to call this boy who returned from the brink Bitshi, Little One. "Watch out, Bitshi, don't hurt yourself. Stay and tell me what you need, Bitshi, let me get it for you. Bitshi, my dear, I know I'm stupid, but remember, I have lived on this earth longer than you have, and I can do things that you can't . . ."

Little by little others begin to use this term of endearment as well; even students as old as Gök and others shorter than he is now call him Bitshi.

One night our Bitshi tells the students at the dormitory the fairy tale of Bitshi Gök Güsge, the Little Blue Mouse. And from then on Gök is called Bitshi Gök Güsge. Bitshi Gök Güsge, how are you? Bitshi Gök Güsge, how are the ants? Bitshi Gök Güsge, please let me pass. Let me ask you a question, Bitshi Gök Güsge. Oh, it's you, Bitshi Gök Güsge!

Day after day we evoke the Little Blue Mouse. These three words form a magic spell; they alone count while the rest can be replaced or left out. More sung than said, each is cradled on the tongue until it almost melts before the next word's turn, and when the whole name has been uttered, one pauses the way the old storytellers pause, as if bowing before the spoken words.

This is how Gök becomes the baby of the class. Even I, a youngest child who never shared this privilege with anyone, gladly let him be. For the first time ever I feel older than someone, and less in need of protection. And while

I'm not sure whether I have always been a pleasant youngest child, Gök certainly is.

He knows many more stories than just the fairy tale of the Little Blue Mouse, but because that one is short and a little different from other fairy tales, he tells it often:

Once upon a time, there was a little blue mouse. It was a restless, hungry little thing. No wonder one day it fell into a trap—and oops, it got stuck! A young boy came along. He had all his baby teeth, a thin neck, two protruding ears, and a tousled head. His first hair had not yet been cut, that's how young he was. He was much bigger than the little blue mouse, though, and he was already a hunter. He carried a club for beating his prey to death and a knife in its sheath for skinning it afterward.

The hunter wanted to kill the little animal, but the little blue mouse did not want to die. So the mouse said, "Dear hunter, please do not kill me. I am so young, my skin is thin, and I have hardly any flesh on my bones. Wait till I have grown into a big fat mouse."

The hunter was astonished to hear an animal, and a tiny little mouse at that, address him in a human voice and in Tuvan. No animal had spoken to him before. Everything he had caught in his trap was mute. He paused before slaying the animal, and the little blue mouse had a chance to slip in one more plea: "It would make me terribly sad to die."

To the hunter this seemed even stranger. He simply could not imagine a creature that lives in a hole in the ground being sad. He wondered aloud, "You talk as though you think you are big and important, don't you?"

The little blue mouse replied, "Do you believe a creature that is smaller and of less value to a hunter has a smaller and less valuable life?"

The hunter laughed and replied, "Of course. How could it be otherwise? Everything around us is either big or small. Just as my body is many times bigger than yours, so must my life be incomparably more valuable than yours."

The little blue mouse asked the hunter, "Have you ever met a bear?"

No, the little hunter had never met a bear.

The little blue mouse thought about his answer and said, "There you are. You are young and you haven't seen much of the world. Because you are so small and weak among the other hunters, you have no greater wish than to grow into a big strong man as quickly as you can. And maybe one day you will. But it is also possible that you will die before you become a big strong man. So let me ask you: Would dying now while you are small and weak be any easier than dying later, when you are big and strong?"

The little hunter became frightened and quickly

asked, "What makes you think, Little Mouse, that I could die soon?"

"You have your own hunters," the animal said calmly. "Cold and heat, floods and storms, evil spirits, diseases, wars . . . the list goes on and on. Sooner or later one of them could catch you, and then you won't be any different from me right now."

The hunter thought about what the mouse had said, and realized it was true. So he let the little animal out of the trap and said, "Go and try to grow into a big fat mouse. I will try to grow into a big strong man. May we both succeed. And may we meet again. Who knows what we will have to tell each other then?"

With these words, the hunter and the little blue mouse parted. To this day they have not met again. And they will not meet again for many more years, for both are still growing.

This is the story. Gök cannot remember who told him. He may have dreamed it or made it up . . .

I ask him why he wouldn't tell me where he was hiding, even though I was his friend.

"My great-grandfather, my mother's grandfather, had a fluttering white beard down to his belt," he tells me. "While you and I grow taller each year, he grew shorter the longer he lived. When he turned ninety-nine, he was the size of a ten-year-old child. At that point he said it was time for him to return home, and that is what he did. But before he left, over one long summer he taught me how to tell stories. He taught me some other things too, and one day he explained that every human being needs to have a little secret. People without secrets are like riverbeds without water or stoves without fire."

I remember hearing about Gök's great-grandfather. My Grandmother with the Shaved Head told me all about him. She always said he was wise, but in her description his white beard reached his chest and not his belt, and he died at eighty-eight instead of ninety-nine, by which time he was the size of a thirteen-year-old and not a ten-year-old. According to her, his name was Erekej and he looked like a gnome. I offer this memory up for Gök.

He listens and calmly replies, "I can tell no one has taught you how to tell stories. All right. Everything was the way your grandmother said. But that's not important. What's important is that he was a very old man, he had a white beard, and he was short. You mentioned a gnome, and in truth he did look like one. I will remember that the next time I tell the story of my great-grandfather. As for his name, this is the first time I've heard it. It's probably true. But in our clan no one is allowed to say -er, little man; we say -ool, young lad. I have always called my great-grandfather Dag Eshem, Mountain Grandfather, and I will continue to do so."

It hits me hard that according to Gök my Grandmother with the Shaved Head didn't teach me how to tell stories. Because I am still not sure why people need secrets, I get straight to the point: "If you'd told me where you were hiding, your feet wouldn't have got frostbite, would they?"

Gök sinks deep into thought and then tries to down-play his bad luck: "Are feet so important that we have to talk about them now? The doctor said they will heal. All I have to do is grow new skin. It would have got really bad if you hadn't found me that day and I'd been left there all night. Then I would have frozen to death. Every day I wonder what good spirit made the teacher think about a stinky place."

I am very tempted to tell him what happened that morn-ing, but just then the spirited youngest child inside the melancholy Gök bursts forth: "Do you think the left-handed ill-tempered bed wetter ever would have turned into Bitshi Gök Güsge if he hadn't got a bit of frostbite in his stupid feet? Not in a million years!" He roars with laughter, and his clear beady mouse-eyes shower me with sparks. This hits me even harder. Something breaks inside me, and the pain lasts until I decide to live with my little secret.

One day the teacher invites Gök and me to visit him at home. Such an invitation is not to be rebuffed, particu-larly if you are Gök and live in a dormitory. Students in the dormitory are infamous for roaming and addicted to eating elsewhere, even if it is only milkless tea and unbut-tered flatbread. So we head off to the teacher's yurt. By the way, while the teacher's official name is Önörmönk, no one calls him that. Instead, he has countless nicknames; people call him whatever comes to mind, and the strange thing is, everyone knows right away who is meant.

We are recognized from a distance, which is not surprising given Gök's crutches. A girl who is about four years
old runs up to us, takes me by the hand, and whispers a
secret: "Mother is kneading noodle dough because Father
said to feed you well."

The yurt shines with mirrors and framed pictures that
completely fill its *dör*. Intimidated, we wait close to the
door before sitting down in the lower half of the yurt even
though both adults invite us to move further up and take
the seats for honored guests. The teacher's wife is nice
and beautiful; her face is bright, her bearing healthy and
upright. She talks with us, even speaks Tuvan. At home
the teacher is strikingly kind, and his little girl is very attached to him. We are fed until we are ready to burst, and
included in the conversation as if we were adults. Both the
teacher and his wife ask me all sorts of things about where
I am from, since neither knows the Black Mountains. I tell
them what I know.

"How is the winter there?"

"Hard."

"And the spring?"

"Harder still."

Suddenly I remember what my aunt said recently. I
relay it word for word: "This time the dragon will come to
us backward, wagging its tail upon arrival. The tail will hit
not only the Black Mountains and the High Altai, but the
whole of Mongolia."

Everyone in the yurt is impressed and looks frightened.
Later the teacher's wife asks me more directly: "Our

daughter has been sick with diarrhea for days. What shall we do, dear child?"

I have heard many questions like this one and know how to handle them. First I ask what happened. I am told she ate too much.

"You must take her to the doctor," I advise.

"We've already done that, but the medicine hasn't helped," the woman says. "There must be something else."

I am not surprised that someone—even one who is grown up and elegant and doesn't herd animals—might need help. But that they would turn to me of all people is incredible. The teacher must have talked about me at home.

I have to think back. My Grandmother with the Shaved Head used to treat diarrhea with *aragy* and salt, whether it was a person or an animal that was sick. So I may know how to help the little girl.

"Do you have any *aragy*?" I ask.

"Of course."

"Fill a small bowl and warm it up. Put in a lump or two of red rock salt, stir to dissolve it, and make her drink it."

As I watch, the solution is prepared and given to the girl. Not surprisingly, she pulls a face and chokes. The lukewarm brine tastes awful. Even animals fond of sour and bitter flavors refuse to drink it. But it always helps, and in the end the little girl finishes the bowl.

The longer we stay, the nicer the wife becomes and, at least in my eyes, the more beautiful. She is so beautiful I am too intimidated to call her "Aunt" as Gök does. This kind, beautiful woman now asks us to come again, and often! She says it mostly to me, and it was me both adults focused on. Bitshi Gök Güsge, who is normally the center of attention, was given less than his fair share, and I feel a bit guilty. I must admit, though, it feels wonderful, really wonderful, to bask in other people's goodwill—and more wonderful still to have a beautiful woman hang on your every word. And when we leave, Gök's and my pockets are bursting with flatbread and sweets.

Before we have gone far, I am struck by something else in their hospitable shining yurt. The teacher, who day after day filled us with dread, seems to be such a quiet, kind man at home. "Teacher doesn't get to say much," I say to Gök, who replies with a story. He tells me how his mother once scolded her niece: "Scandalous woman! To treat your husband like a Kazakh herding boy!" To which the niece replied, laughing, "It wasn't me who courted the son of the yellow-green Hawa. It was he who had the cheek to court me. He's made his bed and now he must lie in it."

But before we talk more about this, Gök shares his latest insights and beliefs. "Now I know who saved my life," he says with a nudge. I play dumb: "It was the teacher, of course, after he nearly drove you to your death."

"No!" he says. "It was you."

"Oh?"

"You're the shaman."

"Says who?"

"Uushum."

"Big Lip says that? Then you might as well forget it right now."

"The *darga* said it, too. When you first arrived."

"Maybe he did. But remember what else he said. And don't tell anyone."

My warning is more lighthearted than serious. It is wonderful to live with a little secret, but more wonderful still to have other people try to discover it.

Gök and I stay friends. But we never get another chance to talk about this question. Nor do we ever go back to the teacher's yurt. One day I run into the teacher's wife on my way home. She recognizes me right away, comes up and strokes my cheek. "Your medicine helped, dear child," she says, and invites me to come home with her. I would love to go, even if just to walk next to her for a while, but I am too shy and quickly decline. When she looks at me surprised and disappointed, I make up a few lies. Having to lie disappoints me, too, and then we go our separate ways.

This occurs on a cold but brilliantly sunny day. As I walk on, memories come flooding back, and I become increasingly aware of my situation: even amid my brothers and sister and my friends from school, I am lonely. Worse, I always have to be on guard, pretending and playing the role of a child or student. I trudge on inconsolably, hanging my head like a tired horse.

The winter drags on mercilessly. Each day the steppe rings more brightly, until it almost clangs like iron. The white mountains rise from the earth like flames, sharp-edged along their ridges and bluish in their shadows, just as they did the morning after the great snowfall. The news reaching us from far-flung families speaks of hardship. In many places people have been forced to change winter camps, and families and herds are on the move. The Black Mountains lie covered beneath an icy-gray armor. Some days the sunshine illuminates them so brightly that we can no longer distinguish the valleys and hollows in the endlessly large icecap. In the mornings, on our way to school, we can just make out a tiny black spot with two bright dots on the slope beyond the far end of the steppe. It is our big winter camp, with the flock of sheep on the left and the yurt on the right. Somehow Father and Mother are managing to stay. But we receive no news from them.

The doctor who sends people to the hospital has news for Gök, and it is not good. In order to find grass for their animals, Gök's parents had to leave their winter camp in one of the sheltered folds of Ak Dag, and move to the exposed steppe in the foothills of Oogar. The news unhinges him. "They can't do that!" he cries. "Mother goes blind in the snow." Then he falls silent. The next morning he has wet his bed again. From then on, the mishap occurs nightly, leaving its trace on Gök's soul as well as his mattress. Even his classmates' acceptance and undiminished love cannot keep the unlucky boy afloat. The youngest, funniest child of the class, Bitshi Gök Güsge, goes back to being the stubborn, tight-lipped Gök.

Still many years later I would not know how he felt toward me in those days. As for myself, I can say in good conscience that even then I felt as drawn to him as to my brothers and sister, although, I must admit, his presence was sometimes hard to bear. But at the time I was devoted to him like a dog to its master, and would have endured anything for his sake.

Gök announces that he is going home during the second quarter break. "I don't care where our yurt is or how I get there. I'm going," he says. "I'll find them." He practices walking without his crutches, using my shoulder as a substitute. I keep close to stop him from falling. Often he is in terrible pain, and though he says nothing, I can feel cutting into my own flesh, which only increases my compassion and admiration for his courage. The day he manages to walk all the way from the dormitory to the school and back without crutches, he is as excited as a child taking its first steps. After this success we smash his crutches and burn them in the stove. "You miserable son of Hunashak!" he scorns himself. "Now you must rely on yourself."

The end of the quarter is approaching, and with it final grades. Any student with a Five will receive an award. I already know what the awards will be because Sister Torlaa has won one at the end of each quarter, and Brother Galkaan won one, too. They got sweets and exercise books, crayons and a little toilet box containing a white face-and-hand cloth, a bar of red soap as smooth and heavy as a stone, a toothbrush, and a round box with tooth powder. This time the award is rumored to be a complete school uniform!

The news makes my heart race. I remember the miserable rags I was given when I first arrived. I'd be much happier with a little toilet box, but I am not allowed to say so. Sister has made the decision for me: "Under no circumstances will you pass up the State's gift again. It's already clear I'll get another award. Brother Gagaa should win one, too. What an honor—and what a relief—for Father and Mother to see all of us rewarded!"

Then we hear that before everyone leaves for the holidays, the whole school will celebrate *jolka*, the Russian New Year. We will have a fir tree and perform the story of the dear Old White Man, who will come with his animal brothers to deliver gifts. Because *jolka* is still so new, no one other than Brother Dshokonaj really knows what to expect. Still, the news creates a stir. The senior students spend many afternoons with their teachers in the building of the District Administration, preparing the club room for *jolka*. The younger students color paper to make chains, bags, and animal masks. Everyone in town watches, makes guesses, asks questions, and gets infected by our burning fever. By the same token, watching the people around us preparing themselves for our *jolka* fans our own zeal, driving us on.

We learn that on the second-to-last day of the year, the day before the holiday, the top student in the first grade will get to light the *jolka* light. But even more awards are waiting for the lucky one. The District Administration will provide an escort to take the student home, and at the end of the holidays that same escort will pick him or her up again—as if the student were a State employee! The anticipation only grows, particularly for Gök and me, for we have done equally well at school.

"It'll be you of course," Gök says. "You're a better student anyway. You've even been my teacher." It is sweet of him to say so, but it is also simply honest. I do think of myself as a better learner than Gök or any of the others, and precisely because this makes me feel good about myself, I have a selfless and noble idea: since his yurt is farther away than ours—in fact, he doesn't even know where exactly it is these days—the State horse and escort would do him much more good than me. And so I disagree: "No way. I am not half as good as you at telling stories. Besides, you are our Bitshi Gök Güsge, and the whole class would love to see you light it."

He rejects the honor; I reject it in turn. As a result, we both get praised by the teacher and admired by the class. Afterward we take dictation. Dictation is not a small thing, but as usual I am doing so well that I know I have done well even before I hand it in. Do I really want to light the light and ride home on horseback with an escort while Sister Torlaa and Brother Galkaan walk behind me? What a dumb idea. Quickly I slip two mistakes into my text, resulting in a grade of Four.

Happy with myself and my grade, I don't care about the consequences. The worst rebuke comes from Gök. "You're dishonest," he says. "If I'd known you're such a sly fox, I would have added two more mistakes to my one honest one." With its single mistake, his work received a Five minus.

The class is delighted, and I feel good knowing my generosity has caused their joy. Without too much trouble we talk Gök, who is more embarrassed than angry, and the teacher, who is slightly stunned, into adding a mouse to the Old White Man's four-legged companions. We sketch out a role and plan a suitable mask and costume for our little blue mouse, taking the character itself from the fairy tale: the hungry little thing that flits about in all directions, trips, sniffs, and slips, and falls into the trap. The other animals arrived in high spirits, but are very discouraged about the little blue mouse's sudden mishap. Then the dear Old White Man comes to the rescue. He frees the little mouse from the trap and carries it once around the fir tree we have decorated with ice and snow. Bitshi Gök Güsge will play the mouse, for by then he will have just lit the light. The teacher likes what we have come up with and promises to include the scene in the *jolka* celebration.

Jolka turns out to be even more beautiful than anyone anticipated. Everyone gets praised, above all Brother Dshokonaj and Bitshi Gök Güsge. The Comrade *Dargas* appear to have forgiven Comrade Principal for at least some of his indiscretions, as later that night the District Administration will award the school a Certificate of Honor. When Gök goes up on the stage, several people in the audience start crying. The mouse boy makes a big effort not to limp, but unfortunately the trap, stuffed with thick cushioning to make it less effective, springs shut with full force. The victim cries out and makes a gesture of such unbearable suffering that many in the audience call for the Old White Man to help. Gök plays his part fantastically well. Bouncing more on his hands than on his feet, his act looks very different from those of the four-legged animals played by his more able-footed peers. In fact, he is the only one whose performance is entirely convincing. We spur him on: "Keep going, Bitshi Gök Güsge!"

The next morning the whole school is in motion. Some students get picked up by their parents or older brothers or sisters, some ride home on horseback, some skate, and others walk. Torlaa, Galkaan, and I are among the last to leave. Along with many other students on foot, we swarm out toward Ak-Hem and the Black Mountains.

I don't see Gök that day because we all leave so early in the morning. Our journey is exciting and wonderful. It would have been a little faster with an escort and a horse, but otherwise it couldn't have been any better. I only hope that Gök and his escort riding the scrawny State horse—there are no fat State horses—left on time. And that he finds his yurt and gets picked up again when the time comes.

We walk across the frozen river. Some students attach flat stones to the soles of their boots to skate on. Galkaan and I have to do what Sister says, and so we can only skate on our flat leather soles. But we are content. We all carry sticks as long as our arms, as do most who travel on foot in the winter. If a rutting male camel or a rabid dog comes charging at you, we are told to simply grab the middle of the stick and push it straight into the animal's gaping mouth. We are pretty sure we won't encounter any dangerous animals, but carrying a thick stick and the very thought of an attack give us goose bumps.

Bigid and Gümbü leave us after our group has passed the island in the lake formed by the merging of Homdu and Ak-Hem. They plan to continue downstream to the next tributary, Terektig, and then to walk upstream on its ice. They have the longest journey ahead, and they will have to hurry in order to reach Hara Dsharyk before nightfall. Their yurts should still be at Hara Dsharyk, unless their parents have not also been forced to move. "What if they're no longer there?" asks one of the other students.

"Then we shall look for them," replies Gümbü, the elder of the two cousins many mistake for brothers. The students whose yurts are in the river valley and who can already see and smell the smoke rising from their homes give Bigid and Gümbü what food they have left. Both boys accept the gifts with outstretched hands and tuck the food into their breast pockets. Then, wordlessly, they go on their way.

This is how Gök, too, will be looking for his yurt, I think as I follow the two boys with my eyes. But it won't be quite as bad with an escort on horseback. I am suddenly over-joyed to have let our Bitshi Gök Güsge have the honor of first place and the right to an escort with a horse.

Soon afterward, Torlaa, Galkaan, and I leave the group and the frozen river and turn toward the mountains. At this hour our Black Mountains, like the entire Altai, are ablaze with the scorching white light of the noon sun. We storm up Gysyl Shat relentlessly. Panting and sweating, we skip from one boulder to the next as nimble and sure-footed as goats. The closer we get to the familiar world of home, the more we long for it. Already we are clambering up the rocky slope of Doora Hara, the soot-black mountain that rises steeply from its surroundings like a barrier to our path. Once we are above the grass line on the awe-inspiring mountain, we finally stop to catch our breath. For the first time we turn and look back at the world of river and steppe we have left behind. It is a restless, busy world, so different from the calm world of the mountains. Steam rises from the mountains above, smoke from the steppe below. Nestled along the bends of the great, dark-gray river, the Kazakh yurts and graves stand out like warts on the back of a hand.

"Do you recognize the island where Bigid and Gümbü left us?" asks Brother Galkaan. Of course I do. It looks like an overstuffed rumen with hardened, bluish veins. "Do you know what it's called?" I know that, too: Eshem-Ortuluk, or My-Grandfather-Island.

"That's what we called it when we were little."

"Does it have another name?"

"Oh yes. It's called the same as our big grandfather with the limp."

Brother looks at me, pleased he knows more than I do, and says what I have been expecting him to say all along: "Admit it, you don't know."

"I know the answer, but I'm not going to tell. That way you can enjoy yourself a bit longer."

The simpleminded Galkaan wants to make sure he comes across as smart: "Hey, you're a student, but you don't know the name of your own grandfather? How's that?"

"What's the word for the hair of a male yak?" I ask, feigning innocence.

"Khyl," he says, realizing only then that I have tricked him. "Man, you're smart."

Sister, who has been listening to our conversation quietly, finally opens her mouth: "Just to set you straight: these days the island is called something different again—Sara Ortuluk, Yellow Island, and it's not just because we aren't allowed to say the name."

I don't have to wait for what is coming. "Grandfather was a *kulak*. He was so rich he owned the whole island. Today, nobody's supposed to remember." I am not the only smart one here, I think. My heart beats faster and harder as I gaze at the hilly island that gleams yellow in the snow-covered ocean of ice. The island looks abandoned and lost, but also invincible and out of reach. Once upon a time it belonged to us—or so the story goes—and was as real a possession as a sheep with its flesh and its fleece.

We scale the mountain's steep, slippery scree as if charging into battle, climb the next mountains with unflagging stamina and courage, and reach home while it is still light, overcome by joy and exhaustion. Sister and Brother and I are thrilled to find our yurt where we had expected it to be. Day after day we had thought about where it ought to be at this time of year. But then we hear what it has cost our parents to keep the yurt in its place and to grant us this joy. The flock is emaciated and already diminished even though this is only the middle of winter and the endlessly long, indescribably difficult spring is still to come.

Even Brother Galkaan, the weakest in our team of three, has managed to finish the quarter with a final grade of Five. Father and Mother are speechless with joy at our achievements, and they have tears in their eyes as they watch us unpack our three sets of awards.

"Knowledge is the flock that each of you has to pursue," Mother says. "While a flock outside remains forever vulnerable and can be hurt in all sorts of ways, a flock of knowledge gathered in your head can never be hurt. Not by heat nor cold, wolf nor thief—not by anything."

Father picks up where she left off: "There are times when a man's bones feel exhausted and his belly is gripped with the fear that his flock might perish, his quota not be filled, and he vanish off to prison. In those moments he may lose heart and wonder, Why not fetch at least one of the children so someone will stand by him? Now I see we have done the right thing by sending you all away and onto the path of knowledge."

The face-and-hand cloths we have won are strung up along the yurt's lattice wall; our little toilet boxes are stacked on one of our chests, and the sweets are displayed in a large bowl, next to the butter lamp like an offering. If people come to visit, Father and Mother explain, they will see that we have won awards. But for as long as we are at home, absolutely no one comes to visit. When we have to leave, the awards remain in place beneath a fine layer of soot and dust.

It is beyond wonderful to walk the paths and do the tasks we are familiar with. From morning to night Sister bustles around the yurt, washing and scrubbing, sewing and mending, cleaning dishes and cooking. She keeps her eye firmly on Galkaan and me, orders us around, praises and scolds us, and decides when we can rest and when we should get moving again. Father and Mother seem to find it appropriate that their eldest child has a good handle on the younger ones.

We learn that on the twenty-ninth day of the most recent month, Father stayed away for the night to attend Aunt Pürwü's shamanizing. Again she foretold hardship for the country and its people. Father repeats what she said: two tears—one carried on the wind, the other welling up from the eye's socket—will meet at the rim of the eyelid when the spring storm begins.

Tending the little flock, I decide to shamanize and smoke a quick-acting, acrid mix of *erwen* and blue-tobacco stems. I get confused when a whirlwind approaches and the flock huddles together. Scared, I interrupt my chant and try to flee from the storm that is now spinning like a drill. The whirlwind ends up racing past us, but more squalls come through and the day turns stormy and cuttingly cold.

Nine days later we must return. This time the journey goes mostly downhill and we have the wind behind us while the sun is up. Brother Dshokonaj welcomes us in a good mood because he has received much praise while we were gone.

Classes start the following day. Some students are absent, mostly the Ak Sayan students, who have the longest way to come. We feel sorry for anyone who has not returned because being back together is such fun. Then we get news that cuts through our hearts' sunny joy like the lash of a whip. The escort who took Gök home on horseback had searched for a full three days before finding Gök's yurt. Gök's mother, he said, was bedridden and determined that no one was to come back and pick up her boy. She was the one who gave birth to the child, she was the one who would make the decisions, and she would keep him right there where his eyes, hands, and legs were desperately needed.

One by one the absent students return, and Gök is not among them. Again his nickname repeatedly comes across our lips, like a wish, an addiction, or a prayer. Sürgündü sobs: "I know I'm old and stupid. And because I'm old and stupid, I can do what I like, when I like, any way I like. I am sick with longing for our Bitshi Gök Güsge!" Then she weeps even more loudly, while the others drop their heads silently, hiding their shining, teary eyes.

Stories are told about him. I add a few, some of which I make up. Made-up stories are always nicer than true ones. Each time I tell a made-up story, it feels as if the story were about someone long gone, someone whom I never want to let go of again, not for anything in the world. Soon we can no longer distinguish between the true stories and the made-up ones, but they keep the class united and in good spirits when otherwise we would have crumbled after waiting in vain too long. In telling stories, I relive in increasingly brighter light the hours of our friendship. We still have each other as friends in spite of, or maybe even because of, the untold secret. I conjure up thoughts and send them on their way to the friend I miss as I would miss the air and the light: We are men now, Bitshi Gök Güsge. We must keep our word and get back together, dear one!

In fact, however, we would never see each other again. Worse, not a single word about him, let alone from him, would ever reach me.

In the end, tired of waiting and weak, I begin to think that maybe there never was a Gök. Maybe Bitshi Gök Güsge was a fairy tale from the start, or a dream dreamed by many.

THE BLACK TAIL
OF THE
WHITE RABBIT

"The White Rabbit is timid," Bajbur said when he last shamanized. "She might just leave the tail end of the year to the Dragon. Her year has already been one to remember."

In this, the last month of winter, the freezing winds blow these words from ear to ear. Though no one would claim that old warty-nosed Bajbur amounts to much as a shaman, everyone is puzzled by the meaning of his words. The Altai remains buried beneath a layer of white, and no one with open eyes would think the Rabbit was on her way out. Just the opposite, in fact. It looks as if the Dragon, no matter how powerful, will have to wait for the Rabbit's snow to clear out before summer begins.

Nevertheless, preparations for *shagaa* are well under way. The more the moon wanes in the sky, the more work gets done in yurts everywhere. Noodles get stuffed with meat and cooked, piles of flatbread fried. The dormitory students are welcome wherever they go because they lend a hand with the extra work. Wood gets chopped, water lugged, and mats beaten.

The old dirt must remain on this side of time's mountain. People settle their debts, return what they have borrowed, and reclaim what they have lent. Everything old must end so the new can begin.

The four of us are under pressure in our brand-new, sparsely furnished yurt. Sister Torlaa has a firm grip on all of us, including Brother Dshokonaj. She is convinced that his reputation is at stake. Given that the Tuvans are stupid, and compulsive gossips, we have to watch out or he will be cut to pieces and destroyed! Brother Dshokonaj does not comment—which is very, very odd.

We want to celebrate *shagaa* with Father and Mother in our yurt in the mountains, and this time Brother Dshokonaj is to come with us. Along with a large bunch of other students, the four of us set out on the last day of the old year.

We have covered a considerable distance in a short time when a rider catches up with us and tells us to turn around on the spot and hurry back to the District Administration. Something tremendously important and serious has occurred. How loathe we are to turn around, and how curious to find out what has happened. And the sight of the rider! His horse steams and pants and trembles under an armor of ice. Obviously the messenger has been riding the horse as if it were summertime. After leaving us, he takes off at full speed toward Gök Meshelik, to catch up with the Ak Sayan students and call them back as well.

"What could it be?" someone asks.

Brother Dshokonaj shakes his head, pale with stress. "Maybe a fire?"

"Or an epidemic?"

"Or a war?"

Some of the girls begin to cry when they hear these words, and our big brother does not order them to stop.

We walk together toward the District Administration, which is in a tall, red structure made of logs. A large crowd is milling around in front of it, and as we stare with growing curiosity, we recognize Arganak, marching up and down on its periphery. He is hunched over, his arms drooping.

"What happened?" Brother Dshokonaj asks him excitedly, before we have even reached the crowd. The men and women must have been standing there for a long time. The snow beneath them has been packed into hard, gray-brown ice by their thick felt boots.

"The worst!" cries Arganak in a muffled, weepy voice. "You'd better hear it directly from Comrade Secretary of the District Party Cell." Although he is an old man, Arganak sobs openly like a child.

Frightened, we stop as if rooted to the spot and watch the shining teardrops run down the wrinkled skin of his gaunt face. It's embarrassing for all of us. There are gloomy expressions all around but he is the only one crying.

Brother Dshokonaj rushes into the building after hearing Arganak's ominous words. When he doesn't return soon after, we realize that our happy anticipation of *shagaa,* the most beautiful holiday of the year, is definitely over. We prepare ourselves for the worst.

At that moment three men and one woman appear, carrying a portrait of Marshal Choibalsan. A thin ribbon of black-and-red cloth is stretched across its lower-left corner. Their bare heads lowered to their chests, the four move slowly, staggering as if under some heavy burden and crying demonstrably. Their rasping breaths, whimpers, and sobs reach our ears still warm from their lungs and throats. I touch one of Sister's fingers lightly and whisper, "Has the Marshal perhaps . . .?"

She pinches the back of my hand in reply, pushing out her lips before quickly pulling them back in such a scary way that her twisted face looks like a yak's hole after a pile of crap has slipped out. I had wanted to add as well that our big brother is not behaving: after all, one may share another's pain, but not their tears. Tears only cause more tears, people say. But instead I keep quiet and do what the people around me do. They are all older than I am, so what they do must be right. And so I am bewildered, but silent for now.

The portrait is to be put up above the entrance. A ladder, a hammer, and several other tools appear, and a lot of people make a big show of helping to drive three nails halfway into the wood. Finally the picture is secured, tilting forward, above the heads of the crowd. Meanwhile more people have arrived, including the Ak Sayan students. Many of them are sobbing, a few noisily like children.

Others cry in a more subdued manner. And some groan and rub their eyes, but apparently cannot produce tears.

No one sheds as many tears as Arganak. And Dügüj, who works in the District Administration office, wails more loudly than anyone else. Brother Dshokonaj, on the other hand, cries in a quiet, unspectacular way. Having returned quietly to the scene, his shoulders tremble, but no other part of his body moves, and his face looks lifeless except for the thin bright tears seeping through the lashes of his half-closed eyes. They leave his gaunt cheeks glistening.

Tears stream from Comrade Party Secretary's nostrils as well—or is it something else? His enormous nostrils quiver, his upper lip shines, and he wipes his face repeatedly with a crumpled, brightly-colored cloth. Soon the area around his nose turns pink, making the man look even more terrifying.

One man climbs on the roof and fiddles endlessly with the slender flagpole on top of which a large, blue-and-red national flag flutters and crackles in the wind. As a result of his efforts, the flag drops and is dragged across the picture and over the crowd's heads. The groaning, gasping, and sobbing grow considerably louder. Arganak and Dügüj seem to be engaged in a wailing duel, reminding me of competing singers at festivals.

Finally the crowd is allowed to enter the building and assemble in the club room where we celebrated *jolka*. In the center of the front wall hangs another version of the same picture with the same black-and-red ribbon. The room is unheated, and it is almost as cold in here as it is outside. In any case, no one sits down and the crowd—by now the whole town seems to have come—stands facing the picture with bowed heads.

Eventually Comrade Party Secretary steps up to the portrait and makes a deep long bow before turning and addressing us. His voice sounds thin and shaky: "Comrades!" At this point, a crying jag gets the better of him and he starts to shake. After a while he emits some deep grunts, which gradually diminish into lighter groans before ending in genuine medium-intensity weeping. Though his tears are not as big as Arganak's, the round, glittering spheres bounce off his huge, protruding cheekbones and drench his hollow cheeks. His crumpled handkerchief no longer appears, and before long the whimpering man with his glistening face resembles a helpless child.

The successful crying of Comrade Party Secretary rouses even more people to tears. Now a second female voice can be heard, and Oksum, who was the last to arrive, enlivens a quiet corner with his stuttering high whimper.

Jadmaj continues his speech. His voice is so quiet and hesitant the teacher would give him a good thrashing if he were a student in our class. Still the Party Secretary does not remember his handkerchief, which should have been used to wipe his tear-stained face and dripping nose. Or has he thought of it and decided to make a point of not using it so the picture of grief will be that much more meaningful? After standing there watching events unfold for at least an hour, Comrade Party Secretary tells us what has happened: our chosen, much beloved leader and father, Marshal Khorloogiin Choibalsan, has died. The whole country is in a state of deep mourning, Comrade Party Secretary says, and now, at this hour, we have joined those who received the news before us. We shall not have *shagaa;* we will neither celebrate nor sing, neither laugh nor indulge in horseplay, nor talk in cheerful, loud voices. Within the hour, he says, delegates of the District Administration will ride off in all directions to inform the people. No one else is allowed to leave town. And all will have to show up instantly when called upon to participate in demonstrations and other ideological and political activities.

"Let's get this room heated right away," the *darga* continues suddenly without groaning and faltering, in his familiar drone. "Workers of the People will be on call day and night. They will mourn and work tirelessly to make sure that our marshal is never forgotten." He says the last words with such fervor that someone in Oksum's corner starts to clap. The *darga* quickly cuts him off: "Comrades! During this time of mourning, applause is forbidden."

Then the teachers and students walk back to the school. We walk in silence, our boots touching the ground lightly. At the school, we have a short assembly. "We no longer have our marshal," says our tear-stained principal. "Our world has turned dark."

By now the sun has reached the fog-shrouded rim of the western mountains, and the sky does indeed look so dark that I briefly wonder how we can possibly continue without the marshal. For some reason the question saddens me.

We're scolded for our earlier behavior at the District Administration building: apparently while others were mourning, not one of the students shed a tear! We should always remember that the Party has its eyes everywhere, and might naturally wonder why a person keeps aloof from the boundless grief of the People.

After the dressing-down, we are sent back to our classrooms, where we learn how to make mourning bands. It is not difficult. We tear strips from two different cloths, the same way we prepare offerings. But while the ribbons we offer at the *ovoo* can be of any length and width and of any color except black, these ribbons can only be black or red. The black ones are the width of three fingers, the red ones the width of two, and both must be as long as two hand spans. They are tied around our left upper arms, first the black one and then the red one, exactly centered on top of the black. The four corners are then tied together. We are instructed to wear these ribbons during all our waking hours until the end of the mourning period.

When we finally leave the school, we find that its entrance has been decorated. There is the marshal's picture, just as it was at the District Administration building. But now lengths of black fabric reach from floor to ceiling on both sides of the picture and of the entrance. On top of each of these hangs, perfectly centered, a length of red fabric half as wide. It all looks impressive, beautiful even, and yet I can't escape the suffocating feeling that accompanies all this seductive invigoration; this sense, that is, that "You, too, belong." On the way back to our yurt, we notice that some homes have been decorated with signs of mourning, though none as elaborately as our school.

In this way, the White Rabbit gets a black-and-red tail and the Black Dragon follows seamlessly. Mute and melancholy, we face the new year, not knowing how life will carry on, and whether we will ever again be allowed to cheerfully welcome the birth of another.

The days of mourning are infinitely long and monotonous. All our lessons are about the marshal. We learn that Khorloo was his mother's name, and that his mother was a poor, honest, brave woman who from day one raised her son to become a fighter. We learn that he hated aristocrats, the rich, and the lamas, and swore to topple their systems. We learn that he wore a blue cotton shirt, and that he unmasked, arrested, and destroyed the enemies who wanted to sell out Mongolia to evil foreign powers, and who were planning to poison our great hero Sükhbaatar, his comrade in the struggle. We learn that he defended the revolution and the fatherland with such wisdom and courage that he was twice named Hero of the State, and that he was promoted to marshal, the highest military rank. And we learned that he worked for us tirelessly until the day he died.

Such stories are lovely to listen to. But they also raise questions. For example, when there is talk about the mother, one would also like to hear about the father. When the blue shirt he wore as a boy is mentioned, one wonders if he wore pants along with the shirt, or scurried across the steppe with a bare ass like the rest of us. However, something keeps all of us from asking these questions — once burned, twice shy.

The days drag on. Living in a state of merciless silence and mourning without having any fun is hard. Yet even during the black-and-red days, different stories emerge. It's just that they have to be whispered more quietly.

Sürgündü is now homeless. The aunt in whose yurt she used to stay got mad and sent her packing after noticing the strange ribbons around her upper arm. "Mourn yourself to death for all I care, but not in my yurt!" yelled her old aunt. Sürgündü moved into the dormitory, where a bed had been empty since Gök's departure.

Ombar taught himself to cry. He soaks a handkerchief with onion juice and wipes it across his eyes whenever tears are called for. Others copy his trick. As a result, copious tears are shed at the great memorial rally, which is attended by representatives of the working herders from all directions. Afterwards, the District Administration praises our school, and so the principal praises our class.

One day we see newspapers with pictures of mourners like us next to a black-rimmed picture of the marshal. One woman in particular stands out because she is young and, as Billy Goat puts it, as beautiful as a witch. Even this woman cries! She must have had her reasons. The teacher knows her name, and tells us she was the marshal's songstress. Later we hear that she held a wake at the marshal's coffin and cried nonstop for days and nights — so overwhelming was her grief! We can't help but wonder whether she, too, had to work on her beautiful, bewitching eyes with a handkerchief soaked in onion juice.

Sometime later, the period of mourning comes to an end, though we are still said to be inconsolable. We are allowed to laugh and be boisterous again, at least occasionally. Now the word is that we must work hard to continue the revolution and change the world, thus gaining strength and filling the gap in our ranks. Everyone comes up with a target. The doctor commits publicly to decreasing the mortality rate by 50 percent. The veterinarian promises to ensure that only healthy offspring are born in the coming spring so the one thousand newborns that perished each previous year will survive and enlarge the People's herds. The District Trade Commissioner promises to procure twice as many commodities as last year for the workers, and to collect raw materials of only outstanding quality for the State. And the District Administration guarantees that all buildings and all *ails* in town will be fenced in, and that all yurts in the countryside will get fabric covers inside and out. Oksum declares himself ready to fulfill the plan by 1,000 percent month after month. And all of the herders commit to increasing their flocks by 50 percent over the next five years.

Morning after morning the teacher tells us of these commitments. And day after day this topic is included in our homework: What more does your fellow citizen want to achieve? The students report on other people's plans and promises. We report on the exact number of wolves, foxes, rabbits, rock partridges, and marmots that will be hunted; the number of willow and larch fences that will be built; and the number of bedsheets and covers that will be sewn. Many of our fellow citizens promise to renounce such remnants of feudalism as drinking, smoking, and taking snuff. Baatar's forty-year-old father, Legshid, is said to have started exercising every morning. The sixty-two-year-old grandmother, Enikej, is determined to wash her neck and feet in the river once a day after the ice has melted. And Mijtik, Seeke's grandfather, will liberate himself from all superstition, never again dismounting at an *ovoo* or making offerings elsewhere.

I would love to include something about Father and Mother at story time. But for the life of me I can't think of anything to share. Finally I come up with something: Father will clear the rocks from all the paths in the Black Mountains, and Mother will clear the bones from all the winter camps. Later I find that my claim about Father is true, simply because he has always picked up rocks. My claim about Mother, on the other hand, misses the mark. She'd be crazy, she says, to rob the earth of its food.

Along with these commitments and promises we hear that the school will soon supply its own firewood, meat, and vegetables. To start the process, the School Collective will go into the woods the following weekend. We think we know what that means: we will walk through the nearby bush and pick up brushwood, break off withered willow or larch branches and, at most, chop up a larch tree felled by a storm.

In fact, much more is about to happen.

On Saturday morning we gather at school at the usual hour but without our bags. Instead, each of us brings an axe, a saw, or a rope. Two older boys arrive with a bright red banner, one fathom long and one cubit wide, with white, glued-on letters. They carry the banner between two poles high above their heads. We march right behind them in rows to the assembly, stamping on the ground and singing the song we have sung several times daily since the mourning period began:

> Heroic Mongolians
> Honored and beloved Choibalsan . . .

The singing ends. The light voice of the leader of the Pioneers' Council calls out: "A—tten—'shun!" We throw our heads back, suck in our bellies, press our palms against our thighs, and stand as rigid as posts. Then the principal addresses the school. He speaks of our beloved leader whose death has left a gap that can never be filled, and of the people's determination nevertheless to fill this gap through ever new triumphs and victories. I know this sentence by heart, along with many others. If I had to, I could rattle off the lot of them. Unfortunately, I am only in first grade. No one allows a first-grader to speak at an assembly or a rally. Again, the question arises: Can that gap be filled or not? Every time it comes up, first, it can't and later, it can!

Should I ask the teacher or Brother Dshokonaj? Should

I ask any one at all? Of course not. By now I am smart enough to remain the good student; actually, I am the top student. And I know that even if Gök, our little blue mouse, were to show up again, I'd still be the best.

We will all contribute to our people's triumphs and victories, says the principal. Fortunately, these triumphs and victories are so easy that anyone can make a contribution to them. Comrade Arganak, member of the Bureau of the District Party Cell, will lead the Collective on the project, continues the principal. What a pity! Or is it? I remember what Sister said some time ago. Perhaps Brother Dshokonaj has listened. The project is to be carried out under Comrade Arganak's direct leadership, and no one is to leave the workplace without his permission.

The same voice as before calls out: "A—tten—'shun! Left turn! Quick march!" The boys with the banner march at the front, flanked by Arganak and the leader of the Pioneers' Council. Behind them we advance in rows of four, flinging our legs into the air in spite of the fact that we can only swing our left arms. Our right arms steady the tools resting on our right shoulders, making us feel like soldiers with guns.

Someone starts up the song. Instantly the rest of us join in and we advance, a mighty, noisy, thundering column. I feel blissful and exhilarated, and imagine I could march this way day in day out, to the ends of the earth without getting tired or bored. For a change I find the man marching violently at the front right corner of our column not only bearable but endearing.

Our formation marches in a straight line toward the first river branch, crosses its ice, and is now fast approaching Hara Alagak, the Black Island. When we get there, we first hesitate, then invade it like a speckled band of predators. Some hold their breath and a few even protest loudly. But this is absolutely nothing compared to what comes next.

"One hundred and eight larch trees are said to grow on this island," says Arganak, marching up and down in front of the rows awaiting their orders. "Everyone knows this number is just a word. It's pretty obvious there aren't that many trees on the island, isn't it? Today we, the Comrade Teachers and Students, will declare war against this bunch of lies that only feeds into the people's superstition. We will mow down these so-called sacred larches and deal a deadly blow to enemy propaganda."

The words were uttered in a fairly low voice. But they impress and shock us nonetheless. The students' faces are anxious and curious, and even the teachers hang back and wait. Then Makaj, the quiet teacher with the broad shoulders, asks in a tone that suggests opposition, "You expect us to chop down the larch grove? And you want us to do it even though there is plenty of brushwood on the ground and whole trees that were brought down during the storms?!"

"The Party Cell has decided, not me," Arganak replies

coolly. Then he turns scornful: "Comrade Makaj! Am I hearing the State schoolteacher speaking here, or his father, the lama teacher? If you think you know better than the Party, then tell the School Collective directly rather than in this backhanded way."

Teacher Makaj looks dismayed and childlike. He mumbles something and then replies in a barely audible voice, "I didn't mean it like that, Comrade Arganak. I just thought these trees are still young and they make such a nice background for the town. But you are right of course."

Herim, who is in fourth grade and one of the school's best students, puts up his hand and turns to his homeroom teacher, the light-skinned Danish: "Teacher! You have always taught us that nature is alive and that we must love and protect it. And now we are to chop down the beautiful larch grove. I don't get it."

"To love and protect does not mean to scrimp," counters Danish. "Read the slogan on the banner, Comrade Herim. Come on, speak up!"

And the student, known in school for his loud voice, reads out: "Do not wait to receive the gifts of nature. Act now and rip them off her! Ivan Vladimirovich Michurin, 1855–1935."

The boy's clear voice seems almost to be echoed by every tree. We all stand rooted to the spot, stunned and surrounded by a great silence. Danish eventually breaks the silence, sounding as if he feels compelled to finish the conversation: "This is the lesson of our great scientist. Besides, chopping down that handful of larch trees has great political significance, as one of the members of the Bureau of the Party Cell has just reminded us on behalf of the District's Revolutionary Leadership."

A shadow passes over Arganak's face. He probably would have preferred to hear his own name. "Enough, Comrades," he says, sounding resentful. "We haven't come here for chit-chat, but rather to work and fight the good fight. Let's get on with it. I have one hundred and ninety-six hands at my disposal. That, divided by four, makes forty-nine trees. Forty-nine trees is my production target for you. If you chop down fifty trees, you will exceed your quota, and I hope you will. Each class forms a division. Your teacher is the leader of your division and may allow you to form subdivisions. Teachers, you will appoint the leaders for any subdivisions. You remain fully responsible for every member of your Collective, for their safety and for their political and work discipline. As leader of the school staff I will supervise our labor front and remain accountable to the District Administration for our overall results."

We remain even more tenaciously silent than before. This silence feels as if it is not based on fear alone, but I am not sure what else may be causing it. Pompousness can be infectious, and I can't help but wonder if some people feel more important themselves when they hear the ragged old Arganak puff himself up. Be that as it may, Arganak seems encouraged by the silence that has descended upon the crowd. He carries on like a man who feels entitled to do whatever he wants: "Comrades, Pioneers, students! Before you throw yourselves into this job, the adults will show you how to fell a tree." He gestures for the teachers to approach, nods toward a saw and a rope, and marches ahead with the teachers in tow. We are paralyzed with shock and slavish obedience, and our hearts hurt as we watch each of his movements, wondering which tree will fall. Arganak is unstoppable. He walks past trees both big and small, crooked and straight, including many larches. The farther he walks, the more we feel awe mingling with fear in our hearts. The ragged, soot-black Arganak grows larger and more sinister with each step.

We soon set out to follow him from a distance. Finally he stops in front of a gigantic larch. It stands in a cloud of blue and white ribbons and strings. We, too, stop and so for a moment do the hearts in our chests. For the larch is a sacred shamanic tree!

Arganak appears calm, then glances at Danish, who is holding the rope, and says matter-of-factly, "Climb up and put a loop around the trunk as high as possible." Then he looks at Makaj and at our homeroom teacher, who are each carrying an end of the gleaming steel saw. "Comrades!" Arganak speaks with heightened authority. "Time to make a different sacrifice to this demented old fogey! Put some bright cold steel to his ankles. Off you go!"

Neither teacher moves. Makaj, with a small voice and timid eyes, turns to the commander: "Is that really necessary, Brother Arganak? Are there not more than enough other trees?"

He fails to move Arganak. To the contrary, the embers burst into flames: "Absolutely not. This is the one. It's not only people who have to learn that the revolution will fight all counterrevolutionary activities. If there is a counterrevolutionary among the trees, rocks, and springs, the larch is surely it. And thus it deserves to be executed. On behalf of the people and their revolution!"

Makaj doesn't reply, but he still looks indecisive. Our teacher, too, seems paralyzed and small. Arganak flies into a rage. He storms at teacher Deldeng, rips the axe from her with both hands, and charges toward the larch tree with its leafless, white-and-blue crown. When he reaches it, he swings the axe with both hands, cutting into the knotted layers of faded strips of fabric that form a cushion as thick as an arm around the tree's knee. The sharp edge of the flat axe penetrates the bark and gets stuck in the wood, while the thick cushion of fabric slides to the ground without a sound. Arganak does not trouble himself with pulling the axe from the trunk. He lets go of the handle, gleefully thrusts his arms and clenched fists into the air, and smirks. His face looks less black and gaunt than usual. He bursts out laughing: "Now you can have a go at the old fogey without shitting yourselves. Its faded thread of life is cut, see?"

Danish stands there motionless, holding the thick rope in his hands. Likewise, the other two teachers, who remain connected to one another by the steel saw, appear to be rooted to the spot.

"The whole Mongolian People are determined to fill the gap they have suffered in their ranks with heroic deeds on the labor front." Arganak sounds angry now. He shreds the tangled ribbons, bunches them up, and flings them to the ground. With the shapeless soles of his much mended dark boots he stomps on the shreds and yells, "You dare to mutiny! You try to pass outmoded superstitions on to the next generation? They're moldy and rotten! You are subverting the revolutionary effort! You know what this means. I'll make sure you'll end up where you belong. I promise. Superstitious riffraff, that's all you are. Poisonous snakes crawling out from the dark caves of feudalism. You are blowflies on the bleeding wound inflicted by the hatred of world imperialism on the back of the revolutionary Mongolian State."

Teacher Deldeng steps forward. She walks up to her two colleagues, pushes Makaj to the side, grabs the saw, and touches its flashing teeth to the tree's trunk. Our teacher has to join in. Danish, too, starts moving again. He flings one end of the rope over a branch and begins to climb the tree. I am so shaken I can hardly take in what follows.

At first I hear a scream. It cannot possibly come from the old tree. Or if it does, it must be the painful sound of the soul leaving its dying body. Next I hear a crash that sounds like a huge heavy ball hitting a hard bone and smashing it to pieces. I hear a chorus of wails that lasts a long time before changing to a sigh. The larch trembles from the first touch of the saw's blade against its thick bark, just as a yak starts when its neck is touched for the first time by the tip of a knife before it is slaughtered. The tremble grows and becomes a bolt, the same way all things grow—a prick becomes a wound, and a flame a conflagration. Then the larch begins to sway. It tries to flee and scratches at the sky with the countless claws its branches with their twigs and pointy ends have suddenly turned into. Finally, the tree falls, never to rise again.

What I hear and what I see don't fit together. These sounds and sights are as separate from each other as ears and eyes in separate places of the head. Thoughts rush to mind, but that must have happened some time later. These people are killing the tree! A tree is our brother, and people who kill a tree will kill anyone, even their own father or mother. This is the thought that recurs, over and over.

Afterward the killing really takes off, and I am lending a hand. It is like the slaughter before the winter. There is a pile of waste here and another one over there. Trees are even more helpless than sheep, which remain mute under the knife and utter a single groan only at the very end, before giving up the ghost. I am not sure if the trees even shiver when the saws invade their trunks. The trees' blood is bright and thick and more like brain or marrow than blood. But a larch tree, like any other tree, makes a terrible sound when it—he, she—falls and dies. The sound awakens and terrifies the whole flock of trees surrounding us in the distant mountains and steppe. All these other trees start and groan and scream in turn, like yaks, who stand roaring with raised tails and lowered heads when they scent their fellow yaks' blood and guts. We quickly get used to the killing, for the shock that first overwhelmed

us all with the felling of the ancient shamanic larch sub-
sides as the screams from all beings near and far subside.
Our fear when the next dying tree screams doesn't stun
and paralyze us anywhere near as much as the first one.

The youngest larches are left to the first grade students. They are tree children, the same age as we, or
maybe our parents, are. Sarsaj, Sürgündü, Galbak, and I
form Subdivision Seven and together attack a young tree.
I am the tree climber and loop tier. Together with Galbak
I pull on the end of the rope in the direction the tree is
meant to fall. The other two have the harder job of sawing. Our larch is medium size, straight at the bottom and
forked at the top. At some point we will have to relieve
Sarsaj and Sürgündü. Sarsaj asks Galbak if her father is
lazy. He's not, she says.

"Why is your saw so rusty then?" the boy flares up. He
is usually one of the quietest students in class, but killing
makes people aggressive. Besides, Sarsaj is our subdivision's leader, and thus allowed to behave a little different
today. He is right about the saw, by the way. It is rusty and
dull, has a loose handle, and is, all in all, completely useless.
I could have come up with a worse comment if I had felt
entitled to voice an opinion on the saw and its owner. But I
am not our subdivision's leader, much as I would have liked
to be. And even if I had been appointed its leader somehow, I wouldn't have made such a cutting remark. Galbak
is a kind girl with fine, blindingly white mouse teeth that
light up her reddish-brown face whenever she laughs, and
she laughs a lot. I am always happy when I'm around her.

Sürgündü and Sarsaj are all right, too; I feel comfortable around them. Who knows how working with the others would have been? Billy Goat, for example, would have puffed himself up and given orders like an instantly full-fledged father: Hey, Little Guy, do this! Hey, Runaway, do that! Or with Big Lip, who would have entertained herself telling us for the tenth time the same old gossip from the hinterland of the Ak Sayans.

At last our hapless larch falls, leaving us with a sense of release. Until this morning I never would have thought anyone could fell a living, growing tree. But now I feel joy, and also pride that my work has contributed to the fall of this young, sky-high larch. How strange. Because we have struggled so long and been frightened by the trees that crashed and fell all around us, we, too, have become heroes, and now stand in the cross fire of appreciative, envious glances. But the fruit of victory is bittersweet. Briefly, I feel an almost deafening blinding rush, which seems triggered less by pride and joy than by remorse and fear. So now you have felled a tree, I tell myself. The thought quickly leads to another. How can I tell Father and Mother? The shaman? How to tell her that a shamanic tree was felled, like an old horse: slowly, mercilessly, and without the slightest expression of respect and gratitude, without the tiniest plea for forgiveness and understanding.

Killing the next tree is easier. And easier still is cutting up their lifeless bodies. Their branches get chopped off, and their trunks sawed into blocks. It is tedious but straightforward work. The young larch's wood is hard and rock solid, with smooth, iced-over grooves. Sürgündü and Galbak do the sawing, while Sarsaj and I take turns sitting on the trunk to weigh it down and give ourselves a break. The person not sitting on the trunk does the hard work of splitting the blocks. The teacher comes by from time to time and helps with his big heavy axe. He is strong, and it is nothing for him to chop up a block that has mocked us by seizing our slim axe and holding fast.

By noon all the trees have been felled. As the leader of the school staff predicted, the target has been exceeded by one tree, the shamanic tree. It is the last tree to be cut up, communal property for the taking.

Late in the afternoon, the leader orders us to suspend work at the labor front for now, and to carry back our booty, the sawed and split pieces of wood. Each of us lugs back as much as he or she can carry. After we have dropped our load in the school yard, we are allowed to relax for the rest of the day. The next morning we are to report directly to the labor front at first light.

"Some people say there are spirits." Sister looks across at Brother Dshokonaj as we eat our soup for dinner. "Others say there aren't any, and doing good or evil makes no difference whatsoever. Now we'll find out who's right."

Then she tells Brother the story of the shamanic larch. Although he listens carefully, he does not think her expectations will come to pass. "Anyway," she says calmly, "I'm glad you weren't there today. Who knows what will happen?" Brother Dshokonaj pretends to be ashamed: "Is that what you think? It was bad luck I couldn't go. I had to help Comrade Jadmaj write a report for the District Administration. Tomorrow I'll come along and fell a larch."

"Don't!" she cries.

"Of course I will!" he replies coldly. "It remains to be seen whether spirits exist or not, but the fact that the Party is all-seeing, all-hearing, and all-powerful is beyond a doubt." Sister has no counter to this, which somehow hurts me deeply.

And so the next morning Brother Dshokonaj comes along. Arganak helps him kill and dismember his larch. His tree is young and straight, its firm bark a reddish brown. It strikes me that the tree and the man may be roughly the same age. The two men accept no additional help, work with a ferocious devotion, and look as congenial as a couple of friends, or even a father and son. Is that how they feel? I find it hard to believe. A few students are absent today, and a number of fathers and mothers have come in their place.

The parents aren't as submissive as their children, and among them Orgush's mother is the fiercest. She is a big, vociferous woman with long heavy braids that lash the air when she waves her arms about. She almost knocks Arganak over when she charges at him, calling him a madman who incites helpless beings to kill other helpless beings. "I know what's inside you," she cries. "Nothing but crap and hot air! I know because I live with a madman just like you! Though at least Oksum has a bright soul and skilled fingers. Whereas you're like your name says: a scrawny, ugly Arganak! Nothing but poisonous crap and hot air!" she cries, shaking her chubby pink fist at his nose.

Arganak cites the Party, the State, and the Law, but to no avail. The woman sneers at him: "Oh well, you and I can go to prison together. I know what I am talking about. Let me remind you of a certain three-year-old yellow mare. And let me tell you: there are more witnesses. They are still around!"

Arganak begins to stutter. Brother Dshokonaj comes to his rescue and orders the woman to stop slandering the man immediately. But the woman only laughs louder and more angrily: "I wasn't talking to you, you little twit. But since you barged in, let me tell you: people like Arganak are bad news. You better watch out. The humiliated and raped larch mother with her murdered children is my witness, and so are all the eyes that watched that disgrace, along with the Blue Sky and the Gray Earth!"

We work hard and in silence, and it takes us till dusk to complete the job. Arganak tells us to clear the area of brushwood. Now that we have listened to the words of Oksum's wife, Arganak seems to us like the leader of a gang of thugs ordering the removal of any trace of blood. No matter how hard we try, we cannot remove all traces of the trees. Traces remain.

A huge pile of light-colored wood sits in the school yard, as if it's there for good. It takes a long time before the eye gets used to it and the heart no longer pounds. Anxious pride begins to sneak into our hearts, but it does not make us any happier. The aftershocks continue, and my chest feels hollow and covered by wounds.

Besides, nothing happens to confirm that Sister was right to be worried. There is no punishment. Neither the sky nor the earth sends one. Arganak lives on and doesn't look sickly at all. Orgush says her mother is still safe at home. No one has come for her, nor has a letter arrived.

One evening Sister Torlaa's patience runs out: "I don't believe anymore what Father, Mother, or the shamans keep telling us. Now I think that the teachers, the *dargas,* and people like him have got it right. If someone were to tell me to puke into a spring, crap on an *ovoo,* burn a shaman's coat, or smash his or her drum, I would no longer hesitate."

I am inclined to think she's right. Brother Dshokonaj sends her an encouraging glance and says cheerfully, "Your teacher is right. You're a smart student, and you'll go a long way. Science has put down deep roots in you."

Brother Galkaan says that for now he will go on believing Father and Mother as well as the teachers. After all, Father and Mother have experience, but the teachers have education.

Big Brother smiles. "Well, well. I can see you want to spare yourself your sister's fate and not get on anyone's bad side."

I keep silent and pretend I am not listening. But I am aware of something that feels like a lump inside me, sitting there like the woodpile in the school yard. It must be the shock given me by the screaming, staggering, crashing, groaning, and whimpering tree. It would be sad if Sister were right and there were no spirits. But I think I can feel them inside me and around me, just as I can feel the wind, the heat, and the cold, even though I cannot see them.

Everyone speaks of the soul that leaves the body. What about the spirits? Can they leave their place? Ever since the day we felled the trees I have been unable to shamanize. I have not once felt the desire to reach inside for a chant that would praise the sky or the earth or one of the spirits. Perhaps the spirits have left with the tree's soul, fleeing from me and everyone else. Perhaps they fled the whole Altai when the great shock stormed through me and through everyone. Is my body—or anyone's body, for that matter—just a bag of skin in which a pile of flesh hangs off a bunch of bones, a hollow bag stuffed with organs, a handful of guts, and a noseful of smelly gases? Is the same true of the sky and the earth? Are they nothing but air, water, sand, and rock? And are the plants and animals also just bundles of flesh, bone, water, air, and earth?

I feel empty inside and dull outside—a soulless bundle in a disenchanted world.

ALL-GOOD
AND HALF-GOOD
DAYS

No punishment ever comes, Arganak remains alive, and everything stays the same. Or so it seems. For there are rumors about things said by the shamans Bajbur, Shalabaj, and Ürenek. Our own shaman is never mentioned. Sister says that has always been the way. In our clan we have always known to keep her predictions to ourselves, while the other clans spread rumors like wildfires in the hope of reversing the course of events. These rumors have also been fueled by some people's dreams.

I have not had a dream worth mentioning for the longest time. I may have stopped dreaming altogether. If so, I really would have lost my soul. But I do well at school and am now clearly the top student in my class. I get quite confused when trying to make sense of these two developments. Sister gets me even more confused. Having loudly announced that she would never again believe our parents or the shamans, now she insists that we not burn anything impure in the stove, nor leave the yurt at night with greasy lips, that we not step on the yurt's doorstep nor break any of the many other rules our superstitious parents have taught us over the years.

Arganak doesn't look as if he is about to fall seriously ill. But his face has grown gaunter, and his eyes pointier. When he looks at us, the piercing light in his gaze drills into us like the tip of an awl. He stands in front of us at Pioneers' Hour. "Not one of my forebears ever soiled himself with wealth," he says. "I, too, have stayed poor. I enjoy being poor, and I am proud of it." More often than not, his words make our freezing hands clap. One day the old man is made an Honorary Pioneer, and a red scarf is tied around the ragged collar of his greasy sheepskin *ton*. It makes him so happy he cries and twitches with excitement.

We often see him go in and out of the teachers' room. While he sits, the teachers stand. At times the principal himself has to stand in front of him. Arganak keeps telling everyone to forge ahead, and "offensive" has become his favorite word. It begins to spread among the teachers and eventually among the students. We yell "Offensive!" each time we enter or leave the school building or classroom, trying to swim to the front of the stream. During recess a group of boys fighting to be first in line to use the outhouse yells the familiar slogan repeatedly.

The logging project was an offensive, we learn, and a very successful one at that. Six more offensives will follow;

Comrade Arganak has dreamed them up while mourning the late marshal—each day he came up with a new one. From now on we will fight one offensive per month. And each of them will enter virgin territory.

By now it is really the middle month of spring. But we must not call it that. The teachers instruct us to no longer call this the Year of the Black Dragon, but rather 1952. When I first hear that number, I wonder how the earth could possibly be that old. When I ask the teacher, he says the earth has in fact existed for even more years than that.

But when I ask how many more years precisely, he has no answer. Nor does he know who started counting and why. "This is the calendar people use in Russia" is all he has to say. I make do with this answer, secure in the knowledge that Russia is called the Soviet Union and that the Soviet Union is clearly more progressive and better.

The current month is not the middle month of spring then, but simply the third month. The night of *jolka* was the start of the year and thus of the first month. The first month, the teacher says, had thirty-one days, but the next one was shorter by a whole two days and nights. Got it, I think, so the third month is going to be three days and nights shorter than the first month. But I am soon to discover that the third month is exactly as long as the first. I wonder if this means that the fourth one is like the second, with exactly twenty-nine days and nights. Wrong again.

I give up trying to figure it out. The Russians are obviously smarter than us. We can only hope they will always let us know how many days there are in which month in any given year, so that when we use their calendar out of sheer love for them, we will get it right.

A month breaks into weeks. Fortunately weeks always have the same number of days, and unfortunately, it is the unlucky number seven. The teachers, who drill us on the new calendar every morning, know that the notion of lucky and unlucky numbers is just superstition. But how can they be so sure? They also number the days of the week, calling the sixth day half-good and the seventh all-good, for on the half-good day we have a half-day of school and on the all-good day, there is no school at all.

On good days people must rest, explains the teacher. Civilized people do. Very soon our parents will also rest for half a day on the sixth day and all day on the seventh. But the teacher does not say when exactly they will start. Civilized people live by the clock, he continues. They get up and go to bed at the same time each day. They sleep wrapped in white sheets that are changed, washed, and ironed once a week, and they eat three meals a day. It is weird to imagine Father and Mother civilized. In the summer they would lie in bed long after first light, waiting to get up at seven o'clock. And in the winter they would sit waiting through the dark evenings, the smoke of an oil lamp wafting around them, until the clock said eleven o'clock and they could finally go to bed. And then every few days they would stay in bed or sit in the yurt, resting. What would become of the sheep, goats, yak cows, and mares? Who would milk them and drive them to pasture? Would Father drive his flocks back to the yurt each day at noon, so he could have his second meal? Or would Mother take a pot and a jug out to the pastures and look for him?

Oddly, the smart Russians appear to have forgotten the names and colors of the years, months, days, and hours. They no longer know the gender of each year, either; their hermaphrodite year consists of flocks of hermaphrodite months, days, and hours.

Rather than calling this moment the beginning of the first quarter of the Snake hour on the Yellow Snake's twenty-ninth day in the Blue Rabbit's middle month of the Year of the Water Dragon called Joy then, Ha! I am simply to say ten o'clock on March 25, 1952.

Admittedly, this new way will be easier. And easier may well be more progressive and better. How did Ombar put it? "Since I no longer have to stare at the moon and the stars in the night sky each evening, I'm so rested I've got a ball of fat in each socket." Billy Goat got it just right.

The teacher also says it is not enough to be civilized. We have to be patriotic as well. Civilized patriots rest doing a different kind of work on the half-good and all-good days. It is called community service. Since the day we went logging, we have done community service each weekend. Arganak decides what we do and for how long. For now we are clearing the steppe of rocks. We pick them up and stack them in hollows. The piles must always be square, as superstitious people might mistake round ones for *ovoos*. The point of clearing the rocks is to create space for growing vegetables. We don't really know what vegetables are, but Brother Dshokonaj has eaten some. They look like wild onions, they grow in soil, and they are supposed to have vitamins. Vitamins are substances one needs to live; they make people's faces handsome, and their bodies and minds strong. We are ugly and weak because we live on meat and milk, neither of which contains vitamins.

In the Soviet Union, says the teacher, people have dug canals that are infinitely long and wide. Whole rivers have been redirected when their waters were diverted through those canals. We partly understand his stories, since we are familiar with the stories of Sardakpan, the Creator, and see the results of his labor all around us. Sardakpan pulled our great river all the way down from Huraan Höl, our Lamb Lake, and past where we are today. Behind Dshedi Geshig he felt like resting a little, so he dug a basin and let it gather the floods following him. It did not take long for the basin to fill, so he took his enormous shovel, plunged it deep into the steppe nearby, and turned it over to let the rising flood rush in. But now that it had been abducted and then allowed to flow, the water would no longer be tamed. It broke through the dam at the foot of the eastern mountains and rushed on from there. Because we can see the sandy bright mountain amid the rocky black mountains, as well as the waterfall where the wide basin tumbles into the steep gorge, and the lake next to the hill thrown up in the steppe, we have unshakable faith in the truth of this myth. But the teacher wouldn't accept this. He says fairy tales, epics, and myths are primitive and dangerous, and distract us from life's truth. "True power comes from

184 • GALSAN TSCHINAG

within," he likes to say. "Everyone is the master of his own fate." We like to hear him say that, for we all would like to have great power, and to be master of a great fate.

One day we, too, will dig a ditch and divert the Haraaty. Before we can start though, the glaciers have to melt and their waters flow past us. Until then, we have to work the soil in the steppe. And because no one knows what working the soil means, we must be patient and wait for someone to come and show us. It has taken us no more than two days to pick up the rocks in a field worked out by the principal with a giant set of wooden dividers. Perfectly straight rows of rocks now mark the borders of our field.

The path is clear for our next offensive: building a root cellar. It is to be dug into the steep slope of Eer Hawak, within sight of the field. At the end of the last week of the third month, work on the cellar starts with a school assembly on site, which features a ceremonial turning of the first sod. We also learn a new slogan: "Earth! We know you are not sacred. We shall tear open your belly and dig into your fat kidneys. We are not afraid!"

The words are meant to chase away our fears. In times gone by, Eer Hawak marked the eastern boundary of a monastery whose lamas used to perform their sacred rituals on the even mountaintop. Its smooth ground reminded people of a saddlecloth and was deeply revered.

Soon it becomes obvious there are simply too many of us. No more than four people can work at one time, and so there is nothing at all for the first grade students to do. The pickaxes and crowbars are too heavy for the senior boys to make any progress in the hard ground. So we set out to find fuel for a fire. We swarm out, collecting anything that will burn: dung, caragana branches and roots, bones, and garbage such as rags, the discarded soles or legs of boots, and bits of dried fur and muddied felt. The pile grows fast, but shrinks even more quickly as it all gets thrown on the fire, which rages impressively. In the end all that is left is a mere pile of embers that we cover with rocks and gravel. It will keep warm through the night and thaw the frozen ground.

The next morning the gravelly ground is covered in soot. But it has indeed thawed, and soon we have dug a hollow that grows to a hole, and then slowly becomes a cave.

We need no fire today, so we stand around, watch the two or three boys working, and indulge ourselves with harmless little jokes behind the backs of the teachers. "The labor front is tight, and not all who burn to work can join. Have a little patience, Comrade Students," Arganak consoles us. "We will open up more labor fronts for you."

And in fact, that does happen soon. We are told to clear a large area around the cellar of any rocks, and to arrange them as boundary markers in the now familiar rows. With so many hands the job is done in no time. Soon we stand idle again, watching the workers and entertaining ourselves with games.

Not long after, we are told to create a path, four steps wide, to bridge the distance between the cellar and the field. This means gathering some of the rocks we had previously removed from the area around the cellar and lining them up in two straight rows to create a long narrow tongue through the steppe.

The distance is considerable, and the floodplains along the river are still covered with snow. In spite of the many hands available, the task keeps us busy for quite some time. The sun is low when we are finally done. We all stand there admiring the bare, lighter-colored strip, which runs as straight as an arrow from the side of the hill all the way down to the eastern embankment of the Haraaty.

Work on the excavation, however, has been slow and laborious. Our leaders decide that work will need to continue daily and full time from now on. Every morning Arganak takes four boys from the senior classes out to continue digging. The rest of us don't get to see the results until the afternoon of the half-good day. But each time we go, the pit has grown deeper.

During the week we all try to guess what job we will get to do next. Arganak has concerned himself with the same question, of course, and decided that we will collect white rocks. Unfortunately, finding white rocks in the steppe between Eer Hawak and Hara Ushuk is as hard as catching fish in meltwater. It would take a very long walk along the dark-brown back of the steppe before you came across anything light, let alone white. There may be a few white rocks closer by, on the mountain, although the crags all stand out dark. But the northern side of the mountain is still covered with snow, and in order to reach its southern side, where the sun has melted the snow, we would have to hike around the broad western slope. And even if we find white rocks there, I have no idea how we would lug them back. In any case, we have no choice but to set out on the long exhausting hike. To make it a little easier for us, the teachers let us play games along the way. We play caravan, walk in single file, and pretend to be camels. To walk like a camel and feel the rays of the sun in every pore of your skin is beautiful. This must be the rest-through-work that people always talk about.

When we finally reach the other side of the mountain, we find no white rocks. Disappointed as well as relieved that we won't have a load to carry back, we soon set out for home. This time we are not allowed to play. The teachers insist we walk faster. They seem to be afraid of Arganak. And, as it turns out, we do get a harsh reception. By now Arganak believes himself responsible for each and every thing that happens, and he explodes with rage when we dare to return empty-handed after having been gone for so long. "So much for 'Our Rich Altai'!" he bursts out. "It doesn't even have white rocks. And as for you scholars with your white paws," he hisses and glares at the teach-ers, "what on earth were you thinking, wasting half the day with these greedy pigs without finding a single rock?"

No one dares to answer. Our teachers look sheepish, like children who have been up to no good. Arganak can't seem to calm down. "Hey, Danish!" he yells in such an ir-ritating loud voice that the teacher jumps. "You're still a member of the Party, right? As a fellow Party member, I'm going to give you an express order. Go fetch a bucket of strong lime. And tell your principal he can work for the Party Cell all he wants at night. But during the day he has to be on-site and join the School Collective's offensive in person." Teacher Danish swallows the speech without arguing. His narrow face shows no sign of resistance. "Yes, Comrade Leader of the Labor Front!" he says before leaving. "As soon as possible."

Next, Arganak commands Makaj to step forward and follow him. He goes to the western slope of the hill, where he orders the teacher to carve the slogan he is fixed on into the ground. Teacher Deldeng is told to fill the carved-out lines with rocks, and our teacher organizes the transport of the rocks to the spot. Finally we all have something to do and, with the teachers spurring us on, we move nimbly and fast. This is an easy job, and we race around like little storms. The Altai steppe is full of black and brown rocks, and in no time we have amassed a big dark pile.

Soon Danish returns. He brings the bucket of lime solution and the principal. The principal delivers to Comrade Leader of the Labor Front a detailed report on why he had been unable to join the front previously. Arganak is unimpressed and replies: "You refer to Jadmaj, the Secretary of the District Party Cell, who apparently held you back. But let me evoke Marshal Khorloogiin Choibalsan. He lives on in my heart, and my heart belongs to the Party. For the marshal, an offensive by the School Collective without its principal is like a thrust from a knife without a tip." Even the principal swallows Arganak's harsh rebuke without responding. Worse, he simply nods.

By now the first letters are rising from the steppe, like wheals on naked skin. Arganak wants them whitened with the lime. And for that we need a brush.

"Why didn't you bring one?" Arganak nags the teacher.
"You only asked for lime," he replies.

"You knew what the lime was for. I thought you were educated. You thought my black worker's hands could be used for any old job, didn't you?" snaps Arganak.

Danish is quick to reply. His voice sounds almost panicked as he turns his lambskin mittens inside out. "Maybe these will do?" he pleads in a thin voice.

"Let's see if it'll work," says Arganak casually.

Danish promptly dips one of his mittens into the bucket, and brushes the solution on a rock with the dripping lambskin. It leaves the rock wet and shiny.

"Couldn't be better," says Brother Dshokonaj cheerfully, and grabs the other mitten. The teacher and the principal work as if they were racing one another. In no time they've painted a letter the size of a yak bull. The upper edge of the first rock is beginning to dry and turns chalk white as the men move on to the next letter. After six letters the bucket is empty.

"How many letters are there?" the principal asks Arganak. But he doesn't know, so the students have to count. Thirty-six letters, two commas, and one exclamation mark, they report.

"Impossible! It will take another six buckets or more. Can't we shorten the slogan?"

"Who is the leader here? You or me?"

"The entire School Collective, including me as the school's principal, stands united behind your leadership, Comrade Arganak."

"Then we do as I've said."

"Lime, Comrade Leader of the Labor Front, lime is hard to come by. We happened to find the first bucket at the hospital. But the hospital doesn't have much left. At most three or four buckets."

"This is not about lime! What's lime anyway? It's made from dirt! Garbage! This is about educating and steeling the young, and the Party's ideology. If the hospital doesn't have enough lime, you will have to find it somewhere else." Disheartened, the principal lowers his gaze.

The next day, when school is out and we enter the school yard, we see white letters glowing on the western slope of Eer Hawak: "Here and now, we shall change your fac . . ." Barely visible, dark shapes that we cannot read follow. There was not enough lime.

A few days pass. The half-finished inscription brightens the spot somewhat, and by now we know what the blind part reads: " . . . e, Altai!" Arganak is in a state. Grandmother often used to say that the fastest horse can't catch up with something that doesn't exist, and it occurs to me now that she must have meant the kind of situation hanging over our heads these days. Brother Dshokonaj says he is trying every day to find more lime, but there is none to be had. Everyone knows that lime comes out of the ground. The problem is no one knows where. Until now, people brought it back from the provincial capital. But the capital is a long way away . . .

In his fury Arganak is driving the work on the excavation with an iron fist. From time to time even the youngest students take turns. As we work in pairs carrying earth on sackcloth to the far side of the rows of stones, the hole becomes a real pit. Dark and smelling of damp earth, it is deep and wide enough to hold several yaks. The plan is to make it even bigger.

As the pit grows, so do the rumors. They started the day of our logging offensive and took off from there. All the stories are about Arganak, Dshokonaj, and Jadmaj and are embellished with true, partly true, and untrue elements. This is the main plot: the principal embezzled State property, and Arganak exposed him. When the principal fired him, Arganak complained to the Party Cell. A commission examined the principal's work and attitudes, and determined that Arganak's accusations were valid, at which point the position of principal would have been vacated were it not for the Party Secretary's interference. Mainly he interfered because he was eyeing the young principal as a potential husband for his cross-eyed spinster of a daughter. The Party Secretary talked Arganak into withdrawing his complaint by promising to get the uneducated but power-hungry man elected to the Bureau of the Party Cell. Soon the school's principal will marry the *darga*'s daughter, and Comrade Arganak will be awarded a medal by the Party and the State. Already the groom has courted the bride, and the receipt for the medal has been signed. The rumors grow as people talk of ambiguous dreams, unambiguous omens, and alarming predictions involving additional well-known names.

One day we hear that Arganak has taken the post van

to the provincial capital to get more lime. In his absence, work on the excavation site is supervised by the principal in the mornings, and by alternating teachers in the afternoons. Brother Dshokonaj seems impatient for Arganak to return. He personally goes to meet him when Arganak returns, and together they carry a heavy bag of lime. Finally the blind letters come to life and the inscription makes sense as it glows on the hillside. Each time I look at it, I feel better. I feel honored and affirmed in my sense of belonging to some larger purpose I cannot name.

Toward the end of the fourth month something occurs that sends shock waves into every yurt and corner of the Altai. Two women and one man—Shalabaj, Ürenek, and Bajbur—are arrested. Uushum sees with her own eyes how Ürenek is taken away. A Kazakh in a green uniform with four stars on each epaulette arrives and tells Ürenek to put on warm clothes and come with him. While she gets changed, he ties black string both ways around both chests in her yurt's *dör*, and seals the knots. No one is to touch them, he says, until the police come and check them. Ürenek is calm but tells her son Uvaj to sprinkle milk behind the man taking her away and to wish him a long life. The Kazakh must understand her instructions, for he says: "This is kind of you, Mother. I can see you realize I'm just doing my duty." Then they both get into the car and leave. Ürenek's son Uvaj does what his mother requested and tells the people standing around that his mother was waiting for this day for months. She knew it would come.

All of a sudden the world seems to have fallen mute. As if a mute sun rose in the morning and a mute storm blew through the day. As if people were mute even when they talked, though their rumors grew louder and traveled farther and faster than ever. People gossip loudly but pray silently, secretly, fervently. Fears that were smoldering are now ablaze. Where people were arrested one by one over the past ten years, now they are taken away in droves.

I live with the all-consuming fear I have felt since I first heard of the arrests. It is a quiet fear, so deep inside me I can almost hide it from myself. But people have taken me aside and warned me to be careful. First it was the teacher, who kept me back during recess, whispering, "Should anyone ask you what I did with you that day in the cellar, please tell them that I interrogated you and forced you to tell me where Gök was hiding. And if anyone asks about the fire, just say I used it to keep warm while I made you stand in a cold corner."

Next it was Sister, who asked me the following evening if I had been blathering about shamanizing again. I said no, I hadn't. She looked at me sternly, and there was no mistaking the doubt in her eyes. Then she told me the story of a boy in Hentej District who, in contrast to me, could truly tell fortunes. "He was much younger than you are," she said, "and still he got shot!" That night I had a nightmare. I was arrested and put in chains, and then shot, over and over again.

One particular rumor seems to become more detailed, more frightening, and hence more convincing each time it is told. According to it, the four-star Kazakh will return to take away more people. When he left last time, there wasn't any space left in his moving glass cubicle. Numbers and names are mentioned. The identity and overall number of people to be arrested is said to be fixed. First the number climbs from three to six, then by another three—people who did not meet their quotas, each known by name—and now settles at nine. The very first name on the list is our aunt's. She is followed by the Party Secretary, which is surprising on one hand, since he is the most important person in the district. On the other hand, it makes sense given that previous arrests targeted mostly state employees. No one knows who the third name on the list is, but everyone knows that there is one. I find all of this terrifying.

One day we see the glass cubicle roll in. My heart feels as heavy and tight as if the box were rolling through my chest. When we hear the next morning that it left without taking away a single person, I am hugely relieved. Until that evening, when I learn that a man wearing the same green uniform but with even bigger stars on his epaulettes called a meeting at which he gave our *dargas* a stern dressing-down. People in our district were clinging to their superstitions, he said. It was high time it stopped, or each and every one of them would feel the hard hand of the revolutionary law. "From now on, the Revolutionary Mongolian Militia will keep its eagle eye on your district," he said. And next time he would come with a van and take away every single offender to eradicate all superstition, root and branch. These words are repeated first in our yurt by Brother Dshokonaj, and later, again and again, by our teachers.

Dügüj shows up at our next assembly. Apparently she is no longer a mere office worker in the District Administration but rather a colleague and member of its Council. She tells us the story of the young Soviet Pioneer Pavlic Morozov, who denounced his own father for counter-revolutionary activities. The father's accomplices took revenge on the boy and murdered him in a most cruel way. But the government of the Workers' and Farmers' State posthumously awarded the brave Pioneer the title Hero of the Soviet Union. Today, schools, streets, squares, and even army units carry the name of the fearless young fighter. "The District Administration believes," adds the young woman whose brisk, pushy voice almost makes up for her tired triangular eyes, "that there are Pioneers in your midst who are just as heroic and dedicated, and just as willing to fight against superstition and for the revolution." She asks us to report straightaway anything we hear about superstitious or counterrevolutionary activities that are out of step with the changing times. And if we lack the courage to do so publicly, we are always welcome to approach the District Administration and tell her or one of the other comrades of the Council. Also, we should drop by in the evenings to listen to the radio programs from Ulaanbaatar, and to learn new songs. She would be in every evening, and would love to see us.

This is impressive. We listen carefully and decide to go find out about the radio programs that very evening. All we know so far is what our teacher has told us: a radio is a gadget that lets you listen to news from all over the world. In the evening we stand dazed in front of a pretty little box that drones and crackles. Dügüj gives us sweets, and explains things. After that evening, we befriend and visit her regularly. I don't remember much of any denunciation.

One evening she tells us not to come the next day. She has to ride out into the country as one of the District Administration's delegates. Would we like to give her letters for our parents and brothers or sisters? None of us has ever written a letter and it sounds like fun. Because she offers paper and pencils, a few of us take her up on it. Once they sit down, though, they can't think of anything clever to write. Embarrassed, several give up after a while. We've heard that letters soldiers send home are always written in stanzas and wonder if ours have to be written the same way. Dügüj says they could but don't have to be that way, and decides to help Uushum, who by this time has become quite close to her. So she dictates to Uushum a few lines meant to be instructive for the rest of us as well.

Under the many-colored blue sky live an infinite number of people I revere. Whom, of all these people, do I revere as much as I revere you, my dear Father? On the many-colored gray earth walk an infinite number of people to whom I feel obliged. To whom do I feel as obliged as to you, my dear Mother?

At this moment, I would like to imagine with my mind's eye that both of you, my dearest parents, and all my younger brothers, sisters, relatives, and friends from near and far continue to be well. I, your thimble-small daughter behind the three rivers and thirty-three mountains, am well. With a healthy body and a determined mind, I tirelessly climb the steep mountain of knowledge. A beautiful calm spring has arrived here at this settlement, with its dozens of fine State institutions and hundreds of sons and daughters of parents from all four corners. The store has many goods, though the people have less money . . .

We are all ears, and try to absorb everything Dügüj says. Her words sound superbly beautiful, and as we listen, she grows into a powerful educated comrade before our very eyes. Then she casually asks Uushum if her parents' yurt contains any sign of religion. Uushum falters before admitting, "A yellow bone that looks like a large wooden ring."

"What kind of bone?"

"Father and Mother say it's our great-grandmother's top neck bone."

"What's it supposed to be good for?"

"Riches will flow through it and into our yurt."

"Do you believe that?"

"Yes, I do . . . I mean I don't know."

"You can't be serious, Uushum! I thought you were a student, and a Pioneer. And what do you say when I call on you as a Pioneer: 'Be prepared!'?"

"Always prepared!"

"There you go! Now, tell me, do you honestly think riches can flow through someone's yellowed neck bone?"

Uushum keeps her head lowered for a moment, then says, "No, I don't believe so."

Dügüj strokes Uushum's head and says gently: "You're a good daughter of the new era. You will be such a good teacher."

Then she carries on with the dictation:

Dear mountainlike Father and dear earthlike Mother, at the State School, your daughter is learning as well as other children. Most importantly, she is growing into a progressive citizen who is shedding her superstitious beliefs. Knowledge, bright as the fire of the rising sun, has taught me that everything about oracles and shamanism is a fraud. There are no spirits, nor is there a soul. And what the shamans and lamas say about the upper and the lower world is also a lie. There is only this one world, and this one life.

Please give the old yellowed bone that supposedly once was a human neck bone to Sister Dügüj, who will deliver this letter to you. The bone will be destroyed under State supervision, together with all the other religious things people are handing in. Incidentally, the bone must not be kept in your chest for it may cause disease. Your daughter, not some old bone, will bring happiness and riches to your yurt.

> Bowing deeply before you,
> Your daughter Uushum

While Dügüj dictates the letter and Big Lip struggles to swallow the steaming stew offered to her, I wonder what ceremonial objects from our yurt would have to be destroyed. I think of the matted strands of each child's first hair; the strung-up pieces of animal ears; our brass butter lamps; and the kneecap—light as sandalwood and soft as birch—that we think belonged to a forefather who lived seven generations ago and was a famous wrestler. I decide not to write a letter.

The next morning the district employees ride off in all directions. Brother Dshokonaj is among them. Later I learn that when he arrived at our shaman's yurt, she was surly. Without returning his greeting, she said she was ready and pointed at the small pile waiting to be grabbed at a moment's notice. It was sitting at the foot of her low wooden bed, and contained a brand-new sheepskin *ton* and equally new boots with white felt lining. Brother Dshokonaj explained that he had not come for her but for her shamanizing tools. "What?" she exclaimed, astonished. "Even the *asalar* have gone soft in the head in these days of the big fist and the shrunken, sickened heart. They have deceived me!" Then she turned to the *ail* women who, having left moments earlier, rushed back when the barking dogs announced the approach of the rider. "And to think that you spent an entire sleepless night struggling with these half-raw hides!" And in the next breath, "Now, at last, with those feebleminded *asalar* and my empty hands, you have more than enough reason to leave me alone."

She looked at Brother and offered him her snuff bottle in the traditional welcome. Then, interrupting her own expansive gesture, she asked, "Or is this bottle one of the outlawed objects that has to be destroyed? If so, put it in your pocket and don't bother with the ritual."

"Oh no," replied the district delegate glumly. "Snuff bottles are not included." He accepted the bottle with both hands, lifted the unscrewed top to his nose, and took a little sniff. Then he passed the bottle back with both hands.

Over tea their conversation slowly got off the ground. "I know you won't respond to what I am about to say," said the shaman. "Still, I have to say it, even if just for the sake of your mother. My sister-in-law might feel hurt if I didn't spell it out. I would have preferred that someone else come, even Hos Haaj, son of Höjük Dshanggy, or, for all I care, that scrawny fox-faced Arganak. The stories you hear about that man make your ears filthy. But it is what it is. It is you who has come, someone from our own family. The things you have been sent to collect are over there, in the chest on the right. I am not going to hand them to you like my snuff bottle and the tea bowl, but you can take them. You simply have to go over, lift the lid, and reach in."

The extended silence that followed was oppressive, until the district delegate broke it: "I'm not allowed to return without the objects, Aunt Pürwü."

"As I said, help yourself," she replied. Brother hesitated, but in the end he got up and walked over to the chest. The women watching the scene trembled and held their breath, retreating into themselves. Brother sensed the quivery silence and the women's oppressive gaze. He lifted the narrow lid and reached inside with his right hand the way one reaches into a sheep's belly during slaughter. Just as one's index and middle finger feel their way forward to find the animal's throbbing thread of life, so did the delegate's hand blindly feel its way forward, eventually snatching a ball of fabric and pulling it out. Then, with his other hand, he seized a corner of the shaman's dark-red cloth. He hurriedly unwrapped the bundle, rummaged through its contents with his rough hands, and said without turning his head: "I've got the headgear and the *shawyd*. Where's the mirror?"

The shaman didn't reply initially. She looked at the hole in the yurt's roof for a long moment, then screwed up her eyes and wiped her palm across them as if to check that her eyelids remained closed. Finally she said, "If you think you need the mirror as well, it sticks in an eye of the grid behind the chest."

The delegate leaned forward, reached across the chest, and helped himself.

Brother Dshokonaj returns home late in the evening, just as we are getting ready to go to bed. We're so happy to see him that all three of us fire questions at him. But we soon realize that he is in no mood to tell us about his excursion.

Disappointed and discouraged, Brother Galkaan and I give up and go to bed. Sister, on the other hand, is more persistent and presses on until she wrings some details from him. The odd fragment reaches Galkaan and me through the veil of sleep that sinks down on us like an anesthetizing cloud, showering us with waves of bright light.

That night my dreams are intense and vivid. I feel as if I am dragged repeatedly through the same dream about my shaman aunt. Naked and bare, she stands surrounded by a roaring, scornful mob. I wake up when I hear her call for me, but even after lying in bed for a long time, my ears still ring from her deep raspy voice calling my name. I have to get up.

The following morning, I am sent to fetch *aarshy* from the shed for tea. I discover Brother Dshokonaj's tack in a corner. He must have lifted it off his horse and dropped it there without gathering in the bridle's long rein and lead, and his half-filled goat-leather bag is still tied to the saddle. I can't help but wonder what is in the bag and so, with snatches of last night's conversation still in my mind, I undo the knots in the saddle strings and open the bag. I immediately recognize the headgear, with its eagle-owl feathers, cowrie shells, and black fringes. My heart begins to pound. Next I pull out the *shawyd* and wave it about silently a few times. The last thing I find is the mirror. It almost bowls me over. As I stand and hold the perfectly round, brightly polished brass mirror with both hands, I see before me the naked shaman, the shape of her body cruelly distorted. And I hear her call again. Then I calmly hide the mirror under the *aarshy*, and tie the goat-leather bag with the headgear and the *shawyd* back to the saddle.

In the evening Brother Dshokonaj asks if anyone outside our family has borrowed the key to the shed. With one voice we say no. Beginning with that moment, an odd change comes over him. He broods, casting a shadow over all of us. We talk little, and life in our yurt becomes quiet. But we make an extra effort with our schoolwork. Even Brother Galkaan, the problem child when it comes to learning, brings home mostly excellent grades.

One day, during the last class of the afternoon, the teacher hands me a small package about the length and diameter of a finger: "Deliver this to my yurt, please. You'd better take your schoolbag with you."

His words leave me feeling curious and excited. The teacher's wife is kind and lively again. She welcomes and feeds me, and remembers to ask about Gök. The memory of that time makes me melancholy and opens the door to my soul. Once again their young daughter is sick in bed. "Dear little Brother! You helped her so much before," says the beautiful woman. "Could you take another look at her?" I agree, and the girl starts coughing as soon as she sits up. I can tell she is suffering from whooping cough. Having had it myself, I recognize the symptoms. I also know a few remedies: in the spring one must swallow a marmot's warm gallbladder just as it comes from the animal's body. In the summer one must eat wild sweet onions, boiled in the milk of a white goat, and stand with one's mouth wide open into the wind; or, better still, ride fast to create one's own wind.

I am supporting the gasping child's back and waiting for the attack to pass when the teacher enters the yurt. Now I can show off my knowledge. The family is impressed and grateful, which pleases and emboldens me. At that moment I remember the mirror and quickly decide to make a move: "I strongly recommend that you check with my aunt first. I could be wrong, and I don't want to give you bad advice. Your daughter seems to be a very serious case."

"Do you think your aunt might see us? We've always heard she's hard to reach. And particularly now that even the last of her tools were taken from her . . ." The teacher is concerned.

"You could take me with you," I say, adding, "I grew up more in my aunt's lap than in my own mother's." This is a gross exaggeration, to put it mildly, but I get what I want when the wife says to her husband, "Go to the boy's aunt right now, and take him with you!"

We leave shortly afterward. The teacher has a good horse with good tack, which makes me think more highly of him. I sit behind him on a rolled-up lambskin coat, which makes for a wonderfully soft seat. So I put my arms around his stout and surprisingly solid waist. Could we ride past our yurt, I ask, so I can drop off my schoolbag and tell the others? "Don't tell them where we're going," he replies. "Tell them we're going fishing." I agree, and fetch the mirror and a handful of *aarshy* in case anyone notices I am carrying something in my breast pocket.

Uncle Know-It-All and my aunt's yurt is within walking distance at Saryg-höl, the Yellow Lake. Earlier I had wondered if I shouldn't just walk over to take the mirror back, but I decided against it because Brother Dshokonaj would have noticed. To welcome me, my aunt sniffs and strokes me as usual, but she is less friendly than I would have expected. She is clipped and gloomy while exchanging greetings with my teacher, and I have to use a trick to lure her out of the yurt. Once we are outside, I take her hand and lead her off into the steppe. "Do you know what I've brought you?" She has no idea, which is somewhat disappointing. But I stay cheerful: "Close your eyes!"

When she indulges me, my initial disappointment wanes. My left hand hangs on to hers, but my right hand reaches deep into my breast pocket, fishes out her mirror with two pieces of *aarshy*, and drops it all into the palm of her other hand. "Open your eyes!"

She begins to tremble even before she looks. Her trembling grows more intense until I, too, begin to tremble. For some time her green eagle-owl eyes stare at the mirror. Then she closes her fingers around it and stares at her fist. Finally she speaks: "Did your brother make you bring it back?"

"No, I stole it."

"You stole it?" She looks incredulous. "Why did you steal it? Why would you do something like that?"

"You were standing there naked, calling me," I say.

"I stood there naked, you say? And I called for you?" She sounds hoarse. "What did I say?"

"First you called out Dshuruunaj," I say. "And then you said 'My dear little lamb!'"

She puts her fist with the mirror on my left shoulder and her other palm on the part in my hair. With her hands on me, I can feel that she is still trembling. Then she asks about the two pieces of *aarshy*.

"Three were stolen from you," I say, "and three should return."

I can feel her hands press harder into me, and the trembling grows stronger.

Back in the yurt, she is nicer to the teacher. Together we drink tea and eat meat. In the end the teacher casually asks our host for permission to get up from the special mat for guests so we can leave. The shaman replies similarly, making light of the situation and not referring at all to his daughter. In fact, the sick child has remained in the background throughout our visit.

"Oh yes, the whooping cough," says the shaman suddenly. "It's been bad again this year. Almost all the lambs have had it. If the poor marmots hadn't provided any fresh gallbladders, no one would have known how to get rid of it. Actually, some of those unfortunate lambs are still coughing and gasping. We can only hope that once summer rolls in and the wild sweet onions grow again, they'll finally recover."

Then they talk about the uphill battle against people who continue to resist seeing doctors. What can the poor shamans and fortune-tellers possibly achieve empty-handed, while a doctor has his knowledge and listening piece? "Nothing!" she says.

We are already outside tightening the saddle girth when

she walks up to me to tie around my neck a piece of white cloth that she has just cut off some larger piece. "When I was young, elegant people carried handkerchiefs. They were made of silk and embroidered along the edges. I don't have any silk. This is the best I can give you, little one. Use it as a handkerchief or, if it's not elegant enough, as a foot cloth or, if you prefer, to wave in front of the marmots to hypnotize them so you can shoot them from up close." She bursts into loud laughter and turns to the teacher. "Brother, I'm sorry I don't have candies for your little one. It's too early in the year; we're short of everything. But here's a little bone for her, a white kiddie for her toy flock. Once she's grown up and become a lady of thirteen, she can come see me and exchange her toy for a real nanny goat."

The teacher receives the gift with both his hands, touches it to his forehead, and then plunges it deep into his breast pocket.

The evening is mild beneath a glimmering wide sky. The stars and the waxing moon bounce along with the horse's trot. The girl will grow out of her illness, I think happily. And I, too, will grow. In fact, by the time we get home I will have grown a little more. My Grandma with the Shaved Head used to say that each day I would grow the width of a blade of grass. Perhaps Galbak will embroider the borders of my cloth with red and yellow yarn. Either way, I have to become a big strong man. The horse is carrying me toward the place where, with great impatience but even greater confidence, the man I will become is waiting for the child I still am.

DAY WITHOUT SKY

Spring still resembles winter, but some of its rough gray days leave behind gifts to the storm-weary steppe—mild evenings that feel like tasty morsels, affectionate winks, and gently teasing swats on the nose. These balmy spells stay with us, along with the Brant geese and the gray ducks that have arrived too early once again, and now have to find and re-create in snow and ice the path that will point toward summer. These mild moments that the gray days have drizzled over the world of the Altai—out of negligence or forgetfulness perhaps, or as thoughtful rewards for our unfailing patience—must stay and swell, nibbling away at the winter as incessantly and tirelessly as mice.

One day hairline cracks show up in the stark, awe-inspiring tableau of the mountain range. Its icy armor is cracking. The steaming fissures darken, and the glistening shards shrink. In the end it takes only a few days for the pallid ocean of ice and snow and its islands of black rocks to give way and let the gray-yellow steppe reemerge, with its roiling, gray-blue streams, rivers, and lakes. The land, on the other hand, stubbornly clings to the vanishing world's last remaining white stripes and patches.

The fifth month opens with a storm. A fiery-red sun starts to simmer early in the morning, its rim erupting into glowing red-veined rings that ripple across the sky before billowing into clouds. They remind me of the epics, in which glowing waves puff and blow over a simmering ocean. I can't help but think of summer bursting onto the scene with great powers. And I like to believe that my bright anticipation is confirmed by the nights that are now filled with the rushing of the migratory birds' return.

Soon the school year will end, says the teacher. His voice is quiet and composed. Then he tells us we have survived the most important but also the most difficult year of our lives. He is speaking from experience; first grade was unbelievably hard for him. He was homesick in the worst possible way, and during the nights both his pillow at the top of his bed and his mattress farther down got wet. "Mind you," he groans, moved by the memory, "that was during the war. And besides, I ended up way too far away from home, torn away from everything familiar. At the time, there was not a single school in this corner of the country. If you wanted to learn how to read and write, you had to go to the provincial capital."

The room falls quiet as we listen with bated breath,

but the teacher does not continue. He finds it hard to think back. Gazing into the distance above our heads, his familiar dreaded eyes don't see us for a change.

The son of a single mother, I think. I can't help but feel sorry for him. Given the look of his eyes and the body he was born with, he probably endured a lot of teasing. Who can say how his life would have turned out if he hadn't been fortunate enough to choose the path of knowledge? Could he have married that beautiful woman? Hardly. A bit of gossip that Big Lip told us flashes through my mind, something the teacher's wife supposedly said about her husband, the father of her child. I feel deeply hurt on his behalf. "Still," the teacher whispers as if awakening from a deep sleep or returning from a long journey, "there is not much difference between what I once was and what you are now. A child is a child, and a school is a school. I am telling you: You have survived the most difficult and the most important year of your lives, and you have survived it well. Better, in any case, than I did some thirteen years ago. And I was a lot older than you. I didn't have to start school until I was twelve."

Again the teacher pauses. Lost in thought, he stares into space. Then he collects himself and says quickly under his breath, "I tell you: You've been good, and you've become very dear to me. You've been a good collective, almost exemplary. You're lively but disciplined, and you get along. That's not a given, I must say; not every class becomes a collective. I hope those of you who've been in other classes will agree."

Sürgündü and Ombar agree. "Right!" the teacher continues, visibly encouraged. "Everyone worked hard. Not with the same results, of course. How could that be? Everyone's different. But I am especially happy that five of you will finish the year with a final grade of Five. And that one of these five will attend Pioneers' Camp for three weeks with three other students from our school. Only the very best of the top students from all the provincial districts get to go to that camp."

I am startled and think: this very best student, that's me! It makes me dizzy. Because of the sudden buzzing and rushing in my ears, I can't hear what the teacher says next, but I do see his lips continue to move, and I think I can read his lips: the youngest one, who arrived late but caught up so quickly and effortlessly, working his way up to the very top of the class, you know who I'm talking about . . .

Then his face goes gloomy. Now he can't possibly be talking about the chosen one. I hear his voice again: "I really don't know what else I could have done for that girl." He looks to be suffering, as if he is about to cry, and then out come the words I thought I heard before: "You know who I'm talking about."

Suddenly a screeching wail rings out from the center of the classroom. It is Sürgündü. I can see her back shake violently and hear her sob more miserably than ever before. Then her lamentations pour out in the familiar hoarse voice with the familiar lisp: "How could an old woman like me sit for another year among the first grade Tom Thumbs next fall? This is my life? This is not a life! Some evil spirit is mocking me! Oh, Blue Sky! Why did you make me so stupid? I wish I could disappear in the Black Earth! Oh, oh, oh . . ."

No one interrupts her. Having triggered this terrible outburst, the teacher, who is normally so strict, just stands there silent, doing nothing. He is watching passively as his student humiliates herself, and looks as if he would let her destroy herself.

"Teacher!" I move quickly. "Teacher! Please, please do not make Sister Sürgündü repeat first grade. We want to have her with us in second grade." Stunned, the teacher stares at me. I realize I have to be fast and continue: "A girl with such skilled hands and such a big heart couldn't possibly be so stupid that we'd have to give up on her. We'll help her. I'll help her. I will do the same as I did for Gök."

The teacher quietly shakes his head, but he appears to be undecided and at a loss for words. I fish for more to say. "I'm willing to move into a yurt with her!" While the words fly out, I am unaware of their consequences. But I am aware enough to notice the shock—or mockery— in the teacher's eyes. Quickly I add, "Next year my sister will no longer live here, so Sürgündü can move in with us. Or if my big brother gets married, I may move into the dormitory."

The teacher doesn't say a word. My words fail to move him to a response that would relieve Sürgündü's suffering. Nothing! Entangled in a hopeless battle, I continue the fight. "Teacher!" My voice sounds funny because I am scared he might not be able to hear me, just as I could not hear him before. "Teacher! Please send her to Pioneers' Camp. Just for once send someone who is miserable, someone who has failed. Let her spend time with all the lucky and successful students. If she could just spend a few days in close touch with what's called good luck and success, maybe she would find her way, who knows . . ."

Tears threaten to drown my voice. But I still haven't managed to say the most important thing, and so I push myself to find the right words: "She needs this more than I do. She has a very strict stepmother at home. I have both my parents, and they spoil me day in and day out. Please send her instead of me, please . . ."

The rims of my eyes are hot, but I am determined not to cry. Clenching my jaw, I give myself a good shake. At that moment my eyes meet the teacher's and I see his shock abruptly become a question. Only then do I begin to realize that he never said I was the one who would be sent to Pioneers' Camp.

I feel dizzy with embarrassment. Fortunately, just then the conch's hoarse roar comes to my, or rather our, rescue. Sürgündü finally stops her whining and whimpering. She is doing me a favor by stopping, and as a result she gains a deeper and more solid presence inside me, as if in a small bright yurt. Moments ago, when I was fighting for her, I sensed her just inside the door; now I feel her presence in the yurt's center, near the stove.

This connection with Sürgündü brightens and warms

me like a fire burning inside. But I still feel uneasy, not so much because of the poor girl but rather because of the premature statement that got away from me, worse than a fleeing foal. Recalling the disaster of the school uniform, I no longer want to go to Pioneers' Camp. In fact, I don't ever want to hear those words again.

As if he has heard my unspoken wish, the teacher silently passes over anything that was said during the previous class, and instead gives us our summer homework. Everyone is to help his or her parents with the housework and the livestock, and to keep a daily record. Also, we all must collect twenty different sorts of grass, flowers, or tree leaves, and catch ten different kinds of butterflies. The leaves and the butterflies must be pressed between pages in a book, and we are to write down what they are called and where we found them. Each girl must dry ten kilos of mushrooms and pick five kilos of berries, and each boy must salt ten kilos of fish and pick five kilos of wild onions.

"Bring all of it with you when you come back for classes on September 1," says the teacher. "By then the root cellar will be finished so we can store all the food." We want to know what the food is for. For the school kitchen, the teacher says. From now on the school will provide for itself in order to ease the pressure on the State and the People. We will form brigades, and we will go hunting. We like this idea a lot.

"Will the girls come along?" The question makes everyone laugh. It comes from Eweshdej, whose real name is

Shut-Up-And-Eat-Up because he never opens his mouth to speak. With his protruding ears he is an attentive listener. Now, on the last day of classes, Mr. Silent, as the teacher once called him, indulges us with the sound of his voice, and general merriment ensues.

"Seriously! Will the girls go hunting with us?"

"Why not?" The teacher enters the game. "They can cook and sew and wash. And they can wash out your mouth with soap and water!" Our sides are splitting with laughter. Names are mentioned, hints dropped. Having put the screws to us all year, the teacher is unusually lighthearted. His round plump face has settled into a kindly smile.

Suddenly the smile vanishes, and a reddish-green sheen spreads across his face. Vestiges of the previous lesson have lingered in the air, and can now be traced across his face.

"I have to tell you something." He begins quietly. "When school starts again in the fall, you won't have me as a teacher. I am leaving because I want to study at a higher school. I may not pass the entrance exam, though; it's supposed to be difficult. But if I don't pass, I'll do some other work. I won't go back to teaching. I know I am a bad teacher. I am simply not cut out for educating children."

His last words come out loud and hard. He scans the room the way he does when he is angry. His eyes narrow, and his face takes on the familiar bitter look. It scares us. Instantly we revert to being his anxious and obedient students, cowering like a flock of trembling starlings in a fold among the rocks. But this time there is more to it, and more in us, than fear. We are sad. In my belly I can already feel the loss that this clumsy, loud, often ill-tempered stranger will cause me by leaving. For better or worse, this oddly kind and understanding man has become part of my life. And now he wants to tear himself from it.

"You obviously don't want to leave anyone behind. One of you has even expressed a willingness to take her hand and carry her along, rather than have her stay behind. To my mind, that's noble and so, out of respect, I want to leave you a gift: it's called Sürgündü. Accept her. But I hope you all know that getting ahead with her in your class may well be a challenge. At that point some of you may think she's dead weight that should have been dumped long ago. But that would be nasty. And another thing: the teacher who will take over your class may wonder and ask, Why didn't she have to repeat first grade? If that happens, speak up and tell the teacher what happened. Show courage and explain who Sürgündü is: not just a fool with a lazy tongue, but a girl with ten nimble fingers and a kind heart."

His words put us back in a good mood, and soon our joy spreads to include him. He refers to himself as a man with a smeared face and a tainted name, but now does so jokingly. "Make sure they won't paint me any worse than in fact I am." Shortly afterwards he adds defiantly: "When I come back, I don't just want to come with beautiful new feathers. I want to come back with more powerful wings, a hawk with feathers as bright as ice, even if it costs me half my life."

Later I hear Big Lip whisper that Gök's father submitted a written complaint to the District Party Cell and that this is why the teacher is leaving.

"How's Gök?" I ask quickly.

Suddenly she knows nothing.

It is on this fifth day of the week, a windless day with low clouds and swarms of buzzing flies, that the school year ends for us. But we still have to spend both the half-good day and the all-good day doing community service. Though the mounts for most of the students have already arrived, Comrade Leader of the School Staff doesn't budge. We have to do our share, if for no other reason than that the work is already weeks behind schedule.

That night Brother Dshokonaj comes home late. He was at the pit where logs and planks have arrived for shoring up the walls and ceiling of the cellar. The work is to begin the next day. We have long finished dinner, and have kept his meal warm by wrapping thick layers around the green enamel pot.

I unwrap the pot and serve up the thin slices of steamed lamb and the grainy rice in Brother's small wooden bowl. With solemn pride I offer it to him. Sister Torlaa has given me this job because she wants me to learn how to serve our big brother. She also wants him and me to be close, and thus has decreed that from now on, I am to sleep only in Brother Dshokonaj's bed so the two of us can maintain our skintight connection. It is important for both of you, she says, though I find it notable that Brother Dshokonaj is not present at the time. Later she explains to me that she, Galkaan, and I are already very close, but that our big brother needs to be brought into the fold. And as the baby, I am most likely to succeed in doing so.

Brother Dshokonaj quickly reaches for his bowl. "Oh, my dear little one," he says with gratitude. "It's still hot, and you've filled my bowl!" I don't reply, but I can't help smiling and thinking how one must never offer older people a half-empty bowl.

While our hungry brother tucks in, I tell him about my homework. "Isn't that great?" he says with pride. "Soon the school will provide for itself."

Sister Torlaa sneers: "Be serious! You don't really believe the students will bring back sacks of dried mushrooms and salted fish and jugs of gooseberries and sallow-thorn berries, do you?"

He glances at her, hesitates, and then insists: "Sure I do. And I also believe that after thousands of years of moving around and being glued to the udders of their animals, our nomads will settle within the next ten or twenty years. They will become farmers, and they will milk the udders of the soil."

"Isn't that nice?" She feins enthusiasm, then adds,

"Maybe they will in ten or twenty years. But in three months, you won't see much more than a handful of measly marmot skins and a few pressed blades of grass and butterflies." Her tongue seems to give vent to her spleen, but Brother Dshokonaj does not react. I admire that and feel closer to him.

Later, in bed, I tell him everything the teacher said. I haven't told Sister Torlaa and Brother Galkaan, and so I whisper, snuggled into the crook of his arm, my face close to his. He remains quiet for a while, and then asks if we like our teacher.

"At first we didn't, but now we do."

"I do too," he says. "Especially because he isn't satisfied with himself and wants to grind off his flaws and rough edges and start over. That takes courage."

A little later I add, "He had a difficult childhood."

"Did he tell you that?"

"A bit. Mostly Big Lip did."

"Who's Big Lip?"

"Uushum."

"I see. Does she really have different lips?"

"Oh no. She just talks all the time. She's a know-it-all and a gossip."

"What did she say about your teacher?"

"That he doesn't have a father. And that his mother is poor."

Brother Dshokonaj holds his breath and then ends the silence with a barely perceptible groan. I feel sorry I said the bit about the father. To get him off the subject and distract him I say, "The teacher was far from home and very homesick. Was it the same for you?"

Brother ignores my question.

"At least he had his mother," he says bitterly. "I only had Grandma, and she was old and frail. She had to eke out a living somewhere on the margins because the rest of the clan left her to her fate. Mind you, she probably brought it on herself, given her moodiness. At times it was hard even for me to get along with her. In some sense I only made it into school because I was born into such misery. Even today some people think sending a child to school is like having to fill a quota. At the time, everyone felt that way. As a result, the first victims were children who got dragged from the poorest, most helpless yurts. No one attended school voluntarily; all the students had to be forced to go. And that's how it was for me as well.

"Your teacher was sent to the provincial capital. Sure, his homeland is along the upper reaches of the Ak-Hem, a long way from here, three *örtöö* if not more. Then it's another three from Tsengel to Ölgiy. All in all, that's six *örtöö* from his home. For me, it was forty. Four days of riding and then four days of driving before you reached Arkhangay and its capital, Tsetserleg.

"Was I homesick? Of course I was. But that wasn't the worst of it. I didn't really understand the language and was shy in general. So I just stood there like a lump, withdrawn into my shell, painfully aware that the other students thought I was a Kazakh. That went on for a few days. Then I understood enough to get by and knew I'd be able to survive. But the worst was the knowledge I'd been carrying with me from day one: I wasn't as good as everyone else. Sure, you're called a ward of the State. But what does that mean, really? So your father is the man with the angry eyes and pockmarked face, and the medals dangling on his puffed-up chest. But your mother? Where is she? What does she look like? And where are your brothers and sisters? Who are they? The boys and girls around you? Including the students who call you a Kazakh and mock your clumsy speech? It's hard when you can't find the answers . . ."

I sense that Sister Torlaa and Brother Galkaan are lying there listening in the *dör*, swallowed by the darkness. My heart thumps against my ribs, the tip of my nose itches, and I snuggle up to my big brother's shoulder.

I don't recall how much longer he spoke and what else he told me. A dream separates then from now. I don't remember what the dream was about, but I know that the following morning I had much more inside me than I did the evening before. I can't be sure what I was told and what I dreamed.

It must have been in Hüpsug. Through the swaying amber heads of the tall, sparse autumn grass I can see the mountain steppe rise at an angle until it ends in a forest. A family of larch trees at the far side of the forest has lifted off the ground and is floating in the sky. Where the plain slopes downward on the opposite side of the mountain meadow, I see a lonely yurt. It looks dark and stuck awkwardly to the narrow end of a gentle mound rising like a breast from the surrounding plain. Grandma, stooped with age, is busy some distance from the yurt. Not far from her a bare-bottomed boy sits in the grass, rocking a baby in a wooden cradle resting on his outstretched legs. The boy is Brother Dshokonaj. I ask who the baby is. "That's you," he says, adding when he sees my surprise, "Grandma is old and on her own. She can't do everything."

Sister Torlaa, Brother Galkaan, and I are at home playing with ankle bones. Mother has prepared milk tea and is pouring it from the cast iron pot into the brass jug. Outside the light is wintry and pale, and a storm begins to blow, making the yurt's scaffolding creak and the flap on the roof flutter. I hear a dog bark and Father shout, "Hey! What are you doing here? Go home. It's late."

"I'm looking for my mother!" replies the bright voice of a child. I jump up to run outside, but Mother says, "Stay put!" Then the boy somehow must have come inside. Wearing a heavy *ton* and a felt hat, he squats on the right side of the stove. Torlaa, Galkaan, and I huddle in front of the bed, to the left of the stove. We are all drinking tea. Mother takes a heart that was left as an offering in the *dör,* and cuts deeper into the slits that are already there. The heart falls into four pieces. She drops a piece into Torlaa's, Galkaan's, and my tea bowl and is about to give the fourth piece to the boy on the other side of the stove when I start whining: "Father always gives me two. I want both!" The stranger is accommodating:

"Give him both. I'll be fine with just the tea." It is Brother Dshokonaj's voice.

Now we lie on our bouncy bed under our soft quilt and are chatting.

"By the way, I accidentally let something slip today."

"What?"

"I said, 'If my big brother gets married next year . . .'"

"How would you feel if I actually did get married?"

"But you aren't."

"How do you know? Everyone gets married."

"True. Some time ago you said that someone might drop by the yurt."

"Did I? I probably meant Teacher Deldeng. I used to think she might become my wife."

"Why not? A family of teachers would be good."

"Things turned out differently. She said she'd marry me if I proved myself as principal and joined the Party. First I thought about it and agreed, but now I've chosen someone else."

"Jadmaj's daughter?"

"Oh no!"

"It was just a joke! I know who she is."

"Who is it then?"

"Dü . . . right?"

"How do you know?"

"I'll drop by her place tomorrow and address her as *Dshenggej.*"

"Don't you dare. I have to ask Grandma and Father and Mother first."

"They'll all agree."

"You think so? A few minutes ago you said, 'If my big brother gets married next year.' But what if I got married this fall?"

"I could move into the dormitory."

"There's no way you'll move into the dormitory. You'll stay here, with me and your *dshenggej*. She'll be kind to you."

"I just thought because . . ." I tell him about Sürgündü. But now I forget what he said about that subject.

During the night it rained. Now the steppe looks washed and polished, and the air is soft and fragrant. Strong, sharp-edged rays come bounding to us from the sun's orb. Equipped with spades, pickaxes, and crowbars we have marched across Eer Hawak to the meadow on the eastern bank of the Haraaty, where the reddish-green, white-capped river crashes and hisses through its narrow curvy bed. As if fired up by the river's powerful energy, we are full of bluster as we launch our attack on the Mother Earth's body. We pry it open, drive our steel tools inside, poke around, and begin to dig a ditch. The tools are heavy, and the work requires a crazy mind. The wet light-colored stones we pull from the earth's insides are like kidneys. The earth's blood appears to be a few shades lighter than sheep or yak blood, but the kidneys we tear from its body look as quivery and helpless as the kidneys of any animal.

Right next to its crashing and hissing artery, I feel as if I can hear the earth weep and wail. Before you touch the belly of a sheep or a yak with a knife and slice it open to sever its throbbing thread of life, you have to tie a solid rope around the sheep's ankles or the yak's legs. Fettered and thrown on its back, the animal will twitch when the blade thrusts through its fur and into its flesh, and it will try to fight you with all its strength. By then it is too late, but at least the animal fought, reminding you that you are a murderer.

The Mother Earth seems tamer and more helpless than even a badly injured lamb, for whom the otherwise cruel blade performs an act of mercy. Not even those lambs will lie still in that fateful moment, gathering whatever strength they have left and convulsing in spasms that only end with the last breath. The powerful Mother Earth, on the other hand, lies still, enduring its violation without a twitch.

Or does it? If I stay very still and listen carefully, I believe I can hear the weeping and wailing behind the crashing and hissing, and I can also feel a quiet but persistent quiver coming from inside the earth. I can also feel something inside myself, something not unlike the feeling I got the day I examined the big belly of a squirrel I had killed. I saw some movement on the other side of the shaggy blue-striped fur, and then discovered the double rows of tits running from the squirrel's lower belly up to its chest. They looked like eyes swollen and tired from crying.

At that moment we suddenly hear many voices screaming in great distress. The cries seem to go on forever, wailing in anguish. We stop our work and look at each other bewildered. Then we run. As soon as we emerge from the high thorny caragana bushes, we see a cloud of red dust billowing above the steep slope of Eer Hawak. Right where the cellar is being built! Fearing a disaster, we race toward it.

The distance is considerable. Soon the group stretches out as gaps open up between the runners. I tear off as if racing against my own strength. Struggling to catch up with those at the front and to escape from those pursuing me from behind, I pass one or two, but also get passed by two, three, four, and then many. I sweat and pant and cough, and I am gasping for air when I finally arrive at a scene that seems so unreal and so distorted that I cannot help but think I am dreaming.

Alas, I am not dreaming at all. The earth has caved in. A crater as big as a large yurt turned upside down has opened up. People crowd around it like a shrill swaying wall. Some people, including Brother Dshokonaj, dig with their bare hands where the entrance used to be, screaming the whole time. Dust rises as they scratch the dirt like dogs pawing the ground. All the tools are apparently buried in the rubble. Brother screams the same words over and over. His mouth is half open, and his thin lips bare his teeth, while the tip of his pink tongue pokes out every so often.

At some point I can make out the teacher's voice even though I cannot see the man himself. He orders the ten fastest students to run back and get our tools from the ditch. Boys from every class are charging off. Far more than ten have already left, but I take off, too, going full tilt.

The distance seems endless, and when I finally arrive at the fresh pile of dark stony earth, other students are turning around to run back with empty hands. The tools are gone. Full of shame and fury, I try to run after them, faster than before. My face is soaked with sweat, and burning hot; stinging tears run down my cheeks, over my jaw, and into my collar in big drops, like round bugs of disgrace and misfortune. Panting and groaning, blinded by tears, deafened by the roar and rumble in my ears, and constricted by the drenched clothes that cling heavily to my body, I am still aware of what is going on around me. The caraganas, such a nuisance a moment ago, are falling behind as I make it to the barren tongue of the steppe between the lined-up rocks, only to see more boys pass me.

I can sense my strength slipping away just as I stumble. I try to catch myself but I lose my balance and fall flat on my face, right on the hot steppe, which lies bright and bare beneath the blazing noon sun.

Too weak to get up from the hot sand and gravel, I remain on the ground, waiting for someone to come and help me. But no one comes. I start to howl, and then eventually I get up and look around. There is no one around. They all must have passed me and arrived at the disastrous cellar, where the crowd has thickened and a frenzied effort is underway with the tools. The deafening noise is punctuated by the clanking and banging of steel and wood. Dust clouds billow into the sky.

Back on my feet, I feel dizzy and decide to walk in the

opposite direction, to wash the tears and dirt off my face and cool my confused head in the glacier water of the river. And so I trudge across the scree and drag myself through the shrubs. Suddenly the river's bank is before me. Bending down and looking into the eddying current, I wonder what will happen if I just let myself drop into the water. You will drown, my mind tells me. The thought gives me such a fright that I jolt back and fall on my bottom. Instantly I feel a searing pain—my tailbone must have hit a rock. I can't help but berate myself inwardly: Cowards like you trip over their own feet, I think. One disgrace after another. You moron!

Slowly I stretch and wriggle back to the river's edge. As soon as my head dips into the river, the cold and the power of the current straining at my neck make me scream. But I keep my head in the water, and when I open my eyes, its rocky bottom lies blurry below me. Dark grooves in the rocks look like writhing bodies struggling for air. I quickly pull my head from the water.

Panting and gasping, I shake myself. Death has come close and touched my skin, cold as ice. I jump to shake it off and scream to free myself, trying to push Death back to where it cannot be seen or felt. And so I rear up and roar:

> E-eh-eej,
> You earthworm,
> Why is the slit of your mouth tied
> And the pipe of your neck throttled
> A-ah-aaj . . .

I allow myself to cry loudly, but it does nothing to calm me. Gripped by a growing anxiety, I tremble until my whole body twitches, suffocated and overwhelmed by a paralyzing fear.

Some time later I find myself surrounded by a crowd of people. I remember neither faces nor bodies, only that they seem to grow tall one moment and wide the next. A hand grabs my arm and pulls me away. I recognize it as my sister's. Then I see her teary twisted face and hear her quivering voice: "A lot of people have been crushed. Brother Dshokonaj will be sent to prison. And so will you if you don't stop right now. Pull yourself together!"

I buck and fight wildly. Through my tears I cry: "Oh Mother Earth, how we have wounded and humiliated you. I heard you groan with pain and I felt you shake with rage. I knew the quake was coming, yet I kept quiet. I am such an ass, such a tiny fart. Oh, oh, oh, why did I keep quiet? Because I was afraid of the people!"

Then I sense Brother Galkaan close by as well. Brother and Sister both try to pull me away. Their efforts double my resistance—I tear myself away from their grip and scream for all I am worth: "Leave my big brother alone. He meant well and had no idea. The person responsible for the disaster is this one here!" I hammer my own chest with my fist. "Report him. Send him to prison. Have him shot. Where is Hollow Nose, Höjük Dshanggy's son-of-a-bitch blood-thirsty son? Now he can drink blood. But if there's going to be blood, it's not because someone has a shaman inside pushing to come out. Nor is it because someone is dabbling with the spirits. Oh no. That's no cause for blood. But that someone stayed silent instead of passing on the message from the spirits—that is cause for blood. He should have run and shouted, 'All of you, come out quick, Mother Earth is angry and wants to quake!' But he did not do that, and so he deserves a terrible death!"

Later I find myself in the arms of the doctor. He is strong and he holds me so tight to his chest that I can barely breathe. He lets go only after he has forced me to sit on my bottom down in the dirt, and only then do I stop bucking. A piece of gauze is held under my nose. It smells sharp and good. I inhale and feel calm. Then I hear the clanking and banging and people's voices again, but they no longer cry and scream. Later I see the crowd again, but they have moved into the distance, where they bustle beneath a cloud of dust as pale and light as a feather. I am overcome with exhaustion.

"Lie down if you like," says the doctor. It feels good to obey. Everything around me blurs and darkens. Where there used to be the sky, there is nothing . . . a day without sky, I think before drifting away, only to come around in the hospital the following day.

A STOVE
GOES OUT

"What is it?"

"Severe shock to the nervous system."

"Is he talking?"

"No."

It is Dügüj who asks and the doctor who answers. Breathing deeply and noisily, I pretend to be asleep. Big Brother must have sent her. The thought of Brother stabs my heart. What did things look like under the earth?

Then it is the doctor's turn to ask a few questions. Judging by Dügüj's replies, it was not Brother who sent her. The disappointment hurts and terrifies me. What will become of my brother and me?

Later the doctor comes in alone, looking stern with his white coat, his even more brilliant white cap, and the listening thing dangling on his chest. He tells me to eat and sleep a lot. And before he leaves, he adds, "If you feel like screaming, go right ahead. But pull the blanket over your head first."

After morning tea with butter-and-sugar flatbread, Sister Torlaa comes to visit. I am sitting up in my bed, holding the rubber ball the nurse brought earlier for me to play with. I have not played with it but I have enjoyed feeling the round soft ball against the tips of my fingers while I try to focus on one thought and one thought only: May Mother Earth be gentle with her children.

Sister Torlaa creeps in on soft soles, sniffs the top of my head, and strokes my neck and back. I look at her questioningly, and she tries to look me in the eye but fails. Still, she manages to ask if I am the only one in here.

"It looks like it."

"Have you been awake for long?"

"Yes. I woke up when Dügüj and the doctor came in."

"Dügüj was here?!" Sister looks straight at me.

"Yes."

"What did she want from you?"

"I pretended to be asleep."

"What did she say to the doctor?"

"She wanted to know if I was talking."

Sister's anxiety is catching my attention. Quickly I ask the most important question: "What happened?"

Torlaa starts, falters, stutters. Once she gets going, though, she can't be stopped. Brother Galkaan is safe and sound, and so is everyone else related to us. Things could have been much, much worse. At times the whole fourth grade class was inside. If it had happened during one of those times . . .

"How many were inside?" I press her. "Tell me."

"Four," she says almost inaudibly.

"Are they all injured?"

She shakes her head.

"No one's injured? Are they all . . . ?" I am close to screaming.

She goes pale and says nothing. A little later she nods softly, as if to herself. All of a sudden I feel strangely calm. The unbearable ache I felt only moments earlier in my chest and my veins has vanished.

"Where is Brother Dshokonaj?"

"People are hiding him."

"Where? And why?"

Sister hesitates. Then she whispers: "In the cellar under the school. But don't tell anyone. They are afraid of the crushed students' families."

"What about Arganak?"

"Don't say his name! He was in there too."

That bit of news surprises me and I think, well, at least . . . Sister notices and interrupts: "It's bad luck for Brother that the man who hatched the whole plot is gone."

"Will Brother have to go to prison?"

"Probably. He has asked the District Administration to arrest him. But the *dargas* want to wait for the militia. The militia should be here sometime soon."

Sister has to leave when the nurse returns. While shooting fear into my heart and a blood-red, stinging liquid into my body, the nurse gives me details that Sister Torlaa kept from me. "Be grateful you're not lying behind that wall," she says, angrily knocking aside the fingers I have spread against her in my panic.

"Do you prick those people behind the wall with an even bigger needle?" I ask once we have made peace.

"Sure I do," she says, full of importance. "Just earlier, I pumped the contents of a bottle this long and this big into each of their bellies."

"Into their bellies?" I am shocked. "Won't that kill them?"

"It probably would if they were alive. But they've been lying there stone cold and crushed black and blue like clobbered and skinned marmots." She laughs out of a crooked mouth. Later she adds indifferently, "I hope the militia gets here before they turn green and start to stink."

I feel nauseous and decide never to let the woman give me another injection. Gone is the calm that had begun to spread inside me like a sunny autumn day or a view of the steppe. Instead I am hot with fever as I lie there trying to avert my eyes from the wall behind, which is a picture of horror. Death lies in ambush for me, coming closer and closer with his rattling breath.

I remind myself of the verse Mother taught us to combat fear. *Om dere düd dere düd suuhaa!* From the bottom of my heart I whisper it three, seven, twenty-one times, and each time I reach twenty-one, I blow at the area around my heart. This seems to help.

"*Dshenggej!*" I say first. And then, "Pürwü! Come and

stand by me. I am scared." My voice sounds depressingly thin and shaky. But it helps.

Dsher dsherni eeleen
Dshedi gök börüm

Next I try to invoke the Seven Gray Wolves who roam different parts of the world. I am not sure how and why I know of them, but I sense that they exist. I know that if they were to show up, the evil spirit terrifying me would take to its heels. This also helps.

The fear reaching for me is so powerful that I feel compelled to call upon more and more powerful beings to fight it. As I am doing so, the door opens and Brother Galkaan slips in. At this moment he is no longer the quiet slight boy who is barely half a head taller than me and only a tiny bit stronger. He now embodies the powerful good spirit I have been trying to invoke; he is the savior I was calling for. I pour my heart out to him.

Quietly he listens and then he says, "Nonsense. The room behind the wall is the doctor's office. There's nothing in there. The dead bodies are kept in the vet's camel shed, where Gök was hiding."

This is a relief. But then I hear something that cancels out the relief and weighs heavily on my soul. The fathers and other relatives of the crushed students have arrived and are looking for the principal.

At that moment we hear a droning. "A car!" we shout as if with one voice and dash to the window. A truck that looks like nothing we have ever seen is arriving. A doctor is squatting next to some bundled-up person on its flatbed. Later we will learn that the truck is a half-ton, and that the bundled-up man is a higher-up doctor. That he would come for the dead later gives everyone much to think about. The truck pulls up to the shed and stops close to the door where it emits two, three, four thunderous blasts from the front end and surging clouds of blue-black smoke from the rear end before falling silent. The passenger door opens, and a militiaman emerges in a uniform decorated with red piping and yellow stripes. Bellowing and waving his hands, he stops the people who come running from all sides. Then two men jump off the back of his truck and disappear into the camel shed. The militiaman follows along behind them, after yelling vague threats in loud haphazard Mongolian at all the onlookers around him.

They take a long time. Slowly but inexorably people inch closer. They reach the truck and the shed just as the three men reappear. The crowd—by now it numbers several dozen, mostly students—seem prepared to retreat, but they stay where they are when the militiaman ignores them.

The truck leaves then, only to return some time later. When it does, I am alone, but glued to the window. Galkaan has left to find out how things are going with Brother Dshokonaj. This time the flatbed is covered with people. They unload four longish, light-colored wooden boxes, one of them considerably longer than the other three. As soon as I see them, I feel in my bones what they are for, in spite of the fact that I have never heard of dead people being put into boxes instead of bags.

Terrified, I watch what is happening only a gunshot away. I can't take my eyes off the boxes. They stand in a row, their lids open like maws craving human flesh, hair, and bones. The fear that Brother Galkaan's protective presence had quelled momentarily returns to life with full force. I struggle feverishly but in vain to find support wherever my gaze happens to land. But soon I am engaged in a bitter fight with what feels like claws throttling my throat.

> In each of my pores
> A gnarly, hungry bird of prey
> Is nesting and watching for lost souls.
> Seizing, hacking, devouring
> Any that dare appear.

One by one, the boxes disappear into the shed. When they reappear, they are visibly heavier. Men load them back on the truck and jump off.

The driver has a hard time breathing life into his truck. He gets out from behind the wheel and jabs a bent iron rod into the mouth of the boxy creature. Finally, provoked back to life, the truck bursts into a furious roar. It exhales an oily leaden smoke that hangs in the air like a filthy curtain and takes a long time to dissipate. By then the shed has been deserted, and stands out tall and lonely against the steppe amid resounding silence and the warmth of early summer.

Meanwhile, I have been rummaging inside me for words that would fit my mouth and could be hurled like rocks at those beings that, like wind or light, cannot be seen but can be felt and heard; those beings that are lying in ambush for me.

Go away, go away
You dreadful creatures.
Follow the path
Of the dust and the roar,
Of the bodies you belong to.

I stretch and turn myself inside out while I continue to listen and wait. Now all that is left to me is a mild breeze with both the fragrance and the stench of this late-summer afternoon. The souls that have left the dead bodies; the flickering lights that have accompanied the souls; and perhaps also the pinching, burning winds; all seem to hurry along behind the cloud of red-hot dust that disappears with the truck beyond the Sholuk steppe. For now they seem to have left me. Then a numbing tiredness spreads to the tips of my hands and toes, and I burrow into my bed.

A heavy sleep overwhelms me so much so that I am almost relieved to be awakened. The nurse is bending over me. When I realize she is holding the syringe, I am struck with panic. In the dim light of the setting sun the syringe looks as long as a spear and as thick as an arm, and seems to have a blood-red glass belly. Screaming, crying, and sweating, I take up another battle.

First the woman tries to break my resistance with force. But when she sees how determined I am to defend myself, she gives up tormenting me and says she will report me to the doctor. Just as she is about to leave me, shadows glide across the window and I hear voices. She opens the door, and I can see more clearly and hear the shuffle of feet.

Instantly I feel alarmed, and my heart pounds in my throat. Will they take me away? If so, they must have already put Brother Dshokonaj in the truck. Have they restrained him? Will they restrain me? Samdar said when he got arrested, they put around his wrists and ankles metal chains that were so tight they would have cut into his flesh if he had tried to break free. Ürenek, on the other hand, was taken away without being restrained.

Later I tell myself that if the militiaman had been among the shadows, he first would have had to return with his truck, and I never heard that. And then he almost surely would have marched in and snatched me the way a hawk snatches a sparrow. But where is my big brother, and what is happening to him? Has he been taken away already, or is he still in hiding in the school prison, terrified that he will be shot, beaten, or stabbed to death? Why have Torlaa and Galkaan not returned? They have been gone a long time.

The voices die down. Darkness thickens fast and threatens to swallow me, and I am retching with panic. I feel as if I can see a tall black person with eyes targeting me like a gun in each corner of the room. Unable to chant and soothe myself, I am stuck in a slag heap of noisy repetitions, with no apparent openings. Words that otherwise carry lights and wind into the world now huddle inside me, paralyzed with fright. My throat quivers and all the tricks I use to escape the dread fail. When I realize I am surrounded by more powerful forces, the blanket I pull up over my head weighs heavily on my feverish body, and stinks of sweat and urine in spite of the disinfectant. I feel as if I will suffocate.

An eternity must have passed. Through the blanket I feel groping fingers. I cry out first with shock, then with joy as I recognize Torlaa's voice: "What's the matter, dear little one? You're drenched and trembling."

I try to calm down, but first I have to cry in order to release the pent-up fear. But Sister has no time for that. She grabs my shoulders and gives me a good shake: "Stop right now. Tell me if anything hurts. If not, shut up and listen. Something terrible has happened to Brother Dshokonaj."

The news sobers me, and instantly I go quiet. I don't have the strength to ask questions, but I am dying to know. Is he dead? The thought flashes through my head. Torlaa's red cheeks look pale and her sharp tongue is unusually sluggish. While I wait, another thought flashes to my mind: If only he's alive! Nothing else would matter then, and before I know what is happening, the longing travels through my body like the echo of an ache.

"He has lost a lot of blood and needs to be bandaged up," she says finally. So he's alive! I am overjoyed. I may or may not hear the details, but they can wait. I am in no rush, and concentrate on the candle that sits on the square tin stove at the center of the room. Its flame casts a quivering light on the ceiling and four walls.

At that moment the door to the adjacent room opens. Above the murmur of deep male voices I make out a bright female voice, probably the nurse's. "They're bringing him in. Keep quiet!" Sister whispers as she dashes to open the door. When she does, the doctor is standing there, swaying and stopping and keeping his upper body very straight as he unhurriedly swings one leg and then the other up and over the doorsill. I haven't seen the doctor since the morning, but I have longed for him and his voice and his firm, soft fingers. Now he comes through the door, as white as milk, and behind him, halfway up, floats a stretcher with the patient, presumably my big brother, wrapped in a white sheet. At the far end of the stretcher is the nurse, also in white. And on her right a third white figure emerges. I suspect that he is the bundled-up person from the truck.

They all enter the room. As the door slowly closes without a sound, I can just make out Brother Galkaan on the other side of the cone of dim light. I look for Sister Torlaa, but can't see her anywhere. She must have slipped from the room just as the group arrived, the way stray dogs vanish from sight. Why did such a terrible fate befall us? Only two days ago, we were brothers and sister living in quiet happiness. How will all this end?

The stretcher is set on a bed in the opposite corner

and then pulled out from beneath its narrow burden. It is hard to recognize this figure as Brother Dshokonaj. The thick bandage around his head makes my heart stop. It reminds me of the pale figure I saw in my ladle that fall day I sat by the river. Brother appears to be either unconscious or asleep, as he is not making a sound. The three white figures surround him. As still and silent as ghosts, they stand there doing nothing. But if they were not standing around him, I think he would float away, for I can see the lightness hanging above him like a gossamer-thin white cloud.

> Any breeze, my little cloud,
> Will blow you away.

Hearing myself think aloud is frightening, and I quickly try to find different words to counter the ones that slipped out. But I can't come up with any on the spot, and before I know it the three people wake from their trance and move toward me.

"Here is the young man who created such trouble for the nurse," says the doctor as he walks up to my bed and puts his hand on my forehead.

"Not just for me," the nurse says. "If you would have heard to the words he was spewing when he was admitted, you'd be shocked. In fact, you'd probably give him a good slap."

"Every nurse either wants to become a doctor or is given to histrionics." The doctor's laugh is short and bitter.

Then he adds, "But basically, you're right. We should have known."

He steps aside and signals for the other doctor to take over. Tall and elderly, the other doctor has deep-seated eyes that he raises with a critical, piercing expression when he takes over. Without a word he grabs my wrist and feels for my pulse. The bony fingers of his big, heavy hand feel cool, but the longer my hand remains in his, the more restless I feel. He takes forever before raising his pinkie, pointing to its nail, and telling me to focus on it. The fingernail moves to the right and to the left, then finally comes closer. I keep my eyes fixed on it, aware that everyone in the room is staring at me.

Suddenly the hand comes down. In a deep rumbling voice the doctor says a Kazakh word I don't understand; obviously it was meant for the others. He then turns to me, speaking in the same voice, this time in a Mongolian that sounds awkward and much clumsier even than the Mongolian we speak.

"Do you feel any pain?"

"Yes."

"Where?"

"In my head."

"Anywhere else?"

"In my belly."

"Any joint pain?"

"Yes. They hurt, too."

Suddenly he wants to know if the earth is alive and

can bleed and has quivering kidneys as sheep do. No, I say, never. The earth holds water and is made up of sand, clay, and rocks. Have I always thought that way? Yes. No. Why?

I pause to think before I say anything else. Then I say that sometimes sick people can't think straight. I ask if I am healthy now. Yes! In spite of the fact that I hurt all over? Darn! I pause to think again. How can that be? And then finally the truth: I am still a little sick, but I am getting better. The man laughs quietly, but somehow it resounds from all four corners of the room. "Smart boy!"

The first doctor, who has seemed a bit uneasy while listening to our conversation, says, "He's the top student in his class. He makes up songs, too."

"I'm not surprised," says the second doctor. "Shamans send out their calls in chants, don't they?"

He says all of this in his own language. Then he switches back to Mongolian and asks me if I understand Kazakh. I say I don't.

Finally the doctors leave me alone and turn to the nurse, who has been busy at the other bed. She is to stay in the room through the night and call them immediately if the patient gets worse. Then the men leave.

At long last I can focus on my brother without distraction. I can't see his face because he is lying on his back and the bandage around his head covers his chin and neck. His body seems long and narrow. The visible-invisible cloud above him has lingered, and now it's getting denser, spinning faster and faster, like a whirlwind approaching from afar. The sound I hear reinforces that impression: each of

Brother's gasps begins and dies equally abruptly against the background of his continuous soft crying.

The nurse goes to the unmade bed next to Brother's and drops on it like a lump. She groans and yawns loudly. The door opens quietly, and first Sister's and then Brother Galkaan's face become visible in the opening.

"Have the doctors left?" the nurse asks in a loud whisper. When she learns they have, she says, "Come in."

Torlaa and Galkaan slip into the room, trying to make as little noise as possible as they step on the creaking floorboards. They close the squeaking door and stop, too shy to go farther, unsure where to look. Brusquely the woman gets to her feet, walks over to them, and in a condescending yet clearly commanding tone says, "You can stay if you like. I have some work in the doctor's office. Call me if anything happens."

She leaves, and Sister Torlaa rushes over to the patient. Brother Galkaan hesitates, then follows with cautious small steps. I am not sure whether to stay put or sneak across to the other bed. I am terrified but can't wait to find out what has happened to our big brother, and to see what he looks like. I sit up in my bed but stay put.

Sister Torlaa calls out Brother Dshokonaj's name several times before he responds. With her ear close to his mouth, she is the only one to hear what he whispers. He asks for cold water. Galkaan leaves to tell the nurse, and after some time he returns with a teapot. Apparently the nurse is sleeping so soundly he had a hard time waking her up. The patient is not to have anything cold, Galkaan reports, or else he will get gas. We are to heat the milkless tea before giving it to him, and we will find chopped wood in the yard. It takes time, but we do as we are told. And yet, when the tea is finally warmed, Brother Dshokonaj refuses to drink it and insists on having cold water.

I find this frightening: thirst that can only be slated with a cold drink is the first of three dreaded symptoms of serious illness. The second symptom is incessant wiping of one's eyes and nose, and the third is the craving to enjoy what has not previously been enjoyed, and to say what has not been said. Every child knows that. I realize that Brother's obstinate craving for cold water has registered with Torlaa and Galkaan as well, and I understand their quiet, painstaking industriousness.

Despite my fear, I feel compelled to approach our big brother. I creep toward his bed in the bleak corner even though the nurse has warned me to keep my bare feet off the filthy floor. Torlaa and Galkaan stare at me, and I can see the fear in their eyes. A thick bandage has been wrapped carelessly around Brother's head. His light skin shines like a peeled onion, his eyebrows jut forth like a forest of black bristles, his eyelids have drooped, leaving two narrow, dark slits that look as rigid and hard as the edge of a knife, the ridge of his crooked nose looks sharper than before, his nostrils flare and tremble with each breath, and his normally thin lips have distinct, dark rims.

"*Aga!*" I cry, scaring myself with my own voice. It sounds helpless and fearful. A light shadow flits across Brother's face. Framed with gauze, it looks as bright and smooth as ice. His lips move slightly, and I put my ear to his mouth. "Dshuruunaj . . . please . . . please . . . something cold."

"*Aga*, please!" I cry. "You're not allowed to have anything cold. Please!"

I hold my ear close to his mouth again.

"Listen . . . carefully," he whispers. "Nothing . . . will . . . help . . . it's my . . . last . . . my . . . very last . . . wish . . . you mustn't . . . deny . . . me."

For Torlaa and Galkaan's sake, and perhaps for my own sake as well, I repeat what I have heard. It's almost as if I need to hear Brother's request one more time before I can even think about it. Silently I look from one to the other, wondering what to do. Torlaa nods first, then Galkaan. "I'll run down to the river," he says.

The open door yawns with a mute heavy darkness. I call after Galkaan, who is already out the door with the teapot in his hand: "Wait! I'll come with you." Hand in hand we race down the hill. The sky is overcast and dull, except in the northeast, where a few stars flicker above Taldyg and Buluktug.

"What happened to Brother Dshokonaj?" I finally ask.

"He was hit by something," says Galkaan. "The families of the people who got crushed were looking for him. That much we know. But no one seems to have seen the actual blow. And no one heard a bang, either. There was only a whirring and rushing."

"When did it happen?"

"When he tried to climb on the truck. The militiaman, the doctors, the *dargas*, they were all standing right there.

Then something came flying through the air, and suddenly he cried out and collapsed."

Strange, but somehow it makes sense, too . . . or maybe it does. Brother Galkaan climbs on a ledge jutting out over the river and dips the teapot into the hissing waves of the angry current. He tries to reach the river's artery, where the fresh glacier water throbs and rushes along, while I hang on to his other hand and cling to the ledge for balance.

When we return, the patient gulps down the water greedily. It sloshes into his throat and gurgles and slaps as it sluices into the depths. He drains the bowl, but still looks desperately thirsty. Torlaa hands Galkaan the bowl for refilling, and the patient empties the second bowl with the same voraciousness. Then he opens his eyes, looks satisfied, and begins to talk. This time his voice is audible, and his words come pouring out clearly.

"My body is weaker," Brother Dshokonaj says, "but my mind is sharper. I see everything with great clarity. I see and feel that Father and Mother are coming. But Erlik's messenger will be faster than their horses, and I will no longer be here by the time they arrive. I will leave behind only my body, which will keep you busy for a while. Do no more and no less than is done for anyone else's body. Father must take it out into the steppe for its last journey no differently than he would with any other body. Tell him I am sorry that I was created too weak to melt the ice inside him. Mother will have a hard time, harder than anyone else. I am well aware of that. Tell her she is still a duck on a lake. If she cannot believe it, remind her to look at all those around her, and then at the three of you. And tell her that I feel infinitely sorry for not having been able to keep alive the healthy body and bright mind she gave me.

"And you, my brothers and sister. Like the three rocks that hold the kettle over the fire, hold tight to Father and Mother and keep them warm. Never abandon the path of knowledge. All the things you read and write day after day are the sheep and the yaks that one day will feed you. Walk on this path that I have only mapped out, blazing a trail for yourselves and for all who will follow you. Your path will be a tidal river connecting our lake with the ocean of the world. Study diligently, become knowledgeable, and avoid the mistake I have made: go along with people, not against them.

"Dear Sister Dosunak," he says, addressing Torlaa with the name Father calls her by. "Give free rein to your mind, your heart, and your fingers, but keep a tight rein on your tongue. You will reach the peak of knowledge and your life's mountain only when you are able to control your tongue. Be a pillar of support for your mother, and a second mother for your younger brothers. My dear and only sister, I want you to keep the yellow box that is in the chest on the yurt's right side. I believe it is made from *dsandan*, sandalwood, and so shares a name with you. It contains things our grandmother left behind. I only glanced at them once and thought they were junk. Be kinder toward them.

"And another thing, Dosunak. Please tell Dügüj that I am infinitely grateful for all the kindness she showed me. Tell her to be a motherly sister to my orphaned brothers and sister. Ask her, above all, to protect my little brother from evil tongues as much as her powers will allow. And give her the red folder, unopened, from the chest on the left.

"And you, my dear, innocent Brother Gakaj," he says, calling Galkaan by the name Mother used for him, "stay as kind as you are but never forget: people like you are easily put at a disadvantage. Stay reliable as you follow in your father's footsteps, and be a wall to protect your little brother from the storms and a skin to warm him in the cold. In exchange, take my black horse. He is not fast, but he is reliable.

"And now to you, my little sparrow. Dearly beloved little Brother Dshuruunaj, listen carefully. Ask Aunt Pürwü to forgive me and, as a sign of her forgiveness, to protect you. You may be a shaman after all. But if you are, you will need to be different than shamans have been in the past. Let your mind be aflame and your heart ablaze whenever you want, but stay on your guard. And keep the things I leave behind. More than anyone else, it is you who shall have the books and papers I leave. Continue on the path that I must now abandon.

"My dear Brothers and Sister, I thank you for the cool clear water. Thank you for not withholding it from me. It has slaked my burning thirst, cleansed my pain, and lit my mind's fire. But even more, I thank you for your love. You have loved me as your brother, and I am grateful I've been allowed to experience your brotherly and sisterly love before I have to go. And one last thing: I have caused Mother

Earth great sorrow. Tell those who will deal with my body not to wake her or hurt her again . . ."

With these last words his voice begins to shake. His face flickers with agitation, and suddenly pales to the color of ash. His lips twitch, and then we hear a scratchy, faint sobbing.

As if we have been given a signal, the three of us cry along with him. Helpless, we cling to each other like three fingers of a hand, huddling beside the bed in which the fourth finger, now severed, is writhing.

At that moment the light dims abruptly. We turn and see that the candle has burned down to a shrinking dot of light, glimmering on the stove lid. Brother Galkaan dashes out of the room, and a draft extinguishes the fading dot. As Torlaa and I suppress our sobs and hold our breath to listen, the sound of shuffling footsteps in the hallway merges with those in the next room. In quick succession, we hear the bright squeak of a door, the sullen creaking of floorboards, a quiet shudder, a gravelly rattle, and a squelching sucking. My sister bends down to hug me and whispers into my ear, "Don't be afraid, little one . . . one mustn't be afraid . . . no matter what . . ."

She is trembling, as is her voice. I try to crawl deeper into her embrace. If only she would talk more loudly, maybe I wouldn't hear the sounds beside me. I am furious with Galkaan. What could he possibly be doing all this time? Can't he just tell the woman to hurry up and give him a candle? After all, right next to us . . .

I am shocked by that thought, and I shake and shiver. Then we hear another squeak and more shuffling, and the door opens. "What kept you so long?" Sister says harshly.

It takes an eternity before Galkaan finds the matchbox he put on the stove lid only so recently, pulls a match out, and drags it over the strip on the side of the box with just the right amount of pressure so it catches fire. And then finally, he lights the candle.

That very moment we hear behind us a quiet drawn-out exhalation, which breaks off abruptly. Torlaa leaps back, pulling me with her; Galkaan jumps to join us. Trembling and mute, we stand there clinging to each other. Then we turn around slowly. Torlaa looks scared. She stares at Galkaan and pushes him forward. He resists, but extends his arm to hold up the candle.

Brother Dshokonaj is still there, but he seems to be asleep. Sister is the first to start calling, quietly but urgently: *"Aga . . . Aga . . .* Dshokonaj *Aga!"* Brother Galkaan and I follow her example and call across, sending him different and increasingly louder calls. *"Odun, agatshaj*—wake up, please, dearest Brother," slips from my mouth.

Again Sister is the first to burst into tears. Galkaan and I follow, and before long the three of us are screaming at the top of our lungs. I wail and screech, call upon the Sky and the Earth, call out their names to call them close, and demand to know why they have robbed us of our brother, our protector, and why they have harmed us weak, defenseless children. Then I am shouting:

There were four of us
Whole and complete,
Like you, Sky,
With your four directions for the light and
    the winds;
Like you, Earth,
With your four seasons.
Now you have robbed us
Of the sunny east
And the warm summer,
And sentenced us
To a sorrowful life as cripples.

Our wailing awakens the nurse on the other side of the clay-covered wall of larch trunks. She staggers into the room and, realizing quickly what has happened, thunders at us to be quiet and to leave the room and go home. She says she will prepare the body for transport, which is required in order to determine the legal cause of death.

Sister Torlaa goes wild. She lifts her arms and spreads her fingers, flings back her head and bares her teeth, and hisses: "How dare you, daughter of Sumashak! You're an old spinster and your father is seventy-times-seven a thief and a liar! How dare you! First you fall asleep until you've killed the patient in your care—you slovenly slut!—and then you can't prepare his dead body fast enough. He's not a piece of meat to be dressed for a feast! You vulture! Nothing but a dead body yourself! You'd like to steam or cook or fry our brother, wouldn't you? Huh? Maybe you think I am just a girl—well, I am a girl. But that doesn't mean that I'm stupid or meek! There's a growing wolf bitch inside me, a devil determined to defend our brother's mortal remains tooth and nail. You touch him, and I will let you have it. You won't know what's hit you. I will scratch your face to shreds, poke out your eyes, and bite through your throat!"

The nurse is speechless with shock. As Sister Torlaa pelts her with words as hard as rocks, she backs into a corner, where she now stands as white as a sheet. Her mouth is open and twitching, but she seems to have lost her ability to speak.

"And as for you two," Sister says, turning to Galkaan and me. "Run home and get the new felt mat from behind Brother's bed, the green bolt of fabric from the left chest, and the sewing box from the case beneath our stack of clothes." We leave as soon as she has finished and trot through the dim light of early dawn, across the rocky steppe. Howling like young dogs, we finally reach the yurt in the *ail* and fight its stubborn lock, and we don't stop howling even when we return to the hospital, just as daylight bursts across the sky. Today we are allowed to howl, I think in my sweet-bitter trance; today we can howl no matter where we are and how things go.

Sister is alone when we return and it looks like she has calmed down and even done some work. Our big brother looks shorter now that he rests under a sheet. "For everything there is a time and a measure," she reminds us. "Too many tears, and they'll add to the ocean that Brother has to cross. Stop howling and crying and give me a hand. Now that it's happened, we have to complete the tasks Brother has left us. He must know that we are here for him, and that we will not let the unworthy play with his body."

We help silently. Sister cuts a disk the size of a grown wether's rumen out of the felt mat. Then she cuts a piece off the bolt of fabric to make a tube with the same diameter as the disk. Using the darning needle and some sheep-wool yarn, she sews a bag, making her stitches as wide as a finger and leaving the ends of the yarn unknotted. Then she slips the bag under the sheet and pulls it up over Brother's feet toward his head.

The bag is too short. "Come help bend his legs," she says. We hurry to help her. As we touch the bag, we feel his shins lying together under the fabric, and push them away from us against the pressure caused by Sister, who is pushing the neck deeper into the bag. The head tilts and finally disappears into the bag.

"One of you, come and help me," she orders. Galkaan rushes to her side and pushes the head down while I push the feet up. I groan and tremble with the strain as Sister sews the bag shut. It looks like an overstuffed rumen by the time we all manage to lift the bag off the bed and place it on the felt mat in the corner.

It is midmorning when the doctors arrive with the militiaman, apparently brought over by the nurse, who must have reported the death. The nurse herself approaches cautiously, waiting at the door the way a startled animal hovers at the edge of the flock, anxiously glancing in all directions. Stunned by what they see, the men stop in their tracks, shake their heads, and quietly whistle through their teeth. Finally the militiaman speaks: "This won't work, children. We must first examine the body."

"There's nothing to examine," snarls Sister. She runs to the corner and stands in front of the bag, as if to defend it with her body. A pair of black scissors flashes in her hand, its white edges gaping wide. "Our brother is not a sheep with a belly to open and a fleece to skin. We won't let you do it."

The doctor interrupts. "I beg your pardon? I am the professional here. It's my job to examine the body, determine the cause of death, and fill out the papers. And no one here is going to stop me."

Sister stomps in place on the floor. A cloud of dust rises around her, and the boards creak and clatter. "You're a scavenger!" she shrieks. "Do you think he is hiding in the bag to escape prison? Do you need to stab and hack him up to make sure he's dead? You're a butcher! There's no way we will let you get near our brother. If you try to use force, well, we have more than these scissors. We have the rocks of the Altai, and our teeth and our fingernails, don't we?" With her last words she turns to Galkaan and me.

"We do!" we yell, stomping along with her.

The other doctor tries to intervene. "Besides," he mutters, "the District Administration won't let Comrade

Principal be thrown to the vultures and foxes in this pathetic bag after yesterday's victims were all buried properly in civilized coffins."

"Ha!" Sister flares up. "You know what a coffin is? It's a prison for eternity. Now that you can no longer take him to prison alive, you want to squeeze him into a prison dead. Our brother is guilty, but not in the way you think. It's because he violated Mother Earth when he was alive that he doesn't deserve to be taken into her womb now that he is dead. If we go ahead and put him into the earth anyway, we'll hurt the earth on his behalf and make his trespass even worse."

By now Galkaan and I are beside Torlaa. We continue stomping and screaming like two young beasts of prey.

The men give up and leave. Neighbors who heard the news begin arriving, and asking when the burial will take place. Torlaa says only that once the body has been undressed and put into the bag, it must be taken away as soon as possible. A few people leave to get a horse and maybe a basket. Waiting for help to arrive, the three of us guard Brother, who has become a bag, as round and as heavy as a rock.

Then I see Father dismounting next to the hitching post. At first I can't believe my eyes, but then I see Mother riding up behind him. "Father and Mother!" I whisper, my voice failing, and leap through the door. As I burst into the brilliant wide world of summer, with its noisy birds and boisterous sheep and goats, I collapse into loud weeping and wailing. Torlaa and Galkaan must have followed on my heels, for I can hear them right behind me. We all huddle right there, a tiny, shivering group.

Entering the scene so noisily gives us a temporary advantage: Father and Mother spend the first few minutes trying to calm us down. They tell us to stop crying immediately, lest our tears create an insurmountable obstacle for the one who has to leave. Tears stream from their eyes as well, but they both know how to cry silently. When we step in front of the bag on the felt mat, Mother somehow manages to ask which kind soul lent a hand to prepare the bag. She utters a little cry and weeps even more when she hears that it was us. Father is standing behind her, and every so often he gives her a gentle nudge. Sister Torlaa describes Brother Dshokonaj's last hour, repeating word for word everything that was said. Father groans several times. Suddenly he makes a sharp banging noise, drops to his knees, and beats his head with his fist. Bright round tears run down his face, drop from his nostrils, and dissolve in his reddish mustache.

Then Mother composes herself and glances at Father with what looks like blissful gratitude. Meanwhile, a number of people appear at the door, some of whom were there before. Sister Torlaa alerts Father, and he gets up and goes over to them.

"How are we going to do it?" someone asks.

"I will carry him across my saddle," says Father.

"It wouldn't take long to get a camel and two baskets," someone suggests.

"No." Father's answer is clear. "We'll follow his last wish."

Someone mentions the need for milk and juniper, and Mother says she has brought some.

"How did you know? Did someone bring you the news?"

"No one did," Mother says. "But for days I have had troubling dreams of the poor man. And then last night, just as I was falling asleep, I saw him lying on the ground bleeding. Around midnight I got a fever, and I could hear him cry and whimper like a young child. He was calling for me. I said to my husband that something terrible must have happened; and if you don't believe me, I said, stay here, but I have to go right now. He said to wait until daylight."

Then someone lights a thick bunch of juniper and holds it up high. Beneath its crackling fire and wavery smoke Father carries the bag and the felt mat out of the building and over to the hitching post, where his white horse is standing still, drenched with sweat. Father gives the bag to one of the two men who have followed, mounts his horse, and sits behind the saddle. The bag and the mat are lifted up and put in place in front of him. The other two men go over to their horses, and one of them says, "We need one more person to come with us so we won't return an uneven number. We can take the sister's horse."

Sister Torlaa makes the decision: "Galkaan, you go."

But Galkaan protests: "Dshuruk, you've earned it more. He was your bosom brother."

I obey wordlessly, run over to Brother Dshokonaj's horse, and jump into the saddle. I cast a quick glance at the people who are staying behind. Short and squat, Mother stands half a step in front of Torlaa and Galkaan, swinging her round leather bag from side to side with both hands. I hear her recite, "*Huraj—huraj—huraj,* leave behind the blessings of all your riches . . ."

"Don't forget to say 'and of your knowledge'!" I shout.

Sister Torlaa is annoyed: "Of course we won't! Now hurry along or you'll be left behind."

I catch up with the riders and stay behind Father, who is between the other two men. The sky hangs low, weighed down by mountains of dark-blue clouds that totter and tee-ter, pushing against each other's bright edges. Up there, storm winds collide, while down here the dying breezes blow thin dust clouds behind the horses' hooves. One mo-ment the air is fragrant with wormwood, the next with fringed sage or saltwort. But all I can see are sparse bluish-green blades of grass and stunted shrubs with hardened gold-glinting bark at the bottom and delicate dark-green crowns at the top. Sparrows chirp around us, but I can't see them either. Instead, I see swallows shoot through the air like pebbles catapulted from slingshots. Ravens, kites, and crows float above them, their unhurried mute shad-ows soaring across the steppe. From time to time a lizard flits across the blue-black gravel or the yellow-brown sand, flickering shadows that emerge from nowhere and return to nowhere. The horses hang their heads as if in a shallow slumber while their hooves move steadily and stubbornly forward, step by step, carrying their riders closer to the edge of the steppe. No one speaks.

Fully alert, I recall the words Brother Dshokonaj said

the day we heard of the marshal's demise. Now I truly feel that one of the world's lights has been extinguished, and some of its stuff carried away.

Sometime later the drifting ocean vanishes, and the shimmering air stands still in places. The edge of the steppe appears in front of us as distinctly as a ditch. Behind it the foothills rise like ramparts with their sandy slopes and dark craggy peaks. On our left, Saryg-höl, the Yellow Lake, lies at the bottom of a deep wide basin, surrounded by tufts of feather grass and mounds of rock salt, like a teary eye in an old furrowed face.

We arrive at last. The men dismount, hurry to help Father, and take the bag as it slides from his horse. Holding it between them at the level of their bellies, they wait for Father to dismount, hobble his horse's front legs with the lead, and turn toward them. Then Father takes the bag and carries it over to a small mound, where he first spreads out the felt mat. He gently places the bag on the mat, as if putting an offering on a plate at the altar.

I, too, get off my horse and stand, with the lead in my hand, next to the other two men. We watch Father crouch before the bag and bow repeatedly, saying his farewell solemnly and loudly:

> You were a son to me,
> A rock of my mountain.
> I was allowed to see you
> Or not see you at times.
> From this hour onward

You will be sky and earth.
You can do with me now
What you felt like doing at your end.
Whatever awaits me
I will repay what I owe
To her who gave life to you,
And to those who came after you . . .

He rises, takes the agate bottle from his breast pocket, and shakes a pinch of snuff onto a flat piece of slate the size of a plate, which rests at the head end of the bag. Then he steps back and turns to me: "Go bow before your big brother, and ask him for his blessing."

I step forward slowly, unsure what to do or say. Suddenly I feel as if the bag is coming toward me. I realize then that Brother, who was tall and straight and full of life at this time yesterday, now lies crooked and stiff in his bag. And that as soon as we ride back, he will be alone, left to the vultures and ravens and to the wolves and foxes, to the wind and the rain . . .

Something inside me rises up. Sinking to my knees, I speak quietly, as if to myself: "My dearest, most beloved mountain of a brother . . . forgive me for not being able to keep you alive . . . I am stupid and cowardly . . . so I may well deserve to be left orphaned in this unfathomable life . . . like a post in the steppe . . ."

Then my voice grows louder and my words become verse:

With you, oh my Brother,
I was a yurt in a valley,
Sheltered from the winds by the mountains.
Without you, my protector,
I am a tent on the steppe,
Naked and exposed to the storms . . .

I rise to my feet and stand there swaying. My head
throbs, my guts burn, my bones are hot and hurt, and I feel
as if I am dying. I scream and try to defend myself from
whatever is besieging me:

Mine was
The arrow
That hit you,
Mine is
The fire
That will cremate you.
Here is the path
You will take.
May your flesh decay,
Your bones fall asunder,
Your soul drift away,
Your spirit rise.
Only then will you become
The sky that stretches out blue,
The earth that springs up green
Through countless millennia . . .

I feel the need to breathe juniper smoke but find out we did not bring any. This disappointing news makes me increasingly anxious: how can we possibly dare to bring a body, its life extinguished, back to Mother Earth without the comfort and offering of warm juniper smoke?

Father comes over, takes my hand, and leads me away. Enough, he says; now the others get their turn. The men keep it brief: each bows three times before the man in his bag, and each moves his lips as he silently pleads with Mother Earth and gives his good wishes to the Earth Child. The bodies of mother and child will once more rest side by side.

Afterward we walk around him once clockwise, with the horses on their leads. Then we walk away a good long distance before we mount them and head back. We ride at an easy trot, talking as we go. Nine of us had left, we say, but just eight return.

I mull over what just happened, and the words that passed my lips: *Mine* was the arrow—did I really say that? If it were true, I would be my brother's murderer. The thought gives me a jolt. And what a pity we didn't have any juniper. If we had burned juniper, a chant that no one, not even Father, could have interrupted would have emerged. I would have been shamanizing long and well, to be sure. Brother so deserved that I accompany him to the other side.

The smoke that we failed to create in the steppe is swirling above the yurt and blowing toward us. Brother Galkaan is waiting for us next to the yurt, holding a water jug in his hands. We dismount without saying a word, hitch our horses to the yurt, and walk over to Galkaan, who has been watching us attentively. We each wash our hands and faces and rinse our mouths. Galkaan is shaking as he pours water over our clasped hands. My turn comes last, and I fear he will ask a question, but he doesn't, and I manage to stay silent as well, even though I would like to know who has gathered in the yurt. As I untie my belt and dry my hands and face with its wide, fluttering end, I feel more grown up than Galkaan, who stands next to me, the water jug still in his hands.

The yurt is full. The neighbors, the teachers, and the *dargas* have all come. Deldeng and Dügüj are busy in the kitchen half of the yurt, and look as if they have been crying.

The pot is as full as the yurt. Hastily dried pieces of meat, as big as piles of yak dung, jut from the fatty broth. As I look at the glistening chunks and breathe in their heavy smell, I wonder if all the meat we have left is now in the pot.

To begin, we are poured milk tea and reminded repeatedly to help ourselves to the fried flatbread and *aarshy* piled high on platters decorated with sugar cubes and candies. We drink and we eat, pausing only to report how, right after reaching the edge of the steppe, we found that slightly elevated, flat and sunny spot. The first one tells the story, the next confirms it, and the third one repeats it. The people around us listen attentively, remarking briefly how good it was that it all came off so easily.

Then people tell stories. Each guest has one, and most

are about our big brother, whom they all refer to as the poor soul. They all have nothing but praise for him. Occasionally, this also touches on the three of us. More than Galkaan and me, it is Torlaa who is praised for having taken care of her brothers like a true mother. If it hadn't been for her forceful interference, they say, who knows what might have been inflicted on the poor soul! Terrible! But she knew to defend her older brother even after his death, like a raptor defending her young.

More people arrive, and we squeeze together until the yurt is filled to bursting. People pass their snuff bottles to Father and Mother with words of consolation and, as often as not, a few bills. *Amysa da höl ishtindeegi ödürek siler jong,* many say; you are still ducks on a lake. Father and Mother sit with their heads bowed, silently accept what is offered, and return the snuff bottles. Once or twice they pass them on to us. We sniff at the loosened stopper and sneeze, which results in no small amusement. We are surrounded by people who eat, drink, and tell stories, and who strive to be good company.

Having eaten the meat and had another round of tea, our guests leave. Some time later, Father departs with Torlaa and Galkaan, who, we are told, have been promoted to the next class and excused from the end of the semester. Mother stays behind with me. Over the next days, people continue to come and see us. Some bring milk from their animals, others goods from the store. Dügüj comes often, and twice she stays for the night. When there are no visitors, Mother and I try to keep one another from crying.

On the seventh day, Mother asks one of the men to climb up a nearby hill and have a look. He returns and says it is still there. The next morning Father arrives with a camel and a lead horse. The teachers come with a few students to help dismantle and remove the state yurt. Brother Dshokonaj's possessions are loaded on the camel, together with the rest of our possessions. The load is so small a horse could have carried it. Before setting out, we cleanse the ground. Mother pours water on the burned spot where our round stove used to stand and then, addressing the Sky, sprinkles the spot with milk:

> Now this stove has gone out.
> In days to come, different people
> May light fires in this place.
> May their lives' fires burn
> For a long, long time

Using our front coattails, Father and I carry gravel to spread on the circle where the yurt and our feet have left the steppe bare and scarred. We work in advance of the wind and the rain, which will once again erase all traces of the yurt and its people.

DEVOURING
THE STONE

Summer proves to be hot and murderously dry. A rusty-red sun rises in the morning and radiates first dust and later flames. Its whole path across the sky glows with fire. Sparks rain down and flames rush at the earth until the spring grass and flowers wilt. For a few days they falter and stand shy and timid. Then their edges grow charred. Finally they crumble beneath the hooves of the flocks, turning to dust and ashes. The sparse meadows between the boulder fields lie black and dead and torn up.

From one day to the next the streams in the valleys vanish into the ground. The puddles left in hollows in the riverbed are soon lapped up by passing flocks. Then the springs dry up. The water table drops and on one sunny afternoon disappears beneath the black stringy clay. Over the course of the following day the clay hardens into rock.

The yurts move up the mountain valleys, struggling to get closer to the glaciers. It is said that the glaciers themselves are disappearing, but at the Alban-Oruk *ovoo* on the northern slope of Haarakan, where our clan has moved along with the flocks and herds, the ice cap stretching across the saddle between the peaks remains as thick as ten yurts stacked on top of each other.

Although the animals produce less milk than in other years, we have more than enough *aragy*. The crowds of roaring riders that in other times traveled night after night from *ail* to *ail* and yurt to yurt, knocking back whatever drink was available in exchange for a song, are nowhere to be found. Now the *ail* people themselves are drinking. Every yurt that distills *aragy* sends someone with a steaming-hot sample for Father, the head of our clan. Invariably the *aragy* arrives in a smoke-stiffened leather flask, accompanied by a half-dried chunk of cheese the size of the palm of a hand.

So Father has no choice but to drink, often early in the day. He drinks merely to slake his thirst, which means he drinks slowly without interrupting his work. The more he drinks, he says, the more he has to move and sweat, and indeed everything inside and around our yurt stays very tidy.

Often Father's younger brother gets his share of the gift of honor, but Uncle Know-It-All throws his head back and downs the contents of the bowl in a single gulp. "You aren't drinking," Father rebukes him, "you're putting it away like a Russian or a Kazakh." Our uncle takes the reprimand with a smile and a wink, says nothing in return, and does not change his nasty habits. Instead, he falls asleep as soon as he has had a drink, dropping wherever he happens to be and staying on the ground as long as his bladder will allow.

Even the women are drinking. In the past, Mother only drank at celebrations. Now she drinks more often, and women who never drank before keep up because they have to. They gather around the eldest among them in what appears to be unheard-of harmony.

Mother cries when she drinks. It is something we all dread. Sister Torlaa would love to take every bowl of *aragy* away from Mother, and one day she actually tips one out. But she gets rebuked for this, and so she drinks the next one herself rather than let Mother have it.

"Let her drink, dear girl," says our shaman aunt.

"There'll be nothing but tears again," replies Torlaa.

"So what? Let her cry. She needs to."

"What if she cries herself to death?"

"Not even a bitch whose puppies have all been clobbered to bits would cry herself to death. The more her tears flow, the more the corrosive and deadly salt gets washed away. Let my sister-in-law cry and dissolve in tears for a summer or two. One day she'll realize that she's following an arrow that has long left the bow, and that she must come back to you. You'll see. She'll start a new life and live twice as long!"

Again the following night, we find no peace. Standing at the edge of the *ail*, almost within reach of the sacred mountain, Mother is drunk. She howls at the sky and at every rock on the mountain. I lie fully awake beside Father, who got drunk as usual toward the end of the day, and who has been panting and snoring exhaustedly for hours. Disgusted by his sour breath, I noisily turn away from him and listen to the sounds outside, where Mother's voice has gone hoarse. Her howling and wailing merge in a chorus with the barking of the dogs, the rushing of the wind, and the groaning and grunting of the herds.

"E-eej, you deaf and aged mountain! You have the ice and the snow of tens and hundreds of thousands of years to melt and run off your sides. Is that not enough? Why do you need the tears of my eyes and the blood of my heart to water the cracked earth and its thirsty creatures? A-aaj, you quivering ancient stars! You have the great flaming sun to heat the sky's cold and infinite space. Is that not enough? Why did you have to set fire to my meager innards? O-ooj, you hundred hungry spirits in the east and thousand thirsty spirits in the west! Did you slaughter my child to satisfy your hunger with his flesh and slake your thirst with his blood?"

First Galkaan goes outside, then Torlaa. Both try to stop Mother from crying and bring her back into the yurt, but they fail. Later the shaman goes and shouts at her. Through sheer force and cleverness she eventually drags Mother back to the yurt. With bated breath I listen to their exchange:

"Stop cursing, woman. Let people and animals get some rest."

"Ooj, my dear, how can you talk of resting when my bones burn and my blood boils?"

"Don't brag about your pain. It's as earned as the happiness you used to enjoy privately, like those yak cows over there."

"Are you suggesting I deserve this? Then tell me, how?"

"Don't ask me. Ask the Blue Sky."

"The Blue Sky no longer listens. He must have gone deaf from old age."

"Stop talking nonsense. You forget you still have children."

"Oh yes, my children, my chicks, my bright little suns— oh my rich Altai!"

"See? You just said yourself you're still surrounded by bright suns."

"I am. But the best of them has gone out. Now it is dark inside me."

"It's a good thing those who still shine can't hear you. There are no such things as better or best. Show me your ten fingers and tell me which one to chop off."

"You're right, Sister-in-Law. But it's true that the Sky no longer listens."

"Do you think the Sky listens to the one who screams the loudest? The one who shouts at the top of her lungs and whines and whimpers like an injured dog?"

"Are you telling me I should be whispering instead of shouting?"

"Maybe. The blue above us is only part of the Sky,

which anyone can see. The greater and deeper Sky, the true Blue Sky, is inside you and will not put up with loud noise."

"I know. I must have heard that before. But if you're born blind, it is hard to see the Sky. By the way, dear shaman, was it an arrow that hit my boy?"

"What a question to ask when I'm sober and don't have my tools. If you really want to know, come see me shamanize on the twenty-ninth. I hope you'll have the courage to ask your question at that time."

Then the door opens and our aunt quietly calls: "Torlaawaj, my dear, light a candle. Sister-in-Law is going to rest now." I watch Mother stagger through the door on our aunt's arm. Mother's hair is disheveled, her eyes are swollen from crying, and she is sobbing. Torlaa helps our drunken mother out of her clothes while the shaman stands nearby and fixes them with her eagle-owl eyes. She orders a full bowl of *aragy* as a nightcap and holds it to Mother's lips. Undressed, Mother drinks greedily, choking after the first swallow. Then, finally, we have peace and quiet.

The twenty-ninth of the middle month of autumn brings a particularly dark and humid night. A foglike veil clouds the steaming peak of our mountain. It approached with the setting sun and now presses down on the *ail*. The shaman starts briskly. Soon the spirits appear and with them many new verses that give me goose bumps.

> On the southern slope of Saryg-höl
> I lie and wither.

A rumen of *bortsha*
On the northern slope of Haarakan
I walk and wither.
A package of *bortsha*
This, I feel, I do not deserve . . .

The burning juniper crackles. When we helped cousin Dshanik pick the bluish-green branches the previous day, we checked the stems for dryness and the berries for juiciness to make sure they would crackle and burst with a pop. Sister Torlaa is responsible for tending the fire in the stove through the night, and she shows herself to be a proud and eager stoker. As always when his wife shamanizes, Uncle Know-It-All tries to meddle. First he complains that the heat is killing him, then he laments that the perfectly good juniper his children labored to collect is being burned to ashes because of the madness of his trickster wife. But like everyone else, Torlaa knows better than to listen to what comes out of his mouth at a time like this.

You are not the only one parched.
The earth is aglow,
The storm has risen.
Too late the question
Who or what is deserved . . .

In the flickering light of the fire our faces look as if blood and milk were pouring over them. Fear is lodged in the flames that dart back from each pair of eyes.

Tea, dark as night
Slake my thirst . . .

Aunt Buja, who is responsible for the sacred tools, quickly fetches the red wooden bowl with the thick, steaming, milkless tea concentrate, ladles of which she tossed at the roof ring only minutes before. She dips a small bunch of juniper branches into the tea and shakes it at the corner of the bed's headpiece, where once a bright-red bag and later the dark-red cloth with the sacred tools used to hang. Uncle Know-It-All, who was the only one trying to sleep, complains, "Ouch, you're scalding me! Do you think I'm one of those dumb thirsty spirits that comes rushing as soon as this madwoman calls upon them, sprinkling them with saltless tea concentrate?" But Aunt Buja knows to ignore the stupid prattle of her younger brother, who turned out badly but is harmless.

"This year even the *asalar* are so parched that nothing can slake their thirst," the shaman says, breaking off her chant. She sits down with her back to the fire. Her head and upper body gently sway from side to side, shaking the *shawyd* made up of only a few, mostly white and blue strips of fabric. It is time for her listeners to ask questions. Everyone addresses her with the traditional greeting: "*Eej tümen eej dshajaatshy!* Oh, you ten thousand spirits!" After each question the shaman lifts her hand, putting the mirror up to her forehead and holding it above her closed hand. Then she resumes her chanting, swaying, and shaking. Mother asks her about our future paths. Will sunshine fall on them, or shadow?

> Go outside and try to make out
> The shadow cast over
> The whole of the Altai . . .
> Your two born earlier
> Will ebb and flow
> With the lakes and oceans.
> But the one born last
> I will carry in the corner of my mouth
> To his destination . . .

More questions follow, and more answers. The fire keeps burning, and Uncle keeps snoring. The yurt seems hotter than ever, and our aunt's shamanizing better than it has been for a long time. Normally she wears a cap embellished with eagle-owl feathers and a multitude of pearls, corals, and cowrie shells, along with the fangs and claws of wolves, bears, and snow leopards. But today she is wearing a simple red cotton bag with black fringes and few buttons and small owl feathers, and using that miserable *shawyd*. Suddenly she interrupts her chant again and says, "Dshuruunaj, my dear little one, come help me!"

Shocked, I look at Father and Mother. They nod in assent. So I leap up and lightly touch the shaman's back. Holding her *shawyd* in her right hand, she puts her right arm around my waist, pulls me down on my knees, and makes me sway with her. I can feel the *shawyd* rhythmically slap my back and my belly like small waves crashing on pebbles, and a soft heaviness bears first on my neck and then on my eyelids, making me drowsy.

"Shut your eyes!" I sense the mirror against my forehead and hear the next command: "Hold it." I obey and feel transported. "Tell us what you see." No matter how hard I try, I cannot see anything. Or maybe I can. Something seems to shimmer. It must be very far away. Something shimmers in the distance, and it appears to be coming closer.

"A cloud," I call out.

"Maybe a mountain?"

It is a mountain. But it can't be from the Altai. High above the clouds in the sky, the mountain is a brilliant white, and every so often it gives off sparks.

"A huge white mountain. Very white and very huge."

"There you are. Hang on to everything. Now run over to the mountain and address it."

The next moment I feel the tightly braided handle of the *shawyd* in my right hand, and so I rise and run, or rather fly, until I stand before the mountain.

> *E-e-ej-eej ewej-im*
> *E-e-ej-eej eshej-im . . .*

I never would have expected such a powerful voice to erupt from me. It awakens and shakes the mountain, and the mountain replies with a manifold echo. Suddenly I realize that I am a shaman the same way each of the stones around me is a stone, and each of the blades of grass between them is grass. And because I am a shaman, I am a stone where a stone lies, and I am grass where grass grows. I am a child of the White Mountain, and I stand before it now.

> Great Father, Grandfather,
> My original flesh,
> My original bones:
> I long to open myself to you
> As you open yourself to me.
> My nine tender springtimes
> Are my nine gifts to you.
> Let me ripen for three more
> Winters, summers, and falls.
> Then I will fly, a meteor,
> Across mountains and oceans,
> And I will carry you, my child,
> To the far reaches beyond,
> To the heights above.
> When I turn eighty-eight
> I will alight and return to you,
> At last a stone again . . .

Some time later I feel a soft hand on my shoulder and wake from my trance. There is our aunt's familiar voice, surging and rising to a chant. As the chant soars, it carries me back to the mountain, which has become an enormous white flame in the sky, casting its light into all corners and recesses inside me.

The east turns blue and dawn arrives.
Everything awakens that is now or will be
    one day.
Wilting grass and flowers, having borne wit-
    ness with us,
Now are eager to rise and bloom.
Streams will water the sand,
Pebbles will roll again.
Release me, oh Spirits!
I want to return to my dear little ones,
To mingle with my flock
And disappear among them,
And with tiny steps to climb
The mountain of life,
And become a mountain myself . . .

With my aunt's arm around my shoulders, I wave the *shawyd*. And then we return, side by side, following the sounds of the pattering ribbons and the peaceful farewell chant. The White Mountain recedes into the distance, gradually reverting back into clouds before disappearing altogether.

Days later the rain arrives with thunder and lightning. But the dusty earth is too parched to absorb the much-longed-for water when it finally comes. In no time a sea of fluttering bright strands spreads across the steep slopes, as if a ravenous giant were choking and spewing foam and mucus from all his pores. The cloudburst stops as abruptly as it started and, rather than easing into the usual fine drizzle, is followed by a windstorm that quickly dries the ground again. And so the drought persists.

Hardly any news arrives from the world beyond, and what little seeps through does not sound good. Eventually we get the feeling that people are avoiding our clan and especially our yurt. "What did we do," Mother asks in one of her nightly outbursts, "to merit the stares of strangers? Are we writhing flesh or stuffed intestines?"

I understand only after some time that her comparison means we are feeling uneasy. But once I do, I feel even more uneasy myself, and so embarrassed I wish I could disappear in a hole each time I encounter strangers, even if the topic of conversation is something as simple as the weather. I feel guilty, almost as if I had single-handedly cut down the trees, torn up the earth, sent people to their deaths, and conjured up the drought that has continued beyond the summer.

And yet I feel blissful and powerful when I am in the mountain steppe, alone with the lively silence that rushes and roars around me. Then I feel inside me the White Mountain again, and beyond it the mountains of the ages, towering above. I know they will move toward me, transformed into hours, days, and nights; and then into springs, summers, falls, and winters. They will pull me into themselves, kneading me first into a grown man, later into an old one, and finally into a stone to be ground into dust, before kneading that dust and giving me shape once more.

No one seemed to notice the arrival of fall. It was as if spring had simply continued, until one day we began to refer to the season as fall. Everything is lean. Our family packs up the yurt and leaves the rest of our clan, who have decided to settle for good at the District Center. Alone, we move westward across the bridge, so that our flocks can graze the earth eyes that stand out slightly darker against the reddish-gray rocks just below the glaciers before the snow arrives. Father decides that we must conserve the pastures in the Black Mountains for later in the season, so that at least part of our flock has a chance of surviving through the coming winter and into the spring. Torlaa, Galkaan, and I accompany Father and Mother to the bridge, where we are put on a raft. The Kazakhs who own the raft promise to drop us off at the settlement in exchange for the butter and cheese Mother gives them, and they do just that.

Galkaan and I are admitted to the dormitory right away, but Torlaa has to stay with us for a couple nights before she can take the post van to the provincial capital. There have been a number of changes. Jadmaj is in prison for embezzling state funds. Tasan, the new Party Secretary, is an older Ak Sayan man who used to have a job at the District Court. The school has two new teachers, both of them Hara Sayan. The older one, Ündük, is the new principal. He has a Mongolian wife and is quiet and tired. Silence reigns. The number of students has decreased to way below one hundred. Some people prefer the quieter school with fewer students. They say having more space means more breathing room. But to me this notion sounds like a retroactive rebuke aimed at our big brother. It cuts deeply into my soul. Fortunately, other voices draw comparisons in favor of the previous principal, suggesting that the school and quite possibly the whole district would really take off if he were still around. Music to my ears!

Sister Torlaa implores us to study harder than ever. After all if our excellent grades were to go down now, everyone would say that we only did well because our brother was the principal.

"Some people are envious and take pleasure in other people's misfortune. Don't give them a chance to throw dirt at our late brother," she says before leaving. I don't particularly feel like working for top grades, but somehow I manage to remain the top student in my class. Because I am now saddled with Sürgündü, I regurgitate the lessons over and over, which fills me with book knowledge the way a bucket is filled with water. Even quiet Galkaan gradually becomes a doggedly ambitious fighter, climbing the ladder until one day he is made Leader of the Pioneers' Council. Among his privileges is the right to be saluted by other students, who must stand at attention until Galkaan returns their salute. This way, neither of us provides any room for the slander of our big brother.

Nevertheless, we overhear rumors that hurt. People say that his body has not yet been touched. This extremely rare phenomenon usually befalls the bodies of only very impure people. It can also be caused by a mistake made during the funeral. When Galkaan and I are alone, we talk about it. We rule out the first possible cause completely, as we know for a fact that our big brother was not impure. This leaves the second possibility, and it does not take us long to identify the likely mistake. "We had no juniper when we said farewell to him," I say, reminding Galkaan of what happened. He immediately agrees.

Then one afternoon, on a half-good day around the middle of the tenth month, Mother appears unexpectedly. Her mount is so loaded down it looks like the horse of a hunter on his way home from a successful outing. Mother's goat bag hangs from both sides of her saddle, each of its legs stuffed to bursting, and another fat bag is tied to the back. After she has talked with the teacher on duty, Galkaan and I are granted permission to leave the dormitory for the night.

Together the three of us go to our relatives' yurt at Hara Dash, which is just under an hour's walk away. We have gone there a few times before, when other yurts from our clan had stayed at Hara Dash. But their yaks kept escaping to the familiar pasture at Ak-Hem, until people finally gave up on the idea of settling in the black steppe on the eastern banks of the great river, and returned instead to their traditional fall pastures. Just Uncle Sargaj and Aunt Buja stay back with their yurt. Nothing, they say, could possibly deter them from taking the side of progress.

As we walk to their yurt, Mother tells us that the shaman has decided to help with the decomposition of the still untouched body. Because the only person able to take the necessary steps is Bagshy, a former *lüüdshing* lama, our aunt rode to see him and ask for his help. He agreed and set the date, which is tomorrow. Father stayed behind to take care of the flocks, and so, for one whole day, the stove in our yurt will be cold.

The next morning, while people in the new world of settlements and all-good days are sleeping in, we rise early, the way people used to rise in the disappearing nomadic world, when they moved their yurts and their flocks. The world is still pitch black in spite of the stars sprinkled across the sky. We start walking after a quick bowl of morning tea, just as a shimmer of blue begins to appear in the east. Uncle Sargaj stays in bed, snoring, and our aunt was unsuccessful in her effort to wake up her nearly grown-up children. No matter how hard she tried to pull back their blankets, her children kept tugging them from her hands, defending deep sleep with their hands and their feet. Mother pleaded: "Buja, my dear, leave them alone. Let them sleep. Maybe they'll even improve with the rest. The Sky knows I wouldn't wish going through this on anyone, not even on those taking pleasure in my sorrow. But as long as you come with us and I don't have to stand there all by myself with these two thimble-sized little things, I'll be just fine."

And so the four of us set out eastward toward Saryg-höl, across the dim steppe crackling with late-autumn cold. We all walk, pulling the horse with its saddle and heavy load behind us. No one wants to ride. Galkaan thinks I should ride because I am the youngest; I think Mother should because her hip and her soul are hurting; Mother thinks our aunt should because if it weren't for us, she could have slept in. And Aunt Buja, who once was one of five children of the wealthiest man around, confesses that she has become used to walking after not riding for close to ten years. "The man gets furious whenever he catches sight of a rider," she says. "He says riding on horseback is a throwback to the old days. He says it's outmoded." By "the man" she means her husband. That she brought this proletarian hopeful— this purultaren, as Uncle Know-It-All fancies himself— into our clan has been so upsetting for so long that no one feels too upset about it now. To the contrary, I am grateful our aunt is talking about something. Walking across the steppe in silence would be far worse.

When we finally reach the edge of the steppe, the ridges of the eastern mountains glow like copper against the flames of the rising sun. A figure on horseback approaches us from the east. It is Bagshy, or Teacher, the great old man whom no one calls by his given name. He is Teacher Makaj's father and was released from prison only a few years ago. Strange stories about him abound. For example, three times he was sentenced to death, but no one managed to kill him, and when he later was asked if the story was true, he is reported to have said there was no point in answering the question: "If I tell you the truth, you won't believe it. If I make something up, you'll instantly fall for it. If you really want to know, try to get rid of me yourself. I'm around."

Bagshy quickly returns brief but deferential greetings, dismounts, ties his horse's lead to our horse's neck, and tells us to spread out what we have brought. He himself has brought a leather bag, dark from grease and scratched with age, which he takes off his saddle, ties around his waist above his belt, and fills with half of everything that Mother has brought: stewed mutton, sliced fresh yak cheese, flat pieces of medium-dry cheese, and bunches of dried juniper. Then he swings the half-filled bag over his shoulder, grabs with his other hand one of the two *dorsuks* filled with *aragy*, and leaves. When he has gone some distance, he calls back to us, "Stay where you are and keep quiet."

He walks toward our hand-sewn bag in a direct line. The bag has faded to the color of the rocks around it, and it seems to have shrunken. I secretly wonder if Bagshy rode out here earlier and took a look, then left again to avoid the eyes of any unwanted witness.

Crouching closely together, a mute huddle in the steppe, we watch with bated breath as the slightly stooped man walks determinedly toward his destination. Each time he walks a rope's length, he stops for a moment and glances to the right and left. He seems to be talking to someone. Shortly before he arrives at the bag, he puts down his burden and gestures like someone arriving at a yurt with a dog: he bends down, picks up a bit of soil, straightens, and tosses one, two, three handfuls of gravel and sand onto the ground in front of him.

We estimate the distance at about five or six lasso throws, and are just able to make out what he is doing. He takes the juniper from his bag, fumbles for his flint, and finally strikes it. It takes forever before we see the first ribbon of smoke. A bit later Galkaan thinks he sees flames. The smoke ribbon pulls behind it teetering blue clouds that rise into the sky. Then, all of a sudden, yellow and red flames flare up. The mutton fat must have caught fire.

Everything is the way it is when we give offerings, until Bagshy hastily empties his leather bag onto the steppe and flings it back in our direction, pours a good jolt from the *dorsuk* down his throat, draws the dagger from its sheath on his belt, and walks up to the bundle. Without hesitating he quickly cuts open the bag, pulls the rags out from beneath the dark-brown something that is now exposed, throws them into the fire, and forcefully thrusts his dagger into this brown something. We hear a blunt thud, much like the sound of a slow bullet entering the chest cavity of a wild animal. Next we hear crunching and creaking sounds and see dark pieces fly through the air. Bagshy has apparently severed them from the brown something and flung them onto the pile of cheese and meat. It makes me think of wood getting split to fit into the stove, and of *bortsha* being broken to fit into the pot.

Soon all the contents of the bag have been cut up and spread out. Bagshy, who was bent over working as fast as a butcher, finally straightens up. He slowly raises his upper body, and after pushing his dagger back into its sheath, he stands still for some time, his hands on the small of his lower back. He looks up and moves his head in slow circles. Then he suddenly squats, raises his arms, flaps them like wings, and starts skipping with childlike ease while simultaneously clicking his tongue, smacking his lips, and cackling like a magpie. Still moving the same way, he starts to crow. Finally, he gets up again and trudges back to us, looking old and tired. When he has come as close as a lasso throw, he scolds us: "Why aren't you burning juniper? Do I have to tell you everything? You're not little kids anymore."

Mother and Aunt Buja reply with one voice: "Dear Brother, we didn't know . . ." They quickly light a bunch of juniper, and it crackles and explodes while Galkaan and I dash off for dry horse manure. Soon we have a clearly visible smoke offering. All the while Bagshy is panting and tottering, and his knees creak as he awkwardly drops to sit on the ground. He pulls his legs into the cross-legged position, as if he had to slowly gather up his pieces and force together what was pulling him apart. When at long last he sits correctly—his knees wide apart and close to the ground, his back straight—he begins to sing. His voice is beautiful and deep. Unfortunately, we can't understand a single word of what crosses his lips. He must be speaking Tangutan.

A magpie arrives where Bagshy did his work a short while ago. It flutters and lands, and skips about with clicking sounds. Soon a second, then a third and a fourth magpie join the first one. Kites, crows, and ravens follow. Brother Galkaan and I copy the adults and sit bending over, our hands clasped in prayer. But we keep our eyes trained on the birds as they cackle and gaggle, coo and caw, every so often screaming and attacking each other with gaping beaks. The entire feathered nation seems to have lost its wits over so many tasty bits.

The singsong swells. Bagshy's voice has grown strong and now booms with great power. Like an epic, his song spills verse upon verse, surging and flowing beyond the steppe and into the hazy distance, awakening the clouds and the winds. Meanwhile the sun, heavy with its bursting bundles of rays, rises to meet the song. With each passing moment, it climbs higher into the boundless Sky, where it will soar unsupported and move closer and closer toward the Sky's misty navel and the shimmering blue heights opening up beyond. Bagshy's eyes are closed tightly and his upper body rocks from side to side. His rugged face with its sharp features expresses a fierce and sublime severity that I recognize from the epics sung through the night in the flickering light of a fire, or from our snow-covered mountains reflecting the white light of an early winter morning, making us shiver with their bracing chill.

Then the song dies unexpectedly. I hear it even after the voice has broken off, as one hears raging storms or galloping riders after they have left, but Bagshy falls silent and sits still again, more exhausted than before. Only his eyes are fully alert, and fixed on the frenzied birds until he finally looks away.

As if he had just awakened, he nods at the food and drink the women have spread on the ground. "Let's get started now, shall we?"

Aunt Buja has filled a bowl with milk and offers it to

him with both hands. He casually accepts it, takes a small sip, and passes the bowl along to us. Next he is given *aragy.* He hesitates briefly, but then empties the bowl in a single gulp. Next he pulls his heavy dagger with its long stag-antler hilt from its sheath, and grabs a shoulder piece of meat. Alarmed, Mother calls out: "*Uj höörküj Aga-uj,* dear Brother, please, let me wipe the blade for you first." Bagshy pauses, looks around, finds a tuft of grass, and carelessly wipes his dagger. "Don't worry, dear Sister," he says defiantly, pulling a face. "I'm a *lüüdshing* lama, remember?" Then he cuts a thin slice, picks it up with his right thumb and index finger, and dangles it high above his wide-open mouth before letting it drop. In spite of his roundabout ways, he eats a lot of food quickly, hardly seeming to chew. And he drinks: each time he empties the bowl he makes a blunt snort accompanied by a light smacking sound.

Bagshy tells us that we, too, must eat and drink. The feast is the last gift the departing leave for those who remain behind. Because we want to believe what he says, we do our very best, but we simply can't finish the mountain of meat. Bagshy, on the other hand, keeps at it. By now the *dorsuk* has run dry. Aunt Buja, who has been pouring the drink, suddenly realizes that we left the second *dorsuk* over there.

"Oh, that's all right," says Bagshy, sounding relaxed. He turns to Galkaan and me: "Boys, run over there and get the *dorsuk.* And since you're at it, bring back my leather bag and your piece of felt." Galkaan and I look first at each other, then at the women. But neither of them will get involved when a lama has spoken. Besides, Bagshy sits there like royalty with his long flashing dagger and his thousands of secrets, and he is close enough to see and hear everything. We get up and walk over.

Birds whir like spirits in front of us. I can't help but wonder if they are spirits, conjured up by someone who speaks their language and may be a spirit himself. I am terrified, and I almost feel like shamanizing on the spot, in order to force the feathered creatures to explain themselves: Why did you come so late? Was it the wound inflicted on Mother Earth? The missing juniper smoke? Or did you, my Brothers and Sisters from the Sky, have another reason? Have your eyes become dull and your beaks blunt?

The birds skip off to the side. They hold bones with stringy bits hanging off them in their beaks. One of the bones has a hole the size of my palm in the middle, and the hole is picked clean. I recognize the bone as a pelvis and wonder if it is from a wether or a man. The felt mat, so brilliantly white at the time, is now dark brown and stained with what must have been some sticky liquid. Brother Galkaan won't let me get close to the mat. He seizes it by a corner and starts beating it. But no matter how much he slaps the mat against the ground, the stain won't go away. Pleased and heartened to find that the *dorsuk* is almost full when I grab it, I catch sight of something round that a kite is rolling in front of itself. It turns but to be the skull, picked clean all the way into the sockets.

I feel like turning to the puffed-up bird with its sunny-red feathers and questioning it to get some clarity. But that very moment I notice Galkaan holding the felt mat in his right hand and moving his lips. Although we are only a few steps apart, I can't hear what he says. Instead I hear Mother's voice: "Please watch over these children, dear Brother." Bagshy's voice replies, "Don't think I'd forget them even for an instant, dear Sister. But I can assure you, they are cared for by better protectors than me." He continues after a brief pause: "Do you remember how loaded down with stuff a lama was when he arrived for a *lüüdshing* in the old days? And how much trouble he had to go to? It was almost like going to war. Now look at me. Though I am shamelessly called Bagshy, as a lama I am bare-naked. And yet the results don't seem to be any different. This is the thing: the cloak, the Sutra, the drum, the bell, the bowls for the butter lamps, and all the rest of it—they're all hidden inside me. Such are the times. But much as kings without crowns or thrones will begin to rule the physical bodies of men, so too will shamans without *shawyds* or mirrors and lamas without drums or bells rule the souls of men."

When Galkaan and I return, we find the three deep in conversation. But while I see their lips moving and their eyes paying vivid attention, I can't hear them. It's as if I've lost my hearing. Only when Bagshy turns to the two of us can I suddenly hear again.

Galkaan takes off the leather bag he had tied around his waist, and Bagshy smiles and slides the felt mat under his crossed legs: "From time immemorial, the mat has been the only reward for the *lüüdshing*. In fact, it's very valuable. If you put it under the saddlecloth, it will quickly heal a festering wound on the horse's back." The *dorsuk* with the *aragy* gives him scarcely less pleasure. But then he asks us to do something unusual: Galkaan and I are to empty a half-filled bowl each. Hesitating and blushing at first, we are encouraged by Mother and Aunt Buja. And so, choking and coughing, we drink it down.

"What were the two of you thinking about when you were over there?" asks Bagshy.

"I thought," Galkaan says without reflecting, "about how I will always need to keep myself alive, mostly for Father and Mother's sake."

I add immediately after him: "I didn't have any time for thoughts of my own because I felt I was hearing voices."

"Did you recognize them?"

"Oh yes. First it was Mother's and then it was yours, Grandfather. And in the end I could hear our big brother."

"What did your mother say?"

"She wanted you to watch over us."

"You heard that?!" Mother starts, alarmed.

"And what did I answer?" Bagshy jumps in.

"You talked a lot. I can't remember. Actually, wait, I can. Something about kings without crowns, shamans without *shawyds* or mirrors, and lamas without drums or bells."

"He said that when you were standing right next to him, dear child," our aunt says quickly.

"And what did your brother say?"

"'She and I were enemies in an earlier life. I came back

to her as a baby, in order first to grow attached to her heart but then to die and tear it apart. My revenge will be complete when I have destroyed her altogether.'"

Everyone stares at me. Mother looks shocked, Aunt Buja trusting, Bagshy incredulous. I overheard the bit about the child and its revenge one day, when I was listening to wise man Dilik Gulak have a go at someone who kept dissolving into tears after having lost a child.

Whether it is the result of feeling guilty or of drinking *aragy*, I can't tell, but I do feel like eating more meat. Brother Galkaan joins me. Having another *dorsuk* with drink, Bagshy is at it again, too. I notice he is chewing now. Between noisily eating and smacking his lips and uttering dull grunts, he turns to Mother: "You've just heard the message your youngest child has brought you from your eldest. Now you know how things stand. You don't believe that all we are doing is drinking *aragy* and eating meat, do you? We are drawing your tears from you and devouring the stone that bears down on you from inside."

Just as I begin to feel full and to wipe my greasy fingers on my bootlegs, I realize that I must not stop. So I carry on and force down a piece I have torn with grim zest off a lower arm, breaking it into chunks. The meat is as crusty and hard as wood, and it tastes of the sun. I can tell from looking at him that Galkaan, too, has grasped what needs to be done. He struggles with a neck bone, and chomps with tensed muscles on a piece of jaw and neck. My tongue is dry and tired. Why aren't we offered more *aragy*? Can't they see how hard it is to have to eat meat dried and coarsened by the sun without anything to wash it down? Don't people say that a two-legged creature mustn't stop after a single drink? If only they would pass me another bowl of *aragy*. I'd drain it in a flash. I'd gladly do so—if that meant I would gulp down and consume for good the transformed tears of our mother. Day after day I would gorge myself on meat, piles and mountains of meat, to devour the transformed stone pressing so hard on our mother's heart and kidneys.

I am choking, but I am determined to do whatever it takes to release Mother from her sorrow. Like a young wolf, I tear from that wretched lower arm its last strand of sinewy muscle meat and the thick spongy skin attached to it. And I whet my gaze on one of the three remaining chunks of meat—dull, black stones with lighter veins— that wait to be devoured.

GLOSSARY

Aarshy dried chunks of cheese, used for provisions in the winter

Aga brother or uncle; used to address an older male

Ail settlement consisting of several yurts

Ak Sayan minority tribe of the Tuvans, living in the mountains and known for their hunting skills

Aragy strong, colorless spirit distilled from fermented milk

Asa, plural *Asalar* spirits that may become dangerous

Baja wealthy man, a prince; traditional,deferential address for a man of higher rank

Bortsha air-dried meat

Darga supervisor, head, person in position of authority; modern address for a man of higher rank

Dör   north side of the yurt, opposite the entrance, considered the place of honor

Dorsuka   smoked-leather bottle used to store liquids

Dshenggej   sister-in-law; address used only for an older brother's wife

Erlikbej   a diminutive form of address for *Erlik*, the Lord of the Land of the Dead, which gives equal rank to the speaker

Erwen   herb smoked by shamans

Gök Mondshak   majority tribe of the Tuvans

Hara Sayan   minority tribe of the Tuvans, living in low-lying areas and increasingly adopting Mongolian ways

Jolka   Russian New Year celebration

Kulak   Russian for "fist"; peasant in Russia wealthy enough to own a farm and hire help, also applied to wealthy Mongolian herders

Lawashak   long, coatlike summer dress

Lüüdshing   lama who takes people on their last journey

Mala   set of Buddhist paryer beads, typically made of 108 beads

Örtöö   thirty-kilometer distance; traditional term for a way station for horses

Ovoo   cairn of sacred stones, erected for the spirits of the respective location and used for offerings and other religious ceremonies

Shagaa   lunar New Year celebration

Shawyd   whisk or bundle made from strips of fabric; used by shamans to evoke the spirits

Sükhbaatar   founder of modern Mongolia

Ton   long, coatlike winter dress

Udarnik   honorary title awarded with a medal and a financial reward to the most efficient laborer

GALSAN TSCHINAG, whose name in his native Tuvan language is Irgit Schynykbajoglu Dshurukuwaa, was born in the early forties in Mongolia. From 1962 until 1968 he studied at the University of Leipzig, where he adopted German as his written language. Under an oppressive Communist regime he became a singer, storyteller, and poet in the ancient Tuvan tradition. As the chief of the Tuvans in Mongolia, Tschinag led his people, scattered under Communist rule, back in a huge caravan to their original home in the Altai Mountains. Tschinag is the author of more than thirty books, and his work has been translated into many languages. He lives alternately in the Altai, Ulaanbaatar, and Europe.

KATHARINA ROUT teaches English and Comparative Literature at Vancouver Island University in Nanaimo, British Columbia. Her translations of contemporary German literature have been acclaimed widely.

Also available from Milkweed Editions:

THE BLUE SKY
BY GALSAN TSCHINAG
TRANSLATED FROM THE GERMAN BY KATHARINA ROUT

The debut of a major voice in contemporary world literature.
The first novel in an epic trilogy of a Tuvan boy's coming of age in communist Mongolia.

"In this pristine and concentrated tale of miraculous survival and anguished loss, Tschinag evokes the nurturing warmth of a family within the circular embrace of a yurt as an ancient way of life lived in harmony with nature becomes endangered."
—BOOKLIST

"Book by book, Tschinag is championing his people and preserving their traditions. He gives a whole new meaning to the power contained in the written word."
—SAN FRANCISCO CHRONICLE

"One of those rare books that even when read in solitude makes you feel as if you've just been told a story while surrounded by family and friends in front of a fire. . . . A book that celebrates kinship, mirrors history and captures the mountains, valleys and steppes in all their surpassing beauty and brutality."
—MINNEAPOLIS STAR TRIBUNE

MILKWEED EDITIONS

Founded in 1979, Milkweed Editions is one of the largest independent, nonprofit literary publishers in the United States. Milkweed's mission is to identify, nurture and publish transformative literature, and build an engaged community around it.

JOIN US

Milkweed depends on the generosity of foundations and individuals like you, in addition to revenue from the sales of its books. In an increasingly consolidated and bottom-line-driven publishing world, your support allows us to select and publish books on the basis of their literary quality and transformative potential.

Please visit our Web site (www.milkweed.org) or contact us at (800) 520-6455 to learn more about our donor program.

Milkweed Editions, a nonprofit publisher, gratefully acknowledges sustaining support from Emilie and Henry Buchwald; the Patrick and Aimee Butler Foundation; the Dougherty Family Foundation; the Ecolab Foundation; the General Mills Foundation; John and Joanne Gordon; William and Jeanne Grandy; the Jerome Foundation; Robert and Stephanie Karon; the Lerner Foundation; Sally Macut; Sanders and Tasha Marvin; the McKnight Foundation; Mid-Continent Engineering; the Minnesota State Arts Board, through an appropriation by the Minnesota State Legislature, a grant from the Wells Fargo Foundation Minnesota, and a grant from the National Endowment for the Arts; Kelly Morrison and John Willoughby; the National Endowment for the Arts, and the American Reinvestment and Recovery Act; the Navarre Corporation; Ann and Doug Ness; Jörg and Angie Pierach; the RBC Foundation USA; Ellen Grace; the Target Foundation; the James R. Thorpe Foundation; the Travelers Foundation; Moira and John Turner; and Edward and Jenny Wahl.

THE McKNIGHT FOUNDATION

MINNESOTA
STATE ARTS BOARD

NATIONAL
ENDOWMENT
FOR THE ARTS
A great nation
deserves great art.

TARGET.

The translation of this work was supported by a grant from the Goethe-Institut which is funded by the German Ministry of Foreign Affairs.

 GOETHE-INSTITUT

The translator thanks Galsan Tschinag for his support and her husband Jonathan, her friend Kathryn Barnwell, and in particular her editor, Daniel Slager, for making this a better translation than it otherwise would have been. She also wishes to acknowledge the asistance of the Banff International Literary Translation Centre and the Banff Centre in Banff, Alberta, Canada.

Interior design by Rachel Holscher
Typeset in Anziano
by BookMobile Design and Publishing Services
Printed on acid-free 100% post consumer waste paper
by Friesens Corporation